ART BOSS

KAYLA CAGAN

CHRONICLE BOOKS
San Francisco

Library of Congress Cataloging-in-Publication Data available.

ISBN 978-1-4521-6037-5

Manufactured in China.

Hand lettering by Luke Choice.
Illustrations by Maria Ines Gul.
Design by Amelia Mack.
Typeset in Prensa.

10 9 8 7 6 5 4 3 2 1

Chronicle Books LLC
680 Second Street
San Francisco, California 94107
www.chroniclebooks.com

For New York City, which gave me
a home

For Meredith and Sherine, who filled it
with poetry

and

For Ricky, who got me there

How can so much happen in three days?

I'm here! I made it! The Dream! I lost my journal somewhere in LaGuardia, I can't freaking believe it. I even called the airport to see if someone turned it in, but nope, so I'm starting new with this notebook. Now I'm drinking an iced coffee and writing on the subway train like I live here or something and I do because this is my life!

This couple balancing against the train pole in front of me is in a fight. She just said, "What did you expect from a new hire? They're never as good as they seem on paper" and he said, "Just once, I'd like you to have my back" and she said, "Nothing's what it seems, I told you that." Now they're glaring at each other and he just turned away to his phone. DRAMA!

Oh, so many good overhears and quotes just by being alive in New York. I love all the accents and funny shit I'm hearing.

"Nothing's what it seems." —Woman on the train

And I'm totally feeling that because everything is weirder than I thought, both good and bad weird and not at all what I've been expecting!

The guy with the dark blond hair that I thought was Jamie Silas, my future soul mate, at the airport? Nope! Just a guy waiting for someone else. Mortifying.

Staying in a big loft apartment? Not even. I mean, not like I was promised that, I guess I just kinda assumed, and as Dad says, "Assume makes an ass out of U and me." Yep, that's me for sure. My apartment at the Webster Residence for Women (that's what it's called!) is super tiny and plain old weird, but um, I also kind of love it. The look is sooo Metro-Retro. I came up with that.

Scheduling an appt. with NYSCFA, the New York School of Contemporary Fine Arts, my dream school that I'm finally going to attend in January, so long as I can get my financial aid figured out? That's what Helen Mundy, my aid advisor, said to do once I was here, but they are all backed up dealing with current incoming students and that kind of made me feel like a loser. I can't meet with Helen until September at least. No big deal, just worrying my brain out until then.

Meeting Carlyle Campbell, the famous modern artist who had discovered my work online and asked me—ME!—to be his assistant developing art to accompany his first-ever fashion line?

(Let's not even get into the fact that my original art piece that had caught Carlyle's attention had been destroyed. Not my fault. But, Kennedy, Carlyle's assistant, knew what had happened and had promised to help me get back on track without Carlyle ever knowing a single thing. Carlyle had hired me for that piece specifically and if he finds out I have to recreate it, plus multiples, from scratch, in less than a month (so help me), he could easily drop me. I can NOT let him know any of that—unless I like the idea of returning to Texas with little chance of coming back or finding some other magical way to pay for school next semester. NO PRESSURE.)

Oh, and bringing enough clothes? Try again, I've already sweated through everything I own. Guess I have to shop. Poor me.

Everything has been a total bizarro version of what I thought. Tonight I go on a do-over date with Silas since our first the night I got here was a disaster. Hoping that things might go better, but that whole online love connection thing? Yeah, I dunno. IRL, not sure either of us is feeling it. Yet.

I need Kit and Enzo to be here to see all of this but that's not gonna happen so I texted them that I'm posting new sketches online so they can check out the local scene whenever they want—and I can keep them all together for me, too, like a little #NYSeen city-sketching home-base collection. That's me, the real-deal real-local now. Ha. Kit, my OG bestie best of all times, said: Thank god. Been waiting for the Piper Perspective! and Enzo, my second-best bestie/greatest hometown heartbreak and newly out main man, wrote: Brilliant! Loves it, Needs it! ☺

Silas is scrawny and curved in, like if a human was a comma, his silhouette is all bow and he has sleek black hair and the greenest eyes and really, really pale skin, like watery skim milk. He's got a cool super-sharp dimple, almost like a scar, that runs up his pale pink cheek. It was like meeting a real live Edward Gorey character. I didn't know how tonight would go, with just the two of us, since Mo (the roommate) came the last time. At least Mo's funny even if he's kind of pretentious. He talks about himself in the third person: "Mo doesn't do that, Mo is happy to meet you." The opposite of Silas, who's real down on himself.

Tonight, Si was wearing a thin black T-shirt, faded black jeans, black Converse, and a tan backpack when he met me in front of the Web. I wore the black dress I wore on the plane—I Febreezed it first!—with my Adidas, and matte red lips. We looked pretty cool.

He looked down at the paper bag I had with me. "Do a little shopping?"

"You'll have to wait and see." I pulled it closer to me, careful not to crush it. I kept sneaking peeks at him. His dimple is cute. Maybe he's cute. He is definitely friend-cute, but I don't know if he is boyfriend-cute. All summer, I had known <u>for sure</u> that he was boyfriend-cute. Dang.

We crossed the gold-yellow safety line painted on the train platform and got on the A train. The line is the same shade of sunflower on the city cabs, marigold-mustard. There were so many people crammed in our subway car and I was trying not

4

to push against anyone, but I couldn't get to one of the bars that were over our heads and he just kind of slid between me and this other dude and moved my hand to the bar and said, "Don't worry, we only have a few stops," which was the first Summer-Silas thing he'd done since I'd met him, which made me happy, even though I was smushed between a guy shouting about how it was "too fucking hot," which was true but don't yell dude we're all dealing with it, and another guy behind me who was taking up way too much room just so he could balance himself while reading an opened-up newspaper. So annoying. Obviously he didn't care about the rest of us squeezed in! Thank god not all rides are squeezy-squeezy like that.

"We're eating at one of my favorite places," Silas said. "But it's not fancy."

"WHAT? Why, I never!" I put my hand to my mouth like, the horror!

I got him to laugh. Victory! Things weren't tense over email this summer but in front of each other, we're both real awkward.

"You know this is on me, right?"

He said it in a way that was both a question and an answer.

"What do you mean?" I thought I got what he was asking but I wasn't sure.

"I don't want to assume—"

"I don't want to assume either," I said.

Then we goofed at each other, kind of waiting for the other person to say the next thing.

He finally said, "I don't know how they do it in Texas, but I would like this to be a date."

"Me too," I said and reached for his arm. Maybe Si had never had a girlfriend before. Huh, I hadn't imagined that until then.

We got to Tavern on Jane and the waiter appeared almost immediately. "Well if it isn't Mr. Sunshine himself. I see you put on your best T-shirt this evening, youngster."

"This is Piper," he said, introducing me to Harvey.

"What can I get started for you guys?"

"Um . . . how are the spaghetti and meatballs?" I asked and he said, "Marvelous" and took my menu. Silas ordered a grilled hanger steak with fries and Harvey went off to put in our order. I could see the POS machine was the same one we used when I was waitressing at the 610 Diner, my old job in Houston, but then I felt Silas watching me and I tried to make my face normal. How could I explain feeling comforted just seeing the same work program we had at our diner back home?

"So, when should I start calling you Mr. Sunshine?"

"Ha. Yeah, no thanks. I've known Harv since I was a kid. When you've lived here your whole life, the city" (Note to self: call it the city, not New York City! The train, not the subway!) "is a pretty small town. Everybody knows everybody, for better or worse."

Harvey was back at the table with calamari. Calamari!

"Chef says have a wonderful night out, guys."

"Mr. Sunshine for the win!" I tapped my glass to his Coke and said, "Cheers, Si."

He smirked or looked embarrassed, I couldn't tell which.

"Here," I said, handing him the paper bag. "Open it!"

A new Silas in two seconds flat: His smile was lit, dimple half his cheek.

"Could it be—" He started to tear through the tissue paper and then sat back. "You didn't."

"You said you wanted one!"

"I can't believe it!" he said, pulling out the brand-spanking-new cowboy hat. I was pretty sure it was the exact midnight blue-black he liked.

"I can't believe I have a genuine cowboy hat from Texas." He put it on his head. "How's this?"

I tipped it down in the front, just a little. "You're the real deal, dude."

He checked himself out in the mirror behind the bar and did a little mosey back to our table. "I belong in this hat. Yee-fucking-haw."

I had never seen anyone so happy to be wearing one. It didn't really match his look, but he didn't care and I was delighted he was showing me anything other than nerves and weirdness! On the first date, he barely talked to me, except to explain why he wasn't at the airport (a last-minute school orientation thing, I understand, I wouldn't want to miss anything cool going on either, but still, really? He could have emailed me! Guess I'm not quite over that yet . . .) and other than that, he and Mo just talked almost the whole time. It was so weird. At least we can text each other now.

Harvey put our dinners down on the table. He straightened Silas's hat and said to me, "Who does he think he is, Johnny Cash?" Then he winked and walked away.

Si was still beaming. It was like it was the first time anybody had ever gotten him anything. Maybe he needed it.

"I wish I had something for you." Something clicked when he said that and he was back to robotic/awkward.

"It's okay," I said. "You'll make it up to me." I was working my eyelashes overtime, trying to flirt again.

"Let's eat."

Okaaaaaaaaay.

I expected to be all nerves around him, not vice versa. Maybe the idea of a New York boyfriend was better over email than over calamari. On the bright side my spaghetti and meatballs were better than anything I had eaten at the Webster so far. It's awesome that the Web comes with free meals, but like . . . the free part is the best part. The meals, not so much.

"So tell me more about Mo," I said, hating to do it but not knowing what else to talk about. "What's his story?"

Silas drained his Coke.

"The thing is," he said, wiping his mouth, "Mo is a really decent guy. He can rub some people the wrong way, but that's just how he is. Honest. He's not afraid to tell the truth. So he'll tell me if I make something that sucks."

"Oh yeah, I got that impression!" I leaned in, relaxing. "But I bet you don't make anything that sucks."

Si winced. "Well. I don't know about that. But anyway, the thing is, he's in a little trouble."

"Like, with the law?"

"What?" Silas snorted, right next door to a smile. "No, at school. So OK, he focuses on food politics. He designs his work out of food, then lets it decay. That's part of the work, the time and the rot. It's his comment on consumerism and commercialism and time and food culture, but sometimes it causes him to miss deadlines. Our profs are kind of sticklers for turning stuff in on time. You'll see."

"Wow. His work sounds epic. And really smelly." I laughed, but it did made me feel like an ounce more cool toward Mo. Like he was doing something semi-thoughtful, in addition to being a know-it-all.

"Agreed, especially when you live with him. But the faculty was really stubborn last semester, and they might have clashed."

"Might?"

"Okay," he laughed, "did. Don't say anything, but . . ."

I put my fork down mid-meatball and held up my Scout fingers.

"He's on probation."

"Whaaat?"

"Yeah."

"They can do that? Just 'cause he's working with food? Didn't they know that when they accepted him? They shouldn't kick him out."

"Don't say any of that in front of him—please. He'll accuse me of dooming him as a failure. I don't really think they're aiming to push him out, I think it's more about him not meeting his deadlines, and his attitude defending his work. They encourage us to stick up for ourselves as artists, as creative warriors—" I must have made a face because Si was like, "School motto. But then when we test it by disagreeing with them, it's like we're messing with the gods. It's all one big pissing contest. They try to break us down to build us back up. Some students practically get away with murder. Mo can't. I can't. Someone like Gillman, for example"—he shook his head—"he could give them an empty water bottle and they'd pee their pants."

"Gillman?"

"Joe Gillman. I might have mentioned him in an email. Or not. I try not to think about him."

"So, he's not good."

Silas shrugged and tried to get another another sip out of his Coke, shaking the ice around the glass. "Depends on how you define good."

"Does Gillman also work with food?" I smirked. "Is it like Iron Chef between them?"

"No, Mo's the only food geek." He smiled and plucked up a fry. "Lucky for us."

"So what's that guy do that's so great the teachers love him so much?" All the talk about Mo's probation makes me nervous. I'll have to up my game when I finally start classes in January. I'm not great with deadlines either.

"The faculty thinks he's changing the world being a 'conceptualist.'"

"What is that?" God, I need school. I don't know any of these terms. Si probably sees the big flashing lights over my head blinking IDIOT-IDIOT.

"You ready for this?" Silas did a drumroll with his fingers. "He has a lot of concepts. And that's his art. His concepts."

"That's it?" He nodded and I have to admit, I had a flash of excitement that we were finally gossiping about art the way I thought we always would. "I don't get it."

"Well, I suppose you're not a genius, then." His dimple popped up.

"That's so gimmicky." We were both laughing.

"Yeah, but he has them wrapped around his finger. He had a 'show' where it was an empty gallery space, and there was nothing inside except for a sign-in book, wine, and cheese. And people wandered around, looking at the white walls, with lights shining where art should have been hanging, and he had just written in really faint script, Untitled Concept 1, 2, 3, etc. . . ."

"And that worked?"

Si was kind of nodding and shaking his head at the same time.

"I wish I saw it just because it sounds so awful. Maybe he's an idiot AND a genius."

"You got the first part right. But anyway, that's why Mo's a little more . . . clingy this semester, why he wanted me to go with him and I missed meeting you at the airport. It wasn't really an orientation. It was a probation hearing for him."

Aha! Well. Si lied for his friend. I can't go back and ask him to fix three days ago but I wish he had just been honest about it. I was going to say something and then he said, "He gets a little paranoid. I know he comes off as confident, but he gets pretty down, and I was worried."

"You're a good friend." Kit and Enzo had come to my rescue too many times to count. I couldn't blame the guy for helping his bud. I was kind of touched by what a true blue he was. Even if so far he was kind of a lame crush.

"Yeah, you get it." Even though he didn't really know if I got it or not, it felt good hearing him say so.

I finally felt relaxed for a second. "Well, that explains why he's so uptight. I'd love to see some of Mo's work and y'know, yours, too."

"Right, yeah."

"Because now I know about Mo's work. And Joe's work. Ha, that rhymes! But um, it's your art that I want to see." Silas finished off his plate, nodding silently. I waited for more of an invitation. "Like before the semester starts?" I said, pushing. "You could come see the stuff I'm making for Carlyle, too. I could use some real feedback. I have to impress him, like kill it, or I could be on some kind of probation with him, too. Or worse, just out, period, back to Texas."

"Nah, he won't fire you. He needs you."

That kind of made me a little pissy. How did he know? Even I hadn't met the guy yet. I had no real idea what I was walking into. "Maybe it's not exactly the same, but we're both making art that's being judged, right? And Carlyle could actually fire me anytime he feels like it. Which would be worse than probation."

He shrugged. "Okay, maybe he will, but I doubt it. Your work is strong. My stuff is all wip."

"Wimpy?" I had never heard anyone call their art wimpy before.

"WIP. W-I-P. Work in progress."

OMG, I need school. I am legit-talk deficient.

"You already know what you're making for Carlyle and you know how it ends."

"Actually, I don't know how any of it ends. I've only talked with him on the phone. We haven't even met face-to-face yet. My job working for him could end this week if he doesn't like my art in real life."

"Doubtful. But you're missing the point."

"Excuse you?" I laughed but I kind of wanted to thump him.

"You have an endpoint and I'm in this endless loop. I'm back in lab at school and all the photos I've been shooting this summer, they aren't telling my story. I thought it would all come to me, match up and make sense, and it's all missing links. Nothing's connecting. No story."

"Well, what is your story?"

He shook his head. "You wouldn't get it."

I narrowed my eyes and crossed my arms. "Because?"

"Oh, shit, don't take it personally. It's not YOU wouldn't get it, it's that I can't explain where I'm headed yet. That's not how I work. I have a while until midterms, but everything I've been making throughout the summer, and now trying to shoot new stuff, I'm just distracted."

"By?"

"The world! The news! Everything going on, my mind can't slow down, it's a tornado in here, and I'm trying to keep it all out of my work."

"Well, maybe you should stop fighting it and use it. Let it in."

He sat back, exhaling hard.

"Oh, come on." I shook his wrist, forgetting I wasn't with Kit or Enzo, and he pulled back quickly. I wasn't being flirty, but he apparently didn't like it. My bad.

"I've been shooting all summer. There's nothing behind my photos. No cohesion, no story. I haven't found my thread. It's boring. You don't want to talk about that and neither do I."

"Yeah, I do," I said. Jeez, I had waited all summer to talk face-to-face with Silas. Of course I wanted to talk about art with him. "It was so hard for me to figure out what I was making in school and every thought I had was, this is bad, this isn't enough, this isn't right. When I was working on my senior project I got so bored sometimes, like just ugh! The day to day? The not knowing, the frustration of trying to make something out of nothing? The drive, the why—besides getting graded. Who's really gonna care? So I had to find my way back into it. And then, people did care. I got reviewed. Kennedy and Carlyle found my work online and then me, and now I'm here. So, I get being stuck. But sometimes it's the only way to get out." Super cheese. But true.

He sighed.

Hello, so rude. I was trying to get him to talk about his art!

"I bet your photos aren't as unconnected as you think," I said. "If you're stuck, you'll find your through-line, right?"

He nodded but I could tell he wasn't feeling it.

BRB—MANDATORY PEE BREAK LIKE RIGHT NOW

So, we rolled out of the restaurant and a breeze was blowing litter around the street, and some crunchy leaves levitated above the sidewalk. Poetry is everywhere. We turned onto another café/tree-lined street and Silas explained we were in Greenwich Village on Greenwich St., not Greenwich Ave. I guess I should learn the differences but I assume they all wind into each other in one way or another.

Kit and I used to dream of coming here together. I was wishing she was in the Village with me, not because I felt lonely with Silas, but because Kit and Enzo and me had talked about it so much. But the NYC3 that was to be is now just the NYCMe, and I have to stop pretending otherwise.

"Hey." He waved his hand in front of my face, breaking my daydream-nightmare. "You okay?"

"Yep. Just spaced for a sec. It's all so new. And old."

"Soooo, if you could go anywhere right now in this new-old place, where would you go?" He held his arms out like the city was ours.

"Seriously?"

He nodded.

"Okay. STUDIO 54! I made a list of all of Andy Warhol's hot spots and that's the top of my list, besides the Factory, obvi."

His mouth pursed together in a smile. He looked like he was going to laugh.

"Studio 54 might be closed tonight. I don't know if we'll be able to go inside or anything, but let's try." His cheeks rose, deepening his dimple. Borderline cute.

"Are you laughing at me?"

"You just . . . like it here so much. It's adorable." I know he wasn't trying to sound condescending, but it sounded condescending.

"I don't like it. I love it!"

He shook his head like, too lame for words, but in a cute way like he liked me, but then just looked at the ground.

Then I realized: maybe he's shy?!? He did like me, does like me, I think, but he's shy! I never thought about it before, because I guess I don't know many shy people. Maybe that's why he felt so different in emails. IRL, he was shy. It wasn't a New York thing, it was a shy thing. Maybe he thought I would be too? Or maybe that's why he likes me? Because I'm not?

It felt like I had decoded life as we kept walking and walking and walking and I was obsessing on every person, every shop, every street we were passing, I had a flash of feeling like everything might be working out. It was the middle of the night and we were running around in the coolest city with the longest blocks and a million people still out eating and drinking and dancing and walking and I was free! Electric! Infinite! I could—can—become a whole new me if I wanted and nobody would ever know who I was before I was NYCMe.

Then Silas stopped us.

"What's this?" I said. The building looked like the front of a movie theater. "Where's the cool STUDIO 54 sign?"

"It's a theater," Silas said. "They do plays here now, like Broadway stuff. My parents are members if you ever want to see a play. We're under where the cool sign used to hang, I think."

"But, the club?"

"It hasn't been here for a long time," Silas said. "I thought you knew—"

"No—"

I hadn't even considered that. I was reading Andy's diaries and looking at his art when he had been here, and he hadn't been here in a long, long time. Duh. Obviously.

"I'm sorry, Piper," he said. "I'm used to it. The city changes all the time. I mourn things that go away, daily, but it's not that big of a deal. It's a city with no respect for the past. Nostalgia just gets swept up with the trash here. New York eats its old."

"I thought you liked it here . . . from your emails. . . ."

"I love it here. It's home. But I can like something and know it's problematic at the same time."

"That's just okay with you?"

I turned my back to him. I felt like such a newbie and he just sounded right about everything. So smart. So New York. I felt like I was going to cry all of a sudden.

"That's always been the great New York way, friend. You'll evolve, trust me. C'mon, you just got here! You love it, remember?" He smiled but it made me feel dumb.

"Just stop."

He pulled out his phone, shaking his head. "Look, do you want a picture with it anyway? This is a big deal for you, right?"

17

"Forget about it," I said.

So clueless. Me about the city and Silas about me.

His voice was soft. "Consider it your first rule of New York. Everything and everyone changes. Disappears. Sometimes they even reappear, if you're lucky. You get used to it."

Okay, I liked that way of looking at it. Not as much as I would have liked Studio 54, but I guess I had to accept it. My senior project got me here and now it was gone, thanks to my sister, but I was here making something new. A New York pattern? Or maybe just an art pattern? A life pattern?

"Do you ever miss anything that was here?"

"Well . . ." He looked thoughtful. "You're an old soul, Piper. We're alike that way. We want the old, but we're here now. And it does suck. For example, I wish I could go back and take pictures with Weegee."

"What's a Weegee?"

"A Weegee is a who, not a what. He was a crime photographer back in the day, in the 30s and 40s, who captured the real New York, the grit and the grime. He held reality up to the people living in it and said, 'Swallow this. This is what you're doing to the world!'" He seemed to spook himself a little bit by being loud all of a sudden. "Yeah, I wish I could go back there. Making art inspired by all of this?" He made circles with his arms, pointing in all directions to the city. "I dunno, but I have to try. And you have to, too. We'll find new originals," he said. "We'll be new originals." He was smiling at me like he had just fixed everything with his great thoughts. He was trying to be nice, but I couldn't just nix my disappointment that quickly.

"I need to see your art," I said/realized/blurted all at once. "And you need to see mine too, not just the photos I emailed you this summer. Okay? Okay?"

"Deal."

"Really? Tomorrow?"

He cleared his throat and looked away from me. "Sure. Tomorrow."

We shook sweaty hands under the hot lights of the Studio 54 entrance and he didn't let go. We were gross and clammy and there were no lightning bolts between us but it was fine. I knew I was in a weird headspace. I really wanted to be with the Silas I had met over email. I felt like I had been searching for him for so long and his brain was so much further away from mine than I imagined when we were first emailing. I thought we were going to be a thing, right away. But maybe this is what it is to "grow up," to have a real adult thing. I couldn't tell what he was feeling exactly, but his shoulders were relaxed and he looked—I dunno, relieved maybe.

The middle of Times Square is soooo different IRL. I had to beg Silas to walk through it even though it was so late I couldn't imagine it would be busy there. But photos really can't explain how it is to be in the crowds moving so slow and fast at the same time, seeing the shops open so late, how tall the buildings are and the billboards stacked on top of each other advertising Broadway shows and cameras and blue jeans and airlines. It's like being alive inside the Matrix. I told Si that I dreamed of spending a New Year's Eve in Times Square.

"Have fun with that," he said in a nice but you're-on-your-own kind of way.

Folks were selling souvenir postcards and I Heart NY scarves and cheapo fake purses and earrings. I bought a pair of fluorescent pink feather earrings for $5.00. People were bumping into us and by the time we got out of Times Square, the main part, I was like THANK GOD. It was INTENSE!

"How often do you go there?" I asked Si, once we were on the other side.

"Almost never. Unless I'm seeing a show with Mom."

"It's kind of fun, like being at a carnival on steroids or something. How do people ride bikes there? I would run into everyone!"

He nodded at me approvingly. "Yeah, me too. Central Park is better for a ride."

We stopped in a place called Kitchen #1 and got egg rolls and Cokes. People in NYC always seem to be eating. Si said it's because it's a 24-hour city, which is so cool. I know they call it the city that never sleeps, and now I get it. Houston is definitely not a 24-hour city.

There were a lot of people—a lot of homeless people—still on the streets between Times Square and the Web. In Houston, when I saw them by the freeway exits, they were almost like a sad blur. But here, on the same sidewalk, I could see their eyes and they could see mine. We could smell and hear each other.

I stopped Silas in front of two people sitting cross-legged on a stack of flattened cardboard boxes and gave them our last egg rolls.

One of the guys opened the bag and started eating immediately. The other one shut his eyes and seemed to pass out or something against the wall.

"You two lovebirds have a good evening," called the eating guy and Si and I walked on.

"That was nice of you," he said.

"Dude, they're on the street," I said.

"Yeah." He sighed. "You'll get used to it. You have to toughen up to this stuff."

"Stuff?" I said. "You help people when they need help." I sounded like Dad. If he was here, he probably would have bought them a full dinner. I didn't know if I wanted to "toughen up." It sounded heartless.

We were about a block from the Web when Silas stopped.

"What?"

Then he kissed me.

My first Silas kiss wasn't exactly what I expected. It was warm and damp and salty. His mouth was open but tight, his lips almost stiff, and it was kinda funny. We kept turning our heads the same way and it just became hilarious disaster time, our noses everywhere. I think we need to practice more or something. Maybe less thinking on my part. Maybe less weirdness on his. Maybe more—or just any—fireworks next time? If there's a next time?

Then we walked to the Webster steps and we kind of stood there awkwardly.

"Well, good night," he finally said, so I kissed him again quickly on the cheek and ran in.

It's a bad sign if I didn't want to try for another long kiss, right? Because it wasn't really awkward-fun, it was just

awkward-awkward. He can't think that was actually good.
I hope not.

Oscar, the Webster security guard, buzzed me in and waved to
me with a rolled-up copy of his newspaper. A couple of drunky-
drunk-drunk girls were sitting next to each other on one of the
old-school pink lobby couches, scrolling on a phone, laughing
their butts off. Si had said, "Everybody knows everybody" and I
would do anything to know somebody—somebody besides just
Silas right now. Where's my Kit? ☹

I took the most perfect shower and thought of Si, wishing our
kiss had been better. I wonder if he did, too. I texted Kit about
our kiss and my #NYSeen drawings. And now I can't write
anymore. Meeting Carlyle and Kennedy IN PERSON and so
excited—I need to sleep so I don't look like a mess! Sketching
then bed.

8/13 9:47 am The Caf

A Webster Breakfast, a.k.a. "the best deal in town": #NYSeen

Mom's voice mail early this morning was all about my sister's new baby, who is by far the cutest member of our family:

"Hi sweetie! How's Day 4? We're heading home with Baby Savannah today. She is so adorable! Ronnie is such a proud father and Marli is on Motrin and still groggy from everything, but, well, she's still Marli. Dad says hi. Call us tonight, okay? Love you!" Marli must be EXTRA EXTRA MARLI now. I'm so freaking relieved I don't have to see that, even if I'm missing quality baby niece time. I hope she's better at being a mom than a big sister.

And a text from Silas at 4:03 am: I had a good time, one of the best I've had in a while. Thanks for the hat. And let's make a date for you to see my art.

Just answered: YES! YES YES YES!

I can't wait to get to see his work IN PERSON! I half-wish I wasn't meeting Carlyle today—but, Si will have to wait!

I like Si. I do. Well, I like this him anyway, the one that writes me—even if in person, I'm not sure how much I LIKE-like him, which is weird. I thought we would be more, that we would get each other more, and faster. Even the text makes me happy, easier with him, than when we are next to each other. I dunno. Last night was nice, but just that. It was like hanging out with a bud. The kiss wasn't horrible, but it was more like a we-should-be-having-a-kiss-kiss than we-want-to-kiss-each-other-kiss. Maybe I'm overthinking it. I wish Kit was here to talk this through. Texted her again, and got this:

It's okay not to be in love with him, girl. You just met!

She's right, but I was dumb and hoping it would just be perfect immediately between us. He's not what he seemed, which isn't bad, but I thought he was different than he actually is. I blame his amazing emails. Or maybe it was how I was reading them. I dunno.

The metal fan that hangs in the ceiling corner of my Web apartment screeched all night and morning in my room, so I didn't hear Mom's call or Si's text. I'd unplug it but it's too hot. This place is a throwback but the fan is throw-OUT. Gotta get a new one. I never imagined living with no AC. We couldn't in Houston.

What I'm wearing (French/old-school hip-hop mash-up)
to meet Kennedy & Carlyle:

❋ cuffed boyfriend jeans

❦ platform wedges

❊ striped shirt

❦ red headscarf

❊ red lipstick

Should have gotten my hair cut before I left Houston.
I'm Shaggytown, USA.

8/13 4:15 pm

We met near Washington Square. I couldn't stop staring at that amazing arch. Students were going into the NYU bookstore with parents and coming out with backpacks and sweatshirts. Never thought I would be jealous of classes and school, but there I was. I wish I could have already met with Helen, I could be working on my financial aid stuff today. Every time I think of how much money I'm going to need for school in January I feel like my whole torso is being wrung out.

Anyway, I met Kennedy, Carlyle's assistant who I've been emailing with since they first got in touch this summer, at the Grey Dog, this funky little café on University Place. I walked there from 34th Street, which was like whatever, too many blocks.

I totally regretted my dumb wedges and didn't wear enough deodorant, I was so sweaty, but hey I got to see A LOT of the city. I don't know how New York girls in their cool summer dresses manage to wear cute shoes and not tear their feet up. The style here is bonkers—extra-good, better than anything I could have imagined or seen on TV or online. You have to be here to really see it and live it and get it. Like the guy in the black leather romper and white tank top rocking zebra-print socks and flip-flops singing opera at the top of his lungs, standing on the park bench. Such a #NYSeen. I had to sketch a quick pic of him and tuck it into his cardboard box that he had on the ground for money. Left a dollar, too.

Then I met Kennedy at lunch. Not Carlyle!!! But long story short: Kennedy is the BEST!!!!

Kennedy's outfit (tropical-beachy-cool AF-professional?):

❀ brown harem pants

❀ tan huaraches

❀ a faded blue tee that you could tell was like $300 or
   something ridic

He is like an even cuter boho Chance the Rapper, if that's possible. He hugged me like we were already besties and when he did, he smelled like plants, like expensive-earthy. Thankfully, he paid for lunch. Mine was 25 bucks!

"OK, now." He sat up straight and pulled a folder from his brown leather messenger bag that was definitely pre-distressed, the scratches were too strategic. "Carlyle sends his regards. He had an investor meeting he couldn't miss since he's missed the last three. You know how it is, bottom-line shit, doll." Bottom line like, how much money Carlyle's making. "Anyway, he's talking numbers at the office, which means we get to talk all about YOU." He wiggled in his seat. "Tell me everything, lady."

I told him about my flight, last night's dinner with Silas, the Webster. I wasn't sure how honest I could be about the Web— and my tiny room there and the whiny fan and the constant smell of air freshener—considering he was my boss and it was his boss footing my bill. But I wanted to say something.

"I like it, but that place has got some seriously . . . out of touch rules. It's very Bell Jar. Like no guys upstairs? 'Beau' parlors—I didn't even know what those were! And that they're Broadway themed?" I started laughing. "I know it's New York and all, and the Hamilton one is at least current, but the rest are so corny. Do people really like Phantom of the Opera?"

He cackled. "Tell me about it, right? The apartment we originally had lined up for you fell through, a space in Donald Judd's old building, but, like, troubles. It's vintage, I know, but it's fabulous. I can't believe they still have the 'NO MALES allowed past the first-floor' rule."

I nodded. "Oh yeah!"

"That is too retro!" We both were laughing.

"My girl Rashida lived there when she first moved here. Not many people get to live there, so it's kind of famous. You're welcome, lucky duck."

"Your girlfriend?" I kind of thought girls weren't his thing.

"Mm, best friend," he said. Winked at me, like, they aren't. "So, this guy, Silas. He's your man?"

"I, uh, don't know. I thought maybe there was a chance, but yeah. I'm not sure now. Maybe?" I swallowed hard.

"Play it aloof, I like it." He leaned in, sipping on his iced tea.

"Mmm . . ." I tried to think how to explain. Distance isn't my thing. If I like someone, I really like him, I'm all in. But that didn't seem like something I could share with him right away without seeming like a clingy freak.

It sucks because the one person I was counting on knowing here was Silas and so far that was weird. I don't feel lonely, but still. Maybe a little. I'm excited for the Web mixer this week. Maybe I'll meet someone else.

"It's just, Silas and I just met in real life, even though we've been emailing since I got my acceptance letter to CFA. He was supposed to be my student mentor. And, real life is . . . different."

"Oh god, the drama." He was clearly loving the goss. "Let me tell you one thing. You seem smart, Piper. Do NOT tie yourself down to someone. Been there, done that. Not worth it. Especially when you first get to the city." He rolled his eyes.

"Oh. Is your ex here?"

"My ex is nowhere. Any more questions, Nosy Nancy?"

He was being funny, not a jerk.

"Um, yeah. So, are you like a native New Yorker?" I tried to put air quotes around "native New Yorker" so he wouldn't think I was a 100% lame newbie. I could seriously not ever imagine a better way of growing up than here, taking the train to school, shopping at the little convenience stores, etc. I always thought NY kids must be the coolest and he seemed like the coolest.

"Of course. I grew up in Washington Heights, now I'm L-E-S. Lower East Side."

"Oh! You grew up right here!"

He gave me a look like what are you talking about.

"Like Washington Square Park!" I waved at the park across the street from us.

He looked at me like he felt sorry for me.

"Different Washington, lady. North Manhattan. Across from the Bronx."

I should find the Bronx on a subway map.

"Then Carlyle discovered me and I've been working with him ever since."

He was def. giving me the short story. "Discovered you where?"

"Downtown. Friend's party on Thompson Street. Girl, things were out of control back then, and I stumbled into him, you know how it is, and like, it was just magique." He waved his fingers like he was a magician.

"Oh." I didn't know how it was. But then I thought of all the parties Andy Warhol used to host. These kinds of parties still happened and cool artists still met at them and like, maybe I was going to be in this world with these people.

"But like . . . how did 'it was just magique' turn into a job?" Also, what was his job? I thought he was just Carlyle's assistant, but if that was how he'd met Carlyle, it seemed like he must be more. "So, you're an artist, too? Right? What kind of artist?"

He chewed slowly and gave me a weird stare.

"Video. Okay?"

"Why wouldn't it be? Is it like porn or something?" I thought I was being funny, and thank god he laughed.

"You." He sighed. "You're exactly right. Of course it's okay, it's more than okay. I directed very short films online. You know Vine?" He winked and poked at his salad.

"The app? Yeah, sure."

He smiled as he chewed and I could tell he liked me when I said that.

"I was making Vines, like serious Vines, like getting paid for Vines for advertisers and a boutique marketing start-up. That was my platform, my preferred medium. I loved the immediacy, the efficiency. A one-two punch." He jabbed his fists. "I was like the Muhammad Ali of Vines, and then overnight, poof! No more. So. I'm still doing video when I want, how I want, but I'm also taking a break from it. Change is all there really is anyway, so why not assist for a while? It shakes up the burnout."

"Sure," I said, trying to be cool and less Nosy Nancy. I really want to know what made him burn out. I can't imagine burning out on art ever. "Change is all there really is." I love that.

"Carlyle offered me a chance to regroup at just the right time. You'll love him. BTDubs"—he handed me a folder filled with papers—"here's your homework. Take this, read it, and put your Jane Hancock and initials on the required pages."

"This is—?"

"Your contract and the copies. You can't get in the studio or do anything with Carlyle until it's signed. It's super basic."

"Yes! I'm dying to start!" I pulled a paintbrush out of my backpack. "See? Always ready! If I sign today, I can start today, right?"

"You'll be busy soon enough." He smiled and I felt like a total overeager nerd trying to be the teacher's pet, but I thought he would like that I was prepared.

I pulled out a pen and started flipping through it.

"You have a few days to get it back to me. So take your time with it, speed demon. It's a contract, it's legally binding, blah blah blah." He looked at his vibrating watch and practically jumped out of his seat. "I need to get back! See you soon, Piper lady— and welcome to New York." He blew me a kiss and was gone.

I got the rest of my iced coffee in a to-go cup and found a bench back in WS Park (not Heights). Read the first couple pages and signed it. Super basic, like Kennedy said.

- Assist Carlyle and Kennedy with general tasks (including picking up supplies, delivery duties). Check.

- Make pieces (replicas of my original piece, 8 total) for his New York Fashion Week show. Check!

- Work and contribute to the first gallery show after NYFW, tentatively scheduled for mid-October (about a month after the show). A billion checks!

Less basic, more scary:

- Carlyle has the option to reject my pieces for the NYFW show. If he doesn't like them or if he rejects them, I pay back the cost of materials, and all the expenses of hiring me (my apartment, today's lunch?!? That's not terrifying at all. I can't imagine not working with him AND having to pay him back AND not being able to stay in NY. My work just has to be extra great).

And:

- He also has the first rights to any pieces I create in his studio for future shows. Yikes. It IS his studio, but still, if I make one extra thing in there, if he wants it, he just automatically gets it? What if I want it? I'm probably overthinking all this but still, I don't see how you can claim something you've never even seen before. I guess I have to find my own studio then—or just make stuff he really hates—because I have to make my own art here, too!

The best parts:

- I get to work with him and learn from him. I can't wait to see how he works. We're going to be working side by side, I bet.

- He pays my rent at the Webster, plus I get a contractor stipend—$800 every two weeks! That's $400 a week to MAKE ART! I'm an official contractor!

Even though I didn't start school this semester, I'm not stuck at home and I am starting my real life in New York, and figuring out the new REAL ME. It's just all so good. And I meet Carlyle tomorrow!

I bought some "cheap" Adidas in a store called Shoe Mania on the way back to the Web. $60 is not my idea of a sale, but my blistered heels are like something out of a horror movie. Drew this on a flyer by an NYU building and added it online for Kit and Enzo.

Texted them: #NYSeen. Streets of desire, feet on fire!

K texted me: Why ya got Hot Feet, Pipes? and Enzo just sent a thumbs-up with StilettoLife. If only. And a few minutes later there were comments from a few users I didn't even know. A smiley-face emoji from @Shoeless&Clueless and some perv @mike1234 wrote Sexy Toes. Ewww—PASS. Someone else wrote U should use pepper-mint oil if your feet r tired! It werks! Okaaay.

So people are liking these posts! Apparently the hashtag is one people actually search on. Huh. That's cool. Maybe I won't change my account to private after all. I thought maybe I should hide the sketches because they aren't 100, but people like them. So okay, #NYSeen stays seen.

8/14 9:15 am

Woke up thinking—maybe I was dreaming—about Mo's probation and my contract. Maybe because now I'm worried about getting kicked out of NYC if I can't make work that Carlyle approves. Now it's serious art focus time.

I grabbed a juice and many coffees in the Webster caf. Everyone must be sleeping in—I don't know how because there must be 50 garbage trucks outside making the worst screechy noises.

Okay, dropping the nervous thoughts for now and getting ready to meet Carlyle and to actually work. My hands need to paint and I'm all hyped up.

8/14 10:18 pm Chillin in the Webster Cats beau parlor because too hot in my room and also why not. Cats R kewl.

Funny NYC moment:

I got to the studio early and couldn't get in without Kennedy/keys, so I went to the convenience store—found out they are called bodegas—across the street and bought an iced coffee, my constant companion. The guy behind the counter gave me my change and said, "We're open 24 hours a day now!"

"Oh? Okay. Congratulations, I guess? This is my first—"

"Yep, yep, everyone wanted us to be 24/7, so now we're 24/7. Must keep the customers happy." He introduced himself. He seemed happy to talk to me, like we were old friends. "Hamid."

"Piper." I smiled back at him, and we did a funny same-side handshake.

"You should meet my son, Freddy!" He tilted his chin up and grinned like, maybe you're interested? "He's single! He works here in the evening." Hamid had a huge grandpa beard and a smiley, wrinkly face. Freddy would have to be at least 30 or 40, then. Maybe since Silas isn't working out . . . JK.

Anyway, I met Kennedy outside of PS 305. It's an old public school, that's what the PS stands for. Carlyle's studio is a rented room underneath two theaters that are also in the building, and it looks like it used to be a mini theater or something because there's a little stage area and those lights we had in our high school auditorium and theater department, I think they're called birdie lights. Really hot and meant for stages, not usually studios.

There was a little natural light creeping in from a rectangular window and it smelled like wet tennis shoes and armpits. Inspiring? No. Perspiring? Yes. Not that it had to be glamorous, but it felt like the wrong kind of space to make art in and way too damp. I have to get some room spray or a candle or something. Now that I met him, I can't imagine Carlyle working in there. And he doesn't, it turns out. It's just a rental for his assistants.

So Kennedy let me in and we walked around the rickety, warped second floor and he was pointing out the other theaters and studio spaces. Everything was musty, rusty, or dusty. He showed me the sinks, where to store materials, the bathrooms in the hallway—what is it with shared bathrooms in this city, that's how the bathrooms are at the Webster, too???—and then we turned the corner right into him: CARLYLE CAMPBELL. The most casually glorious person I've ever seen. He almost definitely has little sunbeams radiating from his face.

Carlyle:

🍂 beat-up red tennis shoes

🍂 dark blue skinny jeans

🍂 black Sex Pistols T-shirt

🍂 short gray-blond hair

🍂 square pink face

🍂 the whitest teeth I have ever seen

Why was I expecting him to look older, or like wearing a cape or something? He sounded so fabulous and important on the phone and here he kind of looked like a younger version of Dad. I thought he would look a lot, lot older, but he looked like he would play the Cool Dad in a movie.

"Hello, Piper." So calm, so relaxed.

"Hi." I tried to stay cool, because even though he seemed more normal than I expected he was still CARLYLE CAMPBELL and I was still just me. I bet he was used to people gawking at him.

"Yes," he said, answering a question I didn't ask. "I am Carlyle Campbell. Welcome to your new home, Piper. Please forgive my absence these last few days. The demands on my time are crushing." Cah-rush-ing. He smiled. His teeth were so white he looked like he had a mouthful of mints. His arms were open, and I went to hug him, because that's what I thought he wanted and also I just felt so thankful for him helping me get here, but he stepped away, closing himself off.

"No touching!" Kennedy said at the same time.

"Oh . . . sorry." Huh? I wasn't going to wipe my hands on him or anything. And my hands were clean anyway. Why put your arms out for a hug if you didn't want one?

"It's wonderful to finally meet the creator of that compelling creation I saw this summer, Piper," Carlyle said. "The one on the computer." Spoken like a man who is not too tech-savvy. "Now, let's have a look at it."

"My art?" I stalled. I didn't bring it with me to the studio because it was broken, but I wouldn't have brought it even if it wasn't broken. What was I supposed to do, just lug it around in the summer heat?

"I thought I was just coming to see the space today. It's not here yet."

"Then . . ." Carlyle's smile dropped a notch. "Why are we here?"

"I thought it was so we could meet. I'm so happy to meet you, seriously! Thank you for hiring me, Mr. Campbell," I said, trying to sound innocent and apologetic.

"I'll need to see it soon," he said, sounding flat and a little irritated. "Next week at the very latest. I'm not coming back this weekend. And it's Carlyle."

It took me a second to realize what he meant, that I shouldn't call him Mr. Campbell. He seemed like someone who maybe had trouble thinking of himself as old.

As he swaggered down the wooden stairs, almost like a little dance, he repeated to himself, all breathy, like a loud whisper that we weren't supposed to hear, "Anxiety is an alien. Anxiety is an alien. Anxiety is an alien." Then loudly, "Coming, Kennedy?"

"I'll call you tonight," Kennedy said quietly. "Don't worry. You can work 24/7." OH, can I? "Here. That"—he pointed down the stairs to a small black box on the corner near the front door—"unlocks the front door and the studio. Security code is 1202."

"Oh! My birthday!" That was a good sign!

He smiled. "Well, look at that. Now I know you won't forget to lock up whenever you leave."

Carlyle cleared his throat.

I whispered, "Does he hate me?" and Kennedy gave a little tsk and said, "Carlyle doesn't hate anyone. Except people who call him Mr. Campbell."

"I was trying to be polite!" I whispered.

"Kennedy," Carlyle called. "We need to leave. Unless you would like us to be late." Kennedy strode down the stairs and they were gone.

So, I started working as soon as they left. Thank goodness the studio was stocked with all the supplies I needed, at least to start. I should be much further along, I should have 1 of 8 pieces already completed, but instead it's all from scratch. How in hell am I going to recreate my heart piece perfectly in days? And give it enough time to dry? Lucky for me Carlyle isn't coming back till next week. His intensely relaxed vibe is weird. So aggro-chill.

I just got to this city. I don't want to give him a reason to tell me to go home. Trying to channel the mindset I was in making my original: graduation, leaving my family, Kit and Enzo and me. Especially me and Enzo. Figuring out how to be friends after we broke up was so tough because all I wanted to do was still hang out and laugh and for it to be as normal as it always was. Maybe some of my original piece was about him too. After all, I was trying to put my broken heart back together. Jeez, I didn't really think about that until now.

But now I'm alone, I already graduated, my family is a whole different family now with my sister's baby and also with me gone, having some space from Marli, not having to see her, or feel her in my life every day. I don't feel desperate for my freedom now. But I do feel desperate to please Carlyle. Those are very different desperations and maybe they make different art.

So much has changed in my actual heart—and life—it feels like that should change in my art, too. I don't know how to keep the heart the same size. Suddenly I want to take up more space. But Carlyle's runway isn't the place for that. This work is for him. My piece has to be the same as it ever was. Even if the artist is different.

I wonder if there's ever been an artist who created the same piece all her life, and how would that piece, or pieces, change as her life changed? Maybe I could do something like that. Maybe I am doing something like that, and I just didn't know. Maybe I'll never be able to do anything but that. I remember hearing that writers tell the same stories and present the same themes over and over in their work; even when they think they're branching out, they never really are.

This is a J-O-B now, not just A-R-T.

My feels are making me hungry for pistachios + licorice, my new salty and sugary fave from the Web vending machine. I hope Maria the manager doesn't mind me just hanging out alone in the beau parlors. Nobody else is using them anyway. I have to buy a real fan for my room. Though the squeaky sound does break up the loneliness a bit.

8/15 9:15 am Nooooo!

I stepped in dog poop on 33rd Street this morning!!! I swear I can still smell poop on my brand-new Adidas in the studio even though I rinsed them in the sink. Yuck yuck yuck. Come on, New Yorkers! It's too early for this shit. LITERALLY.

I gotta paint.

8/15 11 pm

Better tonight, less street poop and more happy news. Breaking Friendship News, actually: I met someone!

#FriendshipFeels #NYSeen

The mixer happened in the Webster first floor community room, the one by the backyard garden. I need to sketch more out there. It's pretty!!!

Maria, our manager, was playing party hostess, jangling her NY charm bracelets and not wearing the same pale-pink Webster polo I had been seeing her wear every day since I moved here, but a white muscle shirt that had NEW YORK CITY printed in big black letters on it.

The so-yummy table spread:

- Junior's Cheesecake—like if a milkshake was a brick

- H&H Bagels—I snuck one in my bag and brought it to my room in case of a midnight snack attack

- Nathan's hot dogs—I had one and a half, mustard only, natch (another gold-yellow!)

About 10 or 11 people showed up. I looked for the yoga girl I see a lot but she wasn't there. One woman in a denim pantsuit and headscarf grabbed a hot dog and left. She looked too cool for the mix anyway. And the two chickies who I always see laughing and texting in the lobby were hanging out doing the same thing up there. I thought about approaching them but it was like jumping into a game of Double Dutch. This girl wearing cool-ass cat's-eye glasses was talking to Maria and as soon as I walked up, she walked away. I was starting to feel majorly dorky, and maybe Maria sensed it, because she said, "Angie just got called to work. That magazine she's temping for is launching next week and they're working her like a dog. Poor thing. This city, the Webster—it's all what you make of it," she said, like some kind of newbie-whisperer. "If you really want to be here, you have to make it yours." She looked past my shoulder at the girl standing behind me, loading her plate. "How 'bout Grace over there? She's new, too."

40

I haven't had to try to make new friends since I was a freshman, not really. It's easy in high school because it's just like built-in. You're in homeroom together. You're in art class together. But a new city and new friends? Hi, I'm Too Desperate, what's your name? I know Carlyle and Kennedy and Silas and Mo, but it's not the same.

I walked over to this chill girl with outta control curly Lorde hair who was digging into her plate of veggies and hummus on a bun.

"No dogs left?" I glanced at the burbling steam tray.

"No dogs allowed." She laughed. "I'm a vegetarian." I tried to casually hide my dog behind the cheesecake and she laughed.

"Oh no, you do you."

"Did you just move in to the Webster, too?" I said.

"A few days ago. I'm Grace."

"Piper." We tapped carrots like they were beers.

"This place is a trip," she said. "The rooms are so small!"

"Here's to livin' that Smurf life," I laughed.

"Where are you from? I hear your accent!"

"I sound Texan?" God, I had no idea. Outside of a few short family trips to Louisiana, I've only lived at home in Houston and everybody sounds the same there.

"So Southern!"

She laughed and I asked where she was from.

"Salt Lake City. Smaller city by a hair." She held a carrot between her fingers like a cigarette and winked. She's funny.

"So, are you going to school?" I asked.

"Nope, I graduated a few years back. I got a gig I couldn't refuse."

"Oh, what?" I said, all excited.

"I'm assisting a writer, she's my mentor and like, she's every-thing. I'm also a writer."

"Who is it? Can you say?"

She moved her big curls over her shoulder and blocked her face, so that nobody could hear her. "Eileen June Haley. Incredible, right?"

Hi, I'm a dummy and I have no idea who that is. "No. Effing. Way."

She was nodding like, I know, right? Another thing/person to know: Eileen June Haley!

As if she could read my mind, she kept whispering. "She's a political activist and a professor, besides being one of the major contemporary poets working today, and I'm a poet, and a lot of my writing has . . . 'an edge' or so I've been told. Anyway, we're a good match. I help her with research, and she pushes me in my work and I get to work with my creative hero. And she's helping me get into grad school. Oh my god, I sound so awful. Sorry, just a HUGE poetry nerd."

She didn't sound awful at all. She was babbling like a crazy person about contemporary poetry. I liked her. "Grad school for poetry?"

"Gender and Media Studies. If she recommends me, I'm as good as in. I'm going to be a part of her reading night series at the Café Angelou, too."

"Angelou, like Maya Angelou?"

"Exactly. Want to come?"

"I loved I Know Why the Caged Bird Sings in school! I think it was one of the only books I actually liked. Cool!" I was excited. A poetry reading in New York just sounded so . . . New York!

"Oh, I'm reading my work there, not Maya's," Grace laughed. "The owner, Lita, who's an old friend of Eileen June's, also knew Maya."

"That's so cool! I'm in!"

"I'm also doing this weekly writing workshop thingy she signed me up for, but at least that doesn't start for another week."

I took a bite of cheesecake. Jay-zus. She was working for someone like I was, PLUS taking a class and planning for more school and doing readings on the side just for fun—and I hadn't even gone to college yet. All I was doing was running around New York trying to figure stuff out and recreating my one real piece of art for Carlyle, then 7x more, and stepping in poop. I'm going to have to up my game if I hang with Grace. Is everyone in this city doing fantastic things? Because it feels like it. And I'm apparently not doing enough.

"What about you?" she asked.

"Um, I'm working for an artist who is having his first show at Fashion Week. I'm an artist, too." I was hoping I wasn't jinxing myself.

She put her empty plate on the table and grabbed my arms.

"Who? Do you get tickets to the shows? Who are you wearing? I've always wanted to ask that! I've been subscribing to Vogue since my bat mitzvah. It's my total Achilles heel—or should I say Achilles kitten heel—and I know there are so many ethical issues with the fash industry. But, le sigh. I love a good look. The problem with being a poet is that you learn to appreciate beauty you can't afford! Total Poet Problem!" She laughed. "So, who's the artist?"

I loved that she was geeking out. I had thought she might be too cool and too smart to care about fashion. I tried to hide my answer with my hair the way she had.

"It's Carlyle Campbell?" I didn't know if she would know who he was or if she would like him once she knew who he was. "I don't know anything yet about how his show will actually work," I said. "I'm just finishing my art."

"What's his line like?"

"Oh, like his clothes? I don't really know about that side of it."

44

She was clearly puzzled.

"So wait, what are you doing for him? What are these pieces?"

I babbled the explanation of Kit posting a pic of my senior project on her website, Kennedy finding it, and Carlyle hiring me to work for them this fall. "Then Carlyle wanted me to make replicas of my senior project, seven copies to be exact, so eight total, and he's using them as props on their runway. I'm his assistant, at least until school starts in January."

"Can I see your piece? Is it still online?"

I pulled up Kit's site on my phone and then clicked to my page and she had a little heart attack—ha!—over my piece.

Now it was my turn to feel relief. We spent the next twenty minutes talking about fashion and how we both have shopping problems and how we both wish we had an extra million or so in our bank accounts and how she wishes she had been a designer but has no skills and then I showed her some of Enzo's stuff too and she liked it. Also, she's engaged to a guy named Evan in Salt Lake! I wanted to ask her a zillion more questions, but she had to take off.

"Wanna meet for breakfast tomorrow? Around 9?"

"Sure!"

"See ya then!" She gave me a giant, mom-type hug and was off.

We both burnt our toast in the shitty toaster this morning. Destined to be friends.

Text from Si: I just ate an egg roll and thought of you. I will spare you the details of what Mo said about the history of the egg roll but Mo has a lot of thoughts on the matter. ☺

Texted back emoji praise/amen hands.

Si: Loaded down with homework. Want to have our art date this week?

Me: Sounds good.

Yay for art dates and new friends! Going to the TV lounge, since there's no TV in my teeny-weeny apartment/room with its tiny bed, tiny bookcase, tiny closet, tiny sink, and tiny, super-whiny

#NYSeen

metal fan hanging in the corner over the bed. TINY for DAYS. It's cozy-cute and oh did I mention, TINY?

8/16 5 pm-ish Just happened, in studio

Carlyle, who I've spent time with officially twice now, was just standing there looking at my original (well, my new original) and the first duplicate piece, circling them, swiping his chin back and forth like a windshield wiper, and sighing a lot. How did he have so much breath? I swear like every breath was a sigh.

"Where is your control? I sense too much urgency. These sloppy edges . . . ?" He trailed off without actually asking a question about the edges, and I stood there in silence with a lump in my throat. Everything about how he looked—relaxed brown leather bomber jacket, black V-neck tee, baggy blue jeans, Stan Smiths—was so casual. But the air around him was tight and suffocating and scary. And all I could think was if he hates them, I go back. If he doesn't pay me, I go back. I have to afford school. How am I going to afford school? I have to get through Fashion Week with him. Repeat repeat repeat.

"Oh, I'll fix them," I tried, attempting to sound just as casual. "They're still WIPs."

C (cutting me off): "Your pieces are infused with a manic quality, momentum, an unexpected energy. I wouldn't have recognized either as the same piece I saw online."

He put his (surprisingly soft) hands around my face. Uh, does the no-touching rule not apply the other way?

"However: Piper, the more I look at it, the more I like it. Maybe even more than the one online. This feels alive. It has energy,

ne new ones will still have to be 100% polished. I trust you'll
ce your newfound enthusiasm with the elegance of the original. Capisce?" Kennedy gave me a secret thumbs-up behind
Carlyle.

"Capisce. Yes!"

Elegance. Elegance. My brain's been repeating it like a mantra.

"And I promise it's not all work and no play, Piper. Don't look so
sullen."

Note to self: "Elegance" as a mantra turns my face sullen.

"It's just Fashion Week! Let's all remember that! We're just pursuing
our dreams here! I'm not going to die at Fashion Week! I'm not
going into cardiac arrest if some critic spits at me, am I? Are we?"

Uh, was he? It seemed like maybe.

"Just don't make any mistakes and we'll be fine," Carlyle smiled
hard at me, his bottom lip curled over his top. I couldn't tell if
he was psyching himself up or trying to psych me out. Then he
whispered something to Kennedy and literally ran out the door.

I get it, being freaked out about art, about his show, about all of
this. I'm also freaking out. My work isn't a total disaster? So I
saved myself for now but I have to focus on elegance, apply
elegance. My plan is now: make a piece a day, dry them, and have
them ready in time for the show. I got this. Inspiration is for
amateurs.

8/16 11 pm

Worked late, so no dinner at the Web for me again tonight. I
grabbed a black-and-white cookie for lunch at the bodega.

Hamid's little gray cat, Daniel, was walking around behind the register like he was the owner. "Piper, I told Freddy about you!"

I gave him $5. "I don't know if I'm ready for Freddy, but thanks."

"Everybody loves Freddy! You'll love him! He's a good boy!" He waved bye with Daniel's little paw and I walked up 2nd Avenue, not crossing back to the west side until I reached 34th. Did a lot of thinking and the Degas quote Ms. Adams, my high school art teacher, wrote on the board last semester popped into my brain. "Art is not what you see, but what others make you see." Okay okay.

8/17 1 pm

I'm in Carlyle's studio and I'm not procrastinating by journaling, I swear, but I'm painting myself into circles. The faces that were in the first piece have changed. I used my cell to stare at photos of the fam for inspiration, since they inspired Map, my original piece. I see my family and I remember how it felt, forming the shape, the memory of it still in my hands. It wasn't that long ago. But I don't feel the now-me anywhere in this new original or the copies. I'm outside of it. I can't inject me into it. Weird. I've never had so much trouble making art, it's never been a source of anything other than . . . safety, I guess. Now it feels scary and unfamiliar and I'm sure if I was Adams I would think this was just GREAT but in real life it's the worst.

I don't know how I'm going to get so many done. Where am I? Seriously. WHERE AM I? I'm not fast enough. Since when do I have painter's block? Is that really a thing? I've always been able to find my way. I'll just mix the reds and blues until I feel it. The paint will trigger it in me. It has to. We're in this together. Time for music, time for movement. Elegance. Work.

Worked all day again and need a break and just in time, Si and I hung out! I was hoping we might find our groove, but we are still just totally in the friend zone. We both had on black tank tops which was dorky-dorky matchy-matchy.

So, I met Si tonight outside of his—OUR!—school! He promised me a full tour, but it was after hours so there wasn't much to see. The campus is a few buildings around the Chelsea neighborhood and a little south. Some of the classes are taught in row houses, actually former stables!!!, that border Washington Square and used to belong to NYU but CFA bought them. Only seniors get to take classes in those. Supposedly Henry James or Edith Wharton lived in them. It's so crazy. They were here once and now I'm here. Andy was here once and now I'm here. The city makes room for new people, but there's all these creative ghosts floating around. That makes me feel more connected to the creators who were here before me, and before them. Such a long line of ancestor-artists who knew: this is the place. I know I am supposed to be here like they knew they were supposed to be here. This is all starting to feel so much more real-real.

"Are you ready?" Si asked when I walked up and I said, "Yes, of course!" He backed up because I was kind of loud and we both laughed. My heart was beating extra fast and I felt like I was about to see my entire future, a flash-forward into everything I have wanted to be. I was taking my very first steps in my dream school, where I was going to study the greats and join their ranks.

I followed him down a long hallway on the sixth floor of the main building. I wanted to see his photos and everything else.

I was all woo-woo before I even saw anything, hoping it would be the stuff that made me finally get the real him. He pulled out a key.

"You get your own keys for classrooms?"

"All second-year photographers get one for lab. For after-hours processing and homework."

He opened the door, and flipped on the light.

There were big tables lining the lab, a darkroom off to the side, and lots of cameras, old and new, displayed in glass cases. He handed me his portfolio. I started flipping through the plastic pages. They were all these cool, overexposed close-up portraits of people. The more out of focus, the more interesting.

- an older man with gray hair and stubble in a park

- a series of a girl with bright red lips wearing what looked like a doll's dress, soft black hair braided and hanging over her shoulder

- another one of her, looking over her shoulder at the camera

- another (!) of her, eyes shut, huge eyelashes

- his eye, his elbow, his knees—I know they were definitely him and his work . . . these were the only things I had been able to find online when I googled him

"What do you think?" He was circling around me like a shark.

"These . . . this girl in the photo? She's special, huh?" I tried to buy some time. What would Adams say?

He shrugged. "I needed a character. What about the rest of the photos? The old guy?"

"They're really . . ." I searched for the right word. "They're really set, y'know? Like rigid? Stiff, cold! But that's what you're going for, right?"

He looked at the ground.

"Am I saying the wrong thing?" Si said he liked the truth, or at least he liked it when Mo tells it.

"You're not the first one to say that." He looked green and so I tried to make it right.

"But what I do know? I'm not even in school yet. And stiff isn't bad. It's just formal, right?"

"Don't dumb yourself down," he said. "Trust your judgment. Tell me what you think of this."

I followed Si to the opposite corner in the back of the room. Here, the walls were covered with black-and-white photos of New Yorkers—the subjects looked staged but Si swore they weren't—with tabloid-y headlines Velcro'd on the top of them. Sometimes the words didn't quite match up with the photos, but they jarred in an interesting way that made you want to look at the pictures closer, like there was a story there.

"What do you think?" He was pacing again. I walked back into the center of the room. The words shaped the photos into more directed stories, something he wasn't achieving with the photos by themselves.

But before I could answer, he said, "I thought about what you said the other night at dinner, when you suggested I should let the world in more, instead of trying to push it away or fight it. So, I'm playing around with the idea of bringing the world to the pictures, but look." He pulled off one of the titles. "What if I let the audience decide to change the art by changing the news, the headlines? The meaning of the photos could be switched in seconds, depending on how people see them? What do you think?"

"I—"

"I just started playing with the idea, it's not refined, obviously."

"No, I know—"

"You hate them. You hate my idea."

"Silas! Shut up for a second!" I laughed. "Lemme get a word in."

He slumped on the stool and clapped his hands like have-at-it.

"I like it."

"That's it?"

"No," I said. "You haven't given me a second to—"

"You're the one who wanted to see my work so badly!"

"Jesus," I said. "I was going to say I think it's amazing, very right now, and still somehow timeless. That I wish I was doing something like this!"

Dude-artists are such babies!!!

"Yeah," he said, breathing hard like he'd run a mile just to hear what I had to say. "Well, thanks. Like I said, they're just my WIPs. I'm not even certain they're worth sharing with anyone else."

"Silas, hello, I'm complimenting your stuff. I want to see more of those photos. The headlines you're choosing are bonkers, dude—in a good way!"

I was serious. I really did like it. I was really happy that this was the work Silas was doing. I think it's smart and maybe important without being pretentious. There's something really honest about it, and not just for artists, but for a regular person too.

I tried to get him to talk about it more, but we called it a night after we got Mr. Softee. (Expensive but really sweet and cold and good!)

He finally lightened up once we started talking about my own nerves working for C and Grace, my new poet friend. I'm guessing this is just another Shy-Si moment. Even I hate when new people see my stuff for the first time. But I hope he knew I was being serious—that I really did think it was special.

8/19 7:28 am Quick sketch

Business dude on bench on 3rd Ave clipping his toenails! I tucked the sketch into the bus bench where he was sittin' & clippin'. I hope he'll get the hint.

I'm sure my followers are gonna have some choice words for this one. So happy they can experience this nasty with me! They loved my sketch of Hamid's cat and someone named Frankie4Paws wrote: Oh, draw my kitteh! and I replied If you want a commission, lemme know. I hope they say yes!!! $$$

8/20 8:30 am

I've got the jumpy jitters. What the hell was I thinking? I'm not a machine. There's no way I can complete four more pieces this week in that hot studio.

54

I'm going to be pulling all nighters until the show. I need some major creative inspiration. Going for a walk. Maybe Grace is around?

I'm back after the most amazing day flying solo—no Si (school), no Grace (work), all me!

I went south and ended up at my new favorite place in the world, the High Line. It's this gorgeous park about the width of a small street, elevated high above the city along old subway tracks and lined with benches and reclining chairs like by a pool, except made of wood, with people hanging out on them, fully dressed with sunglasses—no bathing suits—sipping lemonade. Tourists snapping selfies and a lot of regular New York peeps, walking their dogs and just chillin' with tablets and books. If there is a heaven, this is my heaven. Can't wait to show the world outside of NY how pretty it is here. #NYSeen 4 sure.

And then I went to the Whitney museum. Mind blown.

I have to use a Mom word here. The Whitney is exquisite.

Alexander Calder, Big Red 1959 #NYSeen

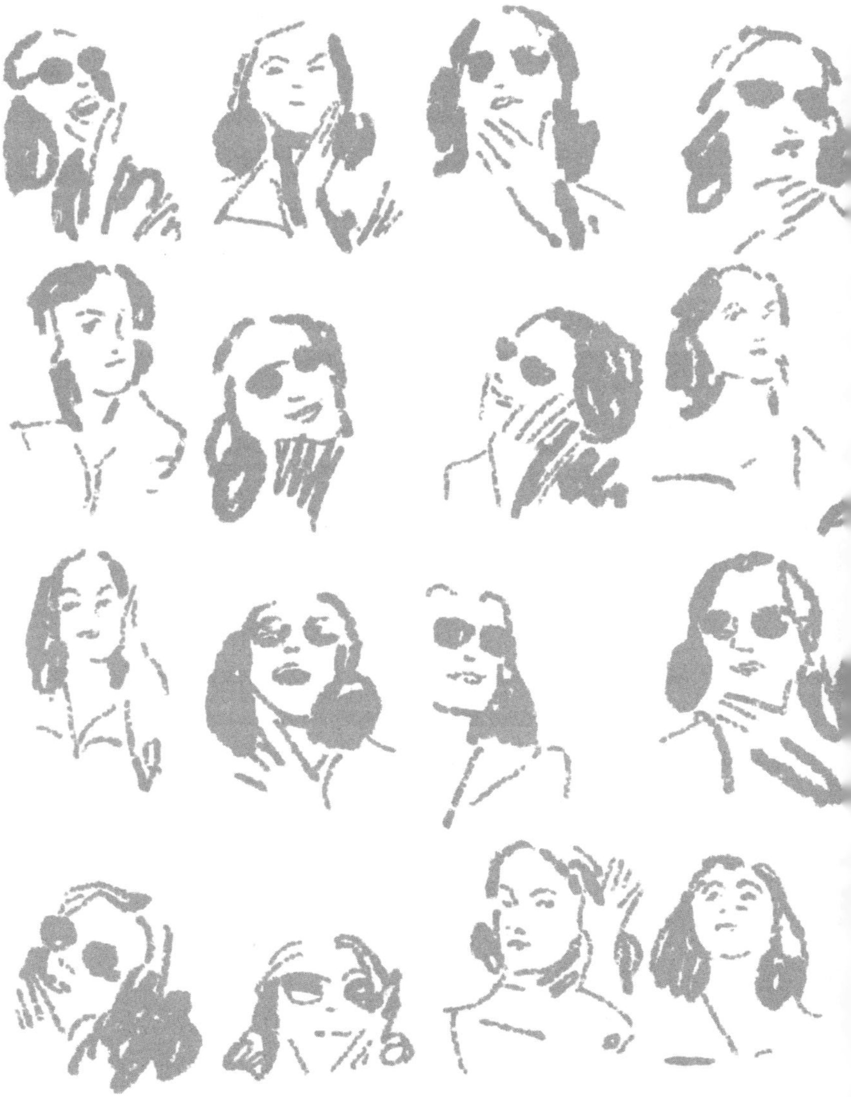

It was in my skin from the minute I was in the lobby. Now I know a soul mate doesn't have to be a person, it can be a place! I walked all the floors (crowded, shiny) and when I got to Floor 6, I stopped.

Right in front of me, an Andy Warhol in New York City: Ethel Scull 36 Times, from 1963. Not on my computer or in a catalogue, but in the actual city where I live now. It was so close I could touch it. Andy and I are both here, at the same time. He did it. I did it. We did it.

My brain started ticking: The Ethels were silk screened, but Andy's soup cans were hand painted originally. Before he was silk screening, he was creating duplicates and had to standardize them by hand. I was doing the same things with my hearts. I clasped my hands together like in a prayer fist and said out loud, "Warhol, be with me." Somebody next to me laughed but whatever. Everything was making sense, clicking.

I sat there forever and couldn't stop sketching. Everything I scribbled is a mess and I don't care, I was just connecting, connected. I didn't know how much I needed it.

Exquisite.

Then I came back to Carlyle's and felt . . . arrrrrgh, not art. Adams used to get on me about practice and technique, how talent without craft was like cooking without knife skills, and I never knew what she was talking about because I was just feeling my way through so much but maybe this is what she meant. When your feelings can't work for you, you can still rely on your technique to get you through. But my technique is wack and I'm a hack, just waiting around for inspiration to strike. I'm going to go broke if I have to pay to see a real-life Warhol every day for inspiration! What if I'm no better than that Gillman guy?

I need to—must—prove to myself that I can do the job I was hired to do.

I'm here to be an artist.

I'm going to be an artist.

I am an artist.

Bought soup at Hamid's for lunch/dinner AGAIN. He only sells vegetarian soups and they are v. good. "Carrot ginger will cure everything," he says, and he's almost right. The soup didn't cure my cruddy work, but it did wake up my brain. I feel connected with my brush, like it's just part of my hand. So much better than yesterday.

I tried to remember the last time I felt like my ideas were coming straight onto the paper, no thinking necessary. Thinking of my senior project, when Kit sparked the idea, how I freehanded the borders of the piece, how I named it Map but it turned out to be a heart. I need a map right now to show me how to get the exact right feel again.

I pulled up photos of the original and searched for the elegance that Carlyle needs me to produce now. What made my original elegant? If I look at it like it's not mine and just disconnect my real heart from it, it's the paint strokes that are elegant, their flow and continuation even where the outer edges are rough. There's the smoothness. It was hard to start that piece too. Is it ever easy to start new art?

This morning when Grace and I were trying not to get electro-cuted by the toaster, she said she was struggling with a poem she had been working on all night. She pulled her burnt toast out with some tongs and scraped the bread. "This is me to a T," she said and I asked, "Dry?" and she snarked, "Crumbling." I thought we were going to sit together, I was hoping for a serious art pity-party, but she was off to get Eileen June's dog, Didion, from the kennel. "Maybe being around dogs will help," I tried and she woofed at me as she left. She's funny even when she's over it. I definitely want to hang with her more.

Finished another heart (yay!), though it took longer than I expected (boo!). I was getting it but it was still missing the real me. I finally left the studio and went to the Met, or should I say the steps of it. I needed some inspiration, some fuel, some something.

I wished Kit or E or Grace or Si were here to talk art with me. It's weird to feel lonely here because, like, I'm surrounded by people all the time, but I'm also alone. I checked my #NYSeen just to have a little company. @ShoelessAndClueless said she loved my Whitney drawing and that she's gonna see the museum on her vacay here. That's cool, I'm spreading the gospel! I also got 14 new followers in the last 24 hours. That cat drawing!

I want someone to discuss my art frustration with more IRL though and I want Carlyle to be more hands-on. I asked Kennedy if I was going to get to work alongside Carlyle one of these days, that's what my contract said, but Kennedy keeps telling me Carlyle is so busy and I get it but still. I need to know if what I'm doing works and I want to watch him work. Even though Marli was annoying as all get-out, she fueled me when she was around. When she freaked me out, I ran to my canvas. When she scared me, I could draw myself away from her. It's not that I'm missing her exactly, but maybe she gave me more inspiration than I realized. I know that when she'd creep into the garage when I was painting, my work always changed. Sometimes worse, sometimes better, but always more intense. My brain is weird. I'm missing the person I couldn't wait to get away from.

I wished I had gotten Grace's number. So I texted Silas instead: Why is art so hard? Why do we do this? and he wrote back, If you can do anything else, why do art? What makes you care?

I was irritated. All I could think is: it's what I know how to do, I don't know how to do anything else, there's nothing I love more. But maybe that's what he was getting at? I didn't write back.

The Met was so much bigger in real life and I didn't end up going in. I don't know what I was expecting, but I didn't realize how busy it would be, how long it would take to get there, and how much it would cost to do all this stuff. I'm going back when I can spend a whole day there. I need to be surrounded by all the amazing art of my ancestor-artists! I could spend my whole life in NY and never see all of it.

When I left the Met, I asked a bus driver for help with directions and then rode the bus all the way to 8th Street. The bus was super slow when we hit traffic, and I loved it because I got to watch the building's silhouettes grow and spread across the streets, watched the city get a cast of gray across it. Also, there are hundreds of taxis, just grays and gold-yellows everywhere. Shadows and shades, eclipsing where they intersect. Where there's light, there's space.

5th Avenue has ALL the tourists—from Central Park all the way down—and I saw the original Tiffany store, the one that's in <u>Breakfast at Tiffany's</u>! There was also a bunch of protestors outside of a Trump building. That was wild. I tried to take a pic but of course that's when the bus picked up speed. My #NYSeen sketch of it is better than that pic.

Kit texted immediately after she saw my post: 5th Ave, right? LOVE!

Yassss! Headed back to studio now. U?

I want to see Carlyle's atelier and YOU! Off to le cinema with DJA. DJA, short for DJ Anonymous, is Kit's true love and on-again off-again boyfriend.

Sooo French.

Oui! Oui!

I miss her.

8/25 9 am In the studio

The Web caf staff reminded me that there is no dinner served on Sunday nights, so tonight Grace and I are going to a place she found right down the street called the Skylight Diner. I'm already ready to pork out on fries and a milkshake.

Sunday mornings are quieter by a smidge in the city so I went for a run. Had to dodge a few crazy cars, and a lot of peeps on bikes, but I did it! I even ran next to another girl for a while, who was also wearing earbuds, and we kept pace and kind of waved/smiled—people are actually really friendly here once you get on their level—but neither of us stopped or broke our stride. It was kind of cool.

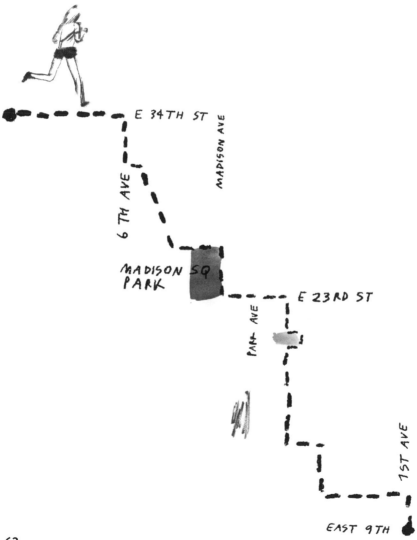

I'm in the studio now and it's too quiet. Going to blast tunes and work and disappear for a while. Time to make some noise.

8/25 10:45 pm The Webster

Finally. Did it.

I was in my zone and found my old fingers, my same hands. HI, HANDS!

Maybe it was the music (Lily Allen, Lorde, Led Zepp, hello the Ls in my playlist). Maybe it was going for a run before I started and my brain just absorbing everything (bus fumes, humidity, life), or hanging with Grace and actually finding a kindred spirit in this place, or seeing a real-life Warhol, or the Whitney settling into my bones. Or maybe it was just really being here, like Maria said, making it mine: all of myself feels here now and when I think of "going home" I picture my little Webster room, squeaky fan and all, not Houston.

I finally stopped worrying about how to do art and being me and I reconnected with my work, and finally it's happened!!! Something's back! The piece, my new heart, was listening to me and I was hearing it and I am EXHAUSTED and happy. I'm not alone and neither is it. I was covered in paint, hello blood-red-blue stained fingers, it's been a long time, welcome home welcome home! I don't feel alone anymore. VIC-TOR-Y. Of course, the new piece needs to dry before Carlyle sees it. Left the oversized industrial fans on in the studio. Wish I could nick one of those for my room, but it probably wouldn't fit through the door anyway.

I kept thinking of Si's question, "What makes you care?" and I realized I'm drowning in answers. Art changes how I see the world, and how people see the world. When I see how they see it and they see how I see it it's like a conversation almost, we get to see how we connect to each other and make sense of the world. Words float into space and are only so accurate, they're just placeholders for what we mean. But art comes from the center of all of us. Art is the physical manifestation of conversations and communication! So it's truer than words. It's the purest way to communicate.

That's my answer. I texted Si about all this, as a friend, as an artist, because I think he will get it. And I brought it up to Grace over our dinner and we talked about the values of words and design and she said, "You think in absolutes, but there's middle ground. There has to be, right? What we can't communicate visually, we explain with words. And when words don't work, we turn to pictures, illustrations. We just try so hard to communicate with each other. Humans are the most imprecise animals. We keep trying, but there will never be real clarity between any of us. Thank god, or we'd be out of work!"

She took a big bite of her veggie burger, and a plop of sauce fell onto the table. "Ohmigod, just call me Grace-less."

I said, "How 'bout I call you genius instead?" and that got a serious eye-roll but she was so inspiring and I was feeling it. I asked her to show me pics of Evan and she showed me one, he's all right but looks boring, and then a bunch of photos of Didion the bulldog, who is way cuter. When I asked to see more of her and Ev, she sighed, and showed me an album she had titled "She and Him," and in every picture she looked like she was about to burst through the frame and he looked like he was bemused by this crazy girl next to her.

I think I know who the star of that show is. Maybe he's really an amazing kisser or something. She asked me if I thought he was cute, and I said, "He looks very solid and . . ." She was waiting. "Even, very even." Then she made crazy eyes and said, "Ohmigod, Even Evan. You nailed it."

Anyway, it was a total A+ FRIENDSHIP NIGHT!

Now I'm back at the Web, about to shower and flop down in my tiny-whiny-too-hot-but-I-don't-care-I-love-it room.

8/26 11:00 am

So Si texted me back last night and I went to his place for the first time. It's small, but bigger than my room or the beau parlors (no surprise). Unfortunately, his place *is* like the Webster in that there is basically no privacy because he shares it with Mo. I forgot about roommates until I saw—and smelled— Mo's works all over the place. Uggs, and I don't mean the boots.

Their kitchen is really . . . vertical. Everything was lined against one wall and about half normal size. A small sink, a small pantry, small shelves. No dishwasher. A stack of matches sat on top of a small microwave that was on a small bar cart. Everything was mini and I loved it. Just perfect, real New York. The noise outside on the street felt like it was right in the room with us.

Mo walked through. I hadn't seen him since my first night here. He came at me for an overly bro-y hug and and a high five, then untwirled his man bun. His jet-black wavy hair hit his shoulders like a hot, hippie Oscar Isaac. Si and Mo are the oddest Odd Couple.

"Yo, Tex, take care of my boy here. Mo's gotta go. Mo out."

"Oh, okay." I gave a tiny wave as he was leaving.

"That was fast! He didn't leave because of me, did he?" I laughed.

"No, that's just Mo," he said. What a weird-Mo.

Si asked me if I "would like a beverage?" which was awkward, and then handed me a glass of water and said, "New York's finest," which was less so. He is funnier when he relaxes. After we ordered Thai food I wandered around the place a bit. Their view is the side of a brick building, but down below I could see people on the sidewalk, sitting at cafés, talking on their phones, girls in cute outfits heading out for the night. It was a really nice, perfect NY apartment. I could live here, I thought.

And then Si walked up behind me and wrapped his arms around my waist. I didn't like it. I tried to like it, but we didn't match up and his bony elbows were in my ribs. He stuck his chin against my shoulder blade and I felt the hairs on my arms stand up. Instead of feeling nervous or excited I felt like laughing because I was really not into it. This was not the way I felt around any of the guys I'd ever hooked up with, not even jerk-face C.J. I tried to relax, but I was thinking NO. It's just not gonna happen with Silas.

"You okay?" I asked, hoping he would casually get the hint that I wasn't interested. His head was still flat against my back and he was leaning against me. I think he thought he was doing the right thing.

"Not really."

I turned to face him.

"I had to see my family, and we got in a fight, as per usual."

His eyes were half-mast, looking down, and he just had this help-me air. I wanted to be focused on what he was telling me, but all I could think about was how it was kind of unexplainable why we were together. Our emails made me feel so connected. I felt bad for him right there, so I kissed him, which didn't really make sense, but I didn't know what to do.

I don't know. I can tell he doesn't really like kissing me, either. Maybe he thinks he's supposed to, like I thought I was supposed to, but it's just. not. there. How much longer are we going to pretend we might be into each other?

It was better when we stopped kissing, thank god, and just started talking. He was going off on his dad.

"He's always breaking everything, or everyone, in his path, and he has to be the center of attention. He's better than he used to be, but he's still him."

"Oh my god, that's exactly like my sister."

"Marli, right? The one you emailed about—?"

I nodded. "Yeah. I would hate it if my parents were like that, too. She's bad enough." I wanted to tell him more about her, how she dominated our entire house and all of us just orbited around her moods and hoped we didn't end up in her crosshairs, but he was clearly in his own headspace. Why talk about my eggshells when he had his own to maneuver.

"It . . ." It was like he was too formal to say "sucks." "It's awful."

"Do you worry you're like your dad? Because I worry that sometimes I'm like Marli. Like, I can get mad. And I think I can get pretty mean, too."

"Nah, I could never <u>really</u> be like him. I don't have his DNA, y'know. He adopted me. The last nice thing he ever did."

"Oh. Wow. Really?" What do you say to that?

He mumbled the rest fast. "My mom had an affair. Of course 'Dad'"—he was sarcastic—"was pissed all the time, he had to raise me, another guy's kid. He used to be worse. When he drank more, when he wasn't funny or charming, just fucking depressing, he and Mom used to really go at it. And Mom's not exactly a pushover."

"Jesus. Was it just because he was mad at her?"

"Would that justify him being an alcoholic?"

"No, no, of course not. That's not what I meant at all. It's horrible, Si."

"It's just kind of hard to unsee that shit. And when I was over there today, he was in one of his fits. And of course, she was just making it worse. It's like they love to get each other pissed off, but I hate that shit. I always have. I leave and they don't notice and I don't care."

I didn't even know what else to say. "I'm so sorry."

I thought I might know a little bit what he felt like, from being around Marli—trapped and small and choiceless. Why did we get stuck with lunatics? Were we just stereotypes of tortured artists?

I rubbed Si's back for a long time. I think he might have been crying silently. I tried to think of what I could say that was just factual data. Something concrete. Something real to help him get out of his mind.

"Did you always know you were adopted?"

"They told me last year."

"What!" I couldn't help but explode. "That's effed up! When you were how old, 18? That's too long to keep a secret like that!"

"I always just figured I was more like my mom. He adopted me when I was 2, so I didn't really have a say in the matter or know any different. But last year, they told me. They had to."

"Why?"

"Because I was starting school."

"So?"

"They . . . had their reasons." Mysterious, but I didn't want to press him.

He looked at me again. Even with just his floor lamps on and the room getting dark, I could tell his face was blotchy. I put my hand on his cheek and he didn't pull away, and I just stood there. I wanted him to know I saw him, I was there for him. Not because this was about me being there, but because I wanted him to not feel so alone.

"Have you told anyone else?"

"Mo knows. A friend of mine from when I was a kid, Astrid. She knows." He sighed and shook out his shoulders. "Sorry I'm such a buzzkill."

"You're not, Silas, not at all. I'm . . . really honored you trusted me enough to tell me. Thank you, okay?"

We hugged like our existence depended on each other. I thought, maybe this is why we found each other. It wasn't about sparks. It was about art, the art of being alive, about feeling squeezed in the place you're supposed to feel safe: home. I'm going to paint us that way. I wished I had a canvas right then.

Over his shoulder, more black-and-white photos on yellowing paper caught my eye. I saw a pair of eyes staring out, with "Lens" underneath them. It wasn't a headline, just a word, final, not temporarily Velcro'd. I held Silas a bit tighter. I was looking at his art without him knowing it and I didn't want to stop. I wanted to see him through his lens.

This was what I felt when he emailed me. This was the reason I knew we were supposed to be in the same place at the same time. This moment and this hug. We weren't supposed to love each other. We were supposed to rescue each other.

Of course, in the middle of this moment, our food arrived.

He seemed to feel better, to feel safer after all that. In the middle of chopsticking his noodles, he paused. "I really appreciate you listening, Piper."

I nodded and said, "You, too." He didn't need to know everything about Marli and me right then. He needed to be heard. He needed to be seen.

8/27 10:25 am Waiting for the N/R train

Late last night/this morning, I went to the TV lounge and Grace was in there, channel surfing. Her window won't open so her room is like a fire pit. Her phone kept blowing up with texts, and she finally turned off the sound, annoyed.

"Somebody's trying to get you!"

"Evan," she said.

"You're not talking to him?"

"Not really." She sighed. "He's being a pain."

Hmm. Is that what it's normally like to be engaged? She wouldn't elaborate, just kept sending his calls to voice mail. We landed on this old-school teenage-hitchhiker-who-had-been-kidnapped movie. The girl survived, and went on to give anti-hitchhiking talks at local schools. The kidnapper was still on the loose.

We're getting fans today, when she's done working.

I texted Si when I was back in my room.

Me: You up?

Si: Working on homework for PHO2.

Me: ?

Si: Photo 2nd year. Influencer v. representation.

Me: Sounds intense!

Si: The camera is taker or maker. That's the thesis; we have to choose one side to argue. I can defend both sides. Major quandary over here.

Me: Camera is taker AND maker! Problem solved.
You're welcome. ☺

Si: Ha ha. Unfortunately Hodges isn't as open-minded as you. She forces us to pick just ONE POV.

What's the difference between influence and representation? Do I have a side? I need to think about this stuff before school starts. Oh school. Oh money. YIKES.

I skipped all that in my text back: I'm on Carlyle Countdown right now. I finished most of the pieces, but I'm still two away and they should all be drying by now. I'm feeling major guilt any time I'm not working.

Si: You'll get there. Be patient with yourself. Problem solved. You're welcome! ☺

Me: OMG, SI—

Si: Seriously, you don't have time for guilt. Get back to work. Remember what Chuck Close said.

Me: Inspiration is for amateurs?

Si: See? I am a fantastic student mentor!

Me: ☺ You're something, all right.

Si: Don't let guilt be an excuse. Go.

Actually felt legit inspired by that.

I'm off to get my paycheck, my first!!!, before I head to Carlyle's studio. Yay money! Train's finally here—

8/27 6 pm

Went to Carlyle's office this morning, and it's like the inside of a hip, modern cabin, with throw rugs and pelts on Lucite chairs and harsh art on the walls, all graffiti and broken glass. There's an American flag hanging in a corner that looks burnt around the edges.

Kennedy handed me my very first paycheck and an itinerary. "This week, besides studio time, your job is to be on call and help Carlyle with whatever is needed. You'll have a bit of rest after Fashion Week, then you're back on call. Cah-peeeesh?"

"Whatever is needed? Like more hearts?" The thought of having to cram even one more of those out made me want to hurl.

Kennedy gave me a weird look. "No, more like he might need you to pick up supplies or call him a Lyft, chat with potential collaborators while he's in meetings . . ." I guess I was pulling a face, because he said, "What?"

"I thought you got him cabs and did the work stuff for him. I'm here for more um . . . artistic assistance, right? I'm working in the studio."

Oops.

He put down his tablet, crossed his arms against his chest, and tapped his elbows slowly with his opposite fingers. "I manage Carlyle's day-to-day operations. I keep this place running. I am not an assistant."

"I mean, and you're an artist—" Tried to eject my foot from my mouth before I swallowed the damn thing.

"Artists have to eat, too, Piper. It's not that confusing. I'm the manager. You're a contractor. We've contracted you for your assisting and artistic services. That includes 'whatever' is needed. Carlyle is THE ARTIST. It's all right there in the contract. Got that?" He went back to his tablet.

I pretend-saluted him. "YES, SIR!"

Kennedy squinted. "Don't let me keep you from the studio, Piper. I'm sure you have much to do."

I like Kennedy better when he's in gossip mode. I'm not messing with Serious Kennedy. Serious Kennedy is Serious.

As I was leaving, Carlyle was walking in. He was getting off his cell and gave me the "one minute" finger so I waited till he said, "Ciao."

"Andre called again," Kennedy said.

"Later!" Carlyle said. "She needs my account number at Soho Art Materials," he told Kennedy. Then to me, "You pick up supplies for our projects there. I had Kennedy stock the studio before you arrived." It did have everything—oils, acrylics, muslin, canvas, and wood. And of course I had my lucky brushes.

"Yes"—the BEST—"and I just tell them I'm with you?"

"Yes." He smiled like, isn't she cute, and raised an eyebrow to Kennedy. "So green," he said and K just kind of shook his head affectionately at me and said, "So true."

Carlyle seemed sincere, not snarky, but my stomach twisted. Like Dad said, back in Houston I was a big fish in a smallish pond, but here I'm just a dang guppy.

"Piper, it's time for me to share something with you." Carlyle kept going without waiting for an answer. "I want to expose you to my vision for your creations. Come here." I walked over to his desk and he opened a file on his desktop monitors. JPEGs of my new piece were spread across the oversized screens.

"You took photos?" I got a little wobbly in the knees. Thankfully the pictures he took, or at least shared, were of two of my best pieces.

"So, these moody reds, the blood clots that are going on through-out the pieces?" Carlyle asked.

"Uh, yeah? Yes?" Mom always said "yeah" was rude. I didn't think of them as clots but I could see what he meant when he said it, the globs of red paint were round and cell-like, something I would see under a microscope in bio lab back in school.

"They work. Your piece, my clothes, there's a fluidity, an extension. Your art could be wearable. Now . . ."

I tilted my head, looking at them as he rotated the images.

"Welcome to the inside!" he announced, and Kennedy gave a small clap. The photos of his designs appeared on the screen. There were bolts of red fabric wrapped tightly around mannequins. They reminded me of arteries. He toggled between his dresses and my piece and I could see how he connected them. It wasn't just about the similar colors, but a textural connection, a fiber that tied them together. I knew if I could touch that fabric, it would feel like my project and vice versa.

"What is that material?"

"Raw silk."

"It looks crunchy, pebbly," I said. "Far away it's smooth but when you zoom in, it's rough. Up close, there's real texture, huh? Like it's almost . . . salty."

"Granular." He closed his eyes for a second and pressed his hands together in prayer (?) against his lips. He nodded gently, but I wasn't sure if it was to me, to him, the computer, or what.

My pieces were definitely the right selection for his gowns, and they did look like extensions of each other. His dresses were the arteries but they needed heart. Without my pieces, they were unconnected. Unalive.

Carlyle lowered his voice and said, "Do you understand why it's imperative that your pieces remain elegant? The connection?

This is all about our interiors, the innermost parts of us. That's why I call it THE INSIDE." Every time he said it, it sounded like an affirmation, like if he said it enough he would believe it.

I nodded, not entirely sure I understood, but he was definitely having a moment.

"This old man"—he cleared his throat—"is finally having his Fashion Week debut, in MoMA of all places." He smiled to a joke he was telling himself. "Even when I try to get away, they pull me back in. Of course my fashion show would be in a museum."

HOLY SHIT, our Fashion Week show is going to be in the Museum of Modern Art? I was shaking. My work, technically, was showing in one of the most important museums in the world! My pulse was off the charts.

"You don't wait this long to do something and then do it half-way. . . ." He drifted off. "Your vision helps me complete mine. I found what I've been looking for. You understand." He smiled a little and his eyes wrinkled at the corners and he looked almost hopeful. Worried. For the first time, I really liked him.

"You're not that old," I said and he looked up at me. Oops. I was trying to be nice. "I won't let you down." I made a snap decision right then and there to switch from oils to acrylics so they'll dry faster and visually won't look too off. I'll just need to add more layers. And I'm NOT going to let him or his show down. No way.

Kennedy said from the table, "Did you tell her about the posing?"

"Oh right," Carlyle said, clapping once. "Kennedy, the other half of my brain. Yes, you should know: the models will be posing on the pieces during their final walk."

"Say what?"

"The pieces have to touch each other. The dresses and your clots."

"They're hearts."

"Okay." He smiled indulgently. "Tomato, tuh-mah-tow, but they need to have a physical connection."

"But people will get the metaphor already. Doesn't forcing the two pieces to connect seem a little literal?" I felt like the battery in my brain had been charged and I was actually adding to our conversation, like two real artists—equals—talking to each other.

"Well, you're giving our audience a lot of credit, aren't you? I appreciate your optimism, but I want the work, for now, to touch."

"So, just so I'm clear, you want the models to just . . ."

"I told you," he said, starting to seem a little less Zen and a little more pissed. "A connection. I want the dresses touching the pieces, the models either sitting on your clots, or leaning on them, or the ones in the longer gowns"—he made quotation marks with his fingers—"'floating' across them. I see the art forming the runway. Everything will touch. Like yoga."

"I don't do yoga," I said. All I could think about was how the pieces had to be able to safely bear the weight of the models. If not they could fall and hurt themselves and, worst of all, destroy my work.

As if he could read my mind, he said calmly, "Don't worry, you'll figure it out. Thank you."

Dismissed.

I waved bye but he was already staring back into his computer, rubbing his temples.

Once Kennedy and I were at the elevator, I said, "He's like, so different, in there. On the phone this summer, he sounded so chill, but at the studio and just now he seemed, I don't know, stressed out."

"It's his private space, where he gets to be Carlyle, not CARLYYYYLE." He swished his hands upward. "His safe space. The demands on him are huge, opening his life's work to fashion. Between the investors, his fans, new clients, it's more pressure than ever."

"So why do it? Why not just stick to the kind of art he already makes?"

He pushed the elevator button.

"Girl," Kennedy said, "you don't tell an artist what they are or aren't going to make. He's wanted to do this for years and this is his time. He decided. It's the big 5-0 this year. The moments are not unrelated."

"When my dad had his midlife crisis he took up golf and sucked at it."

"You're hilarious, Piper, but—" The elevator doors opened and he didn't come in with me so I pushed the open doors button.

"There is big money involved. More than you can imagine. It's not exactly golf. Just because he's been successful in one area doesn't mean that will translate. So his midlife crisis is more like . . . a debutante ball. He's risking a lot in terms of reputation—anything less than total success is going to be laughed at." The doors began to shut and he jammed his hand between them and leaned in.

"So Carlyle cannot under any circumstances fail."

NO PRESSURE.

But in the non-stressful news department, I got paid $800 and I get to go to Carlyle's Fashion Week after-party! Yessss! Must try and sneak in Grace.

8/28 Leaving C's studio

About to walk home to the Web and catch a freebie meal before the caf shuts down at 8 tonight. I forgot to eat today. I was here until now (6:30) from early-early this morning. I'm working faster and the work is . . . working!

Not overthinking it, just making the familiar motions with my arms and fingers. I'll figure out how to make them weight-bearing tomorrow. Can't do more tonight and pieces still need to dry anyway and I'm starving.

Paint paint and more paint. I look like a walking Pollock.

8/29 9:45 pm In the TV room

I was supposed to meet Si but he was held up with a seminar and we just agreed to wait to hang until after Carlyle's show goes up because I'm a mess, even though I would love to talk about weight-stabilizing my work with him. Talking, texting, to him about art is so good. I think we are finally getting each other, like we're just friends. I'm fine being solo because I'm so busy anyway and so is he, and I'm just not feeling guy vibes for maybe the first time in my life. Art first, boys later. I'm okay with that and I'm pretty sure he is, too.

Speaking of, I had dinner with Grace tonight at the Web. During dinner time, it's so dark down there. I forget the caf is actually in the building basement because at breakfast the morning light streams in through the windows.

We loaded up on salad and slices. Cheese pizza is always there for the vegetarians.

She's spent the last two days reading and proofreading Eileen June's latest draft of a new poetry anthology.

"How is it?" I said and Grace's eyes got big and watery. "It's so moving, Piper. I just, I can't really get into the details about any of it yet because it's not public and I signed an NDA, but it's really such tense, important work. I had to take a break and walk Didion around Prospect Park just to breathe. She doesn't allow for pettiness, you know? She's such a RESPONSIBLE artist. God." She put her fist to her heart.

"Wow."

"That's the dream, right? To make stuff that matters like that?"

"Yeah." I nodded.

"You look a little scared." She laughed.

"Oh no, I'm not! That's so cool!"

"I'm not always this dramatic, I swear, but I've been with her manuscript for the last week and I'm just, I haven't talked to anyone about it, really, except her. I called my dad, he's a big reader, and I told him a little, well what I could, and he's so encouraging. He knows Ev and I have been having problems, and he thinks I made the right decision to work with Eileen."

"That's so cool. Does your mom not think that?" I asked, picking up the vibe.

"No, Mom's still a little miffed that I'm not going to be a lawyer like all my brothers, but like, we got that covered. There's five lawyers in the family, they can handle one poet!" She laughed.

"Five?"

"Mom and my four brothers. And then there's me, their freaky poet child. All Mom wants to talk about these days are me and Even Evan. She wants a wedding so badly she can taste it."

"Oh, right." I keep forgetting she's engaged because he only seems to come up as a problem. There's zero talk about a wedding. I was about to ask her more and I think she sensed it because she switched the convo. "Anyway, what about you?"

I told her about my pieces now having to be weight-bearing.

"You should ask someone for help. What about that Kennedy guy?"

"Kennedy is like the office manager. Although he said he was a video artist on break, so I don't really know what that means. He got rude when I asked him about it. I guess it's easier for him to run Carlyle's life than to make his own."

"Burnnn," she said as she dumped a bunch of parmesan on her slice.

"I'm on my own, I think," I said. "Trying to get my friend Silas, the guy who's my student mentor, to help me with ideas."

"Yeah. The last thing you want is a model slipping off the runway or sliding off one of your pieces."

That image had us giggling.

"So, are you going to wear one of Carlyle's dresses?"

I made a BLEH face.

"Nah. I don't have that _it_ thing. I break cameras."

I struck a pose and she covered her eyes.

"Yep, they obviously hired you for your art. I can never un-see that!" she said.

Then she said we were going on a surprise adventure and we put up our trays and I followed her into the elevator. Maria was in there, chatting about her newest nail art (tiny little flecks of diamonds, like confetti) with a few girls.

"Hey Maria," Grace said. She waved to the other girls. Two waved back. Another one was on her phone, loudly saying, "You're crazy if you think we're meeting you in Queens, boyyy!"

The other two were shaking their heads like no way.

"NO THANK YOU! Unless you're talking Long Island City, we're not coming," she shouted into her phone and all of us were laughing as we hit the lobby floor and they ran out.

Then Grace pushed the R button.

The R floor = the roof.

We have a roof! The best-kept secret of the Web. Fact.

We wandered around for a bit and then Grace said, "Ooh!" She pulled me over and we stood against a brick wall with the moon big behind us, and a bright lit-up sign that read NEW YORKER, and the Empire State Building was also lit up, the top part cobalt blue and orange. It was like, the most NEW YORK I had ever seen in one shot. So we took a few selfies, dumb faces then sexy faces then funny faces then serious ones.

"Send them to me?"

"Oh yeah."

We chilled for a few hours and talked about the girls in the elevator and their outfits and what kind of clothes we would buy if we had millions one day—indie labels and Prada and Grace likes Free People A LOT and she really really wants me to get a Carlyle dress for free.

8/30 8 am

Everything will be okay, but my brain won't stop circling and I had panic dreams all night. Now I'm just writing writing and more writing trying to unknot my brain.

How do I make my art safe and secure for the models and still look artistic? Canvas itself isn't sturdy. Their heels will pierce it. I need something underneath the structures, weights I guess, that don't change the color or heaviness or gravity of the pieces and still let them look like themselves and give some pushback or tension to the piece so the models don't feel like they are walking in quicksand.

I wish I had paid more attention in math class. I don't even know how to measure what I really need, don't know the weights of the models. I wish Kit was here. She has the brain I need right now.

Quick break.

I'm back. Just texted her: Kit! I need help with my pieces! Now they have to be supermodel weight-bearing. Help me, Einstein? You're my only hope! ☺

. . .

Are you there?

PIPES! What's the current weight of piece? Why models on it?

I dunno weight! Carlyle wants models to 'model' on them!

Find out current weight and let me know ASAP.

Okay, tomorrow. I have to do this fast. ILU

ILU more!

The idea of one of them walking or sitting or standing on my art is bizarre. Is that what Carlyle's going for, someone walking on your heart literally? Is that how his "need for connection" theme is supposed to play out? My first map, my heart, wasn't about being walked on, it was about claiming space, like owning MY own innermost and outermost territory, like manifest destiny!

And now somebody's going to walk on my art.

What happens when you make something because you wanted to make it, and then it becomes something for someone else, and then you remake it for that person, but based on the one you made for yourself . . . who am I actually doing this for? The answer for now is Carlyle. I'm making my hearts strong enough to carry Carlyle's work. Carlyle's counting on me. And I'm counting on me too. I'm counting on my art.

I have to breathe.

SEPTEMBER

So much people-watching.

Faves right now: the girls teaching the other girl how to draw fake tattoos on their arms with Sharpies and the cute guy with the metal detector walking around on the grass. I don't want to give him my sketch, but I'm gonna leave it on the bench when I leave. Ya been seen, my dude! #NYSeen

Posted my sketch and checked my tag. So many people are liking my #NYSeen posts now, it's cool. I have over 600 followers and they're commenting on each other's comments (mostly funny, a couple of a-holes) and some using the hashtag? Maybe I can meet some of them?!? One girl asked where she can get her own #NYSeen sketched—my second request, though I never heard back from the cat person!!! This is so cool.

I messaged Kit about weight of piece as is and approximate weight of models—100 to 120 lbs before outfits, I'm guessing?

Hope she gets back to me ASAP.

I've been working in the studio since 5:30 am till now. I couldn't sleep anyway, so why not. And I'm starting to feel badass. Last pieces happening, not done completely. I did run out of the acrylics because now I'm using more, and ended up going to that Soho Art Materials store where Carlyle has an account. It's on Wooster, and the street is paved with bricks. I thought they were cobblestones but a guy inside Soho Art told me they're actually called Belgian blocks because they have a smoother finish. I took pics of the street, also sketched it, because we don't have streets like this back in Houston. Definitely a NEW YORK street!

#NYSeen #WoosterStreet #Bricks #SoOld #SoCool

I just wanted to play hooky in Soho Art and look at all the tools. I had to resist more brushes, especially this goat hair brush that actually made my mouth water when I picked it up, it was the perfect weight, but I kept my head down and came back with the paint I need and only one new fan paintbrush that I don't exactly need, but whatever, I love it. I'll go back to dream-shop later. I should have said unlimited art supplies when G and I were playing what would we do if we were millionaires. I mean, of course I always want more supplies. Oh and it would be GREAT not to worry about student loans and just straight up have enough money to go to school. I'm so relieved it's finally September so I can just get the sitch on my financial aid and really know what more I have to do. I'll be all over it.

I also stopped by Carlyle's office with a list of questions that Grace helped me prep last night.

Kennedy was on the phone, madly scribbling something down. "Uh-huh. Huh. Yes, yes. We'll make that happen. Yes, got it. We'll get the Syrah. Not a problem. Well, I'm sure we can up the order. Yes. Yes. Yes. Yes."

He hung up the phone, shaking his head and whispered to himself, "Mercy me, mercy me, mercy me."

There were envelopes stacked on the desk. He was stuffing them with flyers and samples of red fabric that I just KNEW was for our show.

"Ooh, can I see those—"

He snapped up.

"Don't you know how to knock?! They're for the show attendees. Your fingers have <u>oils</u> on them. You'll ruin them. Why do you think I'm wearing these?" He held his hands up. He was wearing latex gloves. "How can I help you?"

He was looking at me like HURRY UP.

"I just had a few questions." I held up my question list and he snapped his fingers for me to come over and took it from my hands. "No. No. Yes. Maybe."

"What?"

"No, you can't invite anyone to the show. No, you don't get one of Carlyle's dresses to wear. Yes, Carlyle will see final work beforehand. Yes, you'll have a seat but it'll be backstage. Now OK, sweetheart, unless you're here to tell me the pieces are complete, scoot. I'm in the middle."

"Thanks. One last thing, what should I wear?"

"It doesn't matter," Kennedy said, tapping numbers on the phone. "It's not about us, lady."

"Thanks a lot."

"You ask, I answer." He spoke into the phone while putting on his earpiece. "Hello? It's Kennedy McEnroe calling on behalf of Carlyle Campbell. We have a problem."

He waved goodbye.

I let myself out.

Sent Grace a message: bad answers > no answers?

G texted back immediately: Let's discuss at dinner. See you in Caf.

WTF Si is here, in Washington Square Park, with pretzels. YAY! SURPRISE!

Oh, Mo, too. Of course.

Bye!

9/1 11:50 pm On bed, too hot for sheets

Kennedy stopped by the studio tonight. He was with his friend Rashida, who looked like she could have been his sister. She has dreadlocks down to her butt, and a nose ring, and was wearing the coolest harem jumper thing. Super on point.

Kennedy was in a tank top and jeans, but his basics always look so money. How does he pull that off? I just look like a model for Costco.

"Dang, Piper, it's hot in here," Rashida said. "You're smart, wearing that."

I was wearing my pajamas—old cotton pants and a tank. I have to do laundry.

"Do you need water?" Kennedy asked. He wiped his forehead.

"I'm okay," I said. "It's hotter here in the evening than in the morning. Dunno why."

"Open the windows," Rashida said, trying to lift a big one.

"No!" I jumped. "We're below street level. Rats!" I made a barf face at them. "I found out the hard way."

They looked super icked out.

"They live for the paint," I said, "but it kills them."

"I'm pretty sure there's a lesson in that," said Rashida, and Kennedy laughed. He seemed a lot less stressed with her.

"All right," he said, running a finger over one of the dry pieces. "Looks like we're getting our work done here."

"They'll be ready. I'm still working on figuring out the supports, since models have to sit on them. If you have any ideas . . ."

"That's why we hired you," he said. "I'm busy handling a to-do list that's more demanding than my mama—the least you can do is handle the physics."

I wanted to say something nasty about to-do lists not sounding very artistic but I didn't.

"Six days until they're picked up, right?"

"Use 'em while you got 'em." He looked at his watch. "We gotta go if we're gonna be on time." They were off to see The Graduate at Film Forum. I passed that place on one of my runs. I like how it looks like it belongs in NY, tiny and indie. I don't really get how Kennedy has time to go to the movies if he's so busy, but whatever. Not my job to lose.

Back at the Web now, going downstairs to grab some ice for my wrists.

The best part of the work right now is being too tired to be anxious. That means I'm working. Thinking about the work makes me anxious, but work always makes my anxiety disappear. Are all artists this way?

I wish my dreams would stop being creepy. I walk into places like hotel rooms, with bathtubs overflowing with paints and I can't stop them from flooding the floors. I had one weird Beethoven dream. He wasn't deaf and he was telling me that he could hear the trains screeching. Then he made that screeching noise and I woke up grabbing my sheets.

Too hot to fall deep asleep, and when I did, more crazy dreams. Dreams of models going to a fashion shoot on a rooftop, stepping out of the elevator, and falling through the hollow buildings. I was supposed to warn them, but every time I opened my mouth red paint spilled out, down my chin, over my clothes. Spooky.

I'm running before I do anything this morning. Maybe I can get Grace to go with me. I'm tired as all get-out but I need to pump up for the studio.

I'm still in NEW YORK and still an artist in NEW YORK! And if I can keep doing this, I can stay here until school starts and not leave NY, which reminds me I still haven't heard back from the Financial Aid office. I called the other day but the scheduler was at lunch so I left a message. Now it's September. They may not be stressed, but I'm a mess. Come through, Helen Mundy!

Eating fries with Grace—my savior!—after she helped me all day. She's answering some emergency work emails about an In Conversations event with Eileen June right now. So, I'm doing this.

G went running with me, even though I found out she hates running, and we ran all the way to Union Square. We almost got tagged by a cab, and we were in the bike lane! The cyclists and messengers were hating on us, too. G made me promise her that if we went running again we would have "a real route." Fine. Besides, I want to run in some of the parks and on the Brooklyn

Bridge anyway and she's super into going on the bridge, but she doesn't want to run it. Fine, fine.

We walked the rest of the way from Union Square to the studio and I read back Kit's email to her. I didn't give K enough info to calculate the precise answer, but G helped me, the best she could. We stabilized the dry pieces with braces and screws. They're a little bit heavier now but not unmovable—each about two pounds heavier. We did our best and I'm praying there are no fashion disasters! Fash-asters!

G: Which one is our test model?

I pointed to one in the corner, away from the fans.

G: Can I?

She perched her butt over it.

I shrugged and said, Go ahead.

Grace is very muscular—more than any model—and I figured it would be way better and safer to see if they break in the studio than during the show.

She held her breath and hesitated.

"Prayer hands," she said and I made them at her.

"No matter what, it's going to be fine." Then she sat.

She was right, it was fine. Sculpture 1 held her easy-peasy. She even rocked back and forth carefully to see if it would move. It didn't! It had to remain balanced because if it slid or moved, that meant it wasn't level and that could cause an accident, too. Pure friggin' relief.

"Can you stop shaking now and help me?" she asked, holding her hand out so I would pull her up. I did and cracked my neck and exhaled.

"You okay?"

"It's just, my art's been broken before and I guess, I don't want to go through that again."

"How'd you break it?"

"Uh, how'd my sister Marli break it? She drove a car through it." Saying it made me feel like I was in our backyard again, watching our garage collapsing on the car and my art. I didn't know how much that was living inside of me.

"Shit. I'm sorry. Accident?"

"Unfortunately, no."

"Oh. Oh? Some sister."

I nodded but then looked at the art on the floor around us and tried to remind myself I was here now, not back in Texas, not with Marli. She side-hugged me and that helped.

"It's still weird that some of them will be stepped on." I don't like the metaphor, even if I feel less connected to these pieces than if I'd made them for myself.

"They'll do the job," she said. "They're sturdy."

"Putting them out in the real world means they're gonna be judged and I guess it's just all hitting me."

"Right. That's what you signed up for." She shrugged at me.

"Using them as furniture?"

"Well, you didn't know what he was planning on doing with your pieces. What if he had decided to . . . destroy them on the runway? Would that have been okay?"

"I'd hate that."

"But you signed them over to him, and to the public. That's what we do when we make something," she said. "Art, poetry. It's not ours anymore."

"Why does that sound so painful to me?" I wrapped my arms around my waist.

"Oh, I didn't say it was EASY! I'm not a masochist," she said, wiping the dust from her hands onto her yoga pants. "But Carlyle's paying you for these, right?"

I nodded.

"So, you have to let your art go. Your art is paying for you to be here, right? Fair's fair. You are being fairly compensated. You need to detach."

I nodded.

"Nobody—NOBODY—is going to see them like you do. That's like, literally impossible. So why worry about it?"

I felt less nervous than I had all month.

"You're going to survive this, I promise! You're just ripping off your baby-artist bandages, okay? You'll be even stronger for your next projects. You'll have scar tissue."

"I guess," I said. She has a way of making me laugh while telling the truth, which is kind of amazing.

"So, since you couldn't get me in"—she mugged at me—"you've got to take photos of everything. Backstage. Onstage. All of it!" She's also really good at changing the subject.

I asked G how I could ever thank her for helping me all day and she said buy me a beer.

Me: That's the one thing I can't do!

She always forgets I'm not 21. Which is flattering. But frustrating on days like today.

G: Well, how about how some fries? I'm dying for something salty.

Me: Deal.

I had read about Shake Shack before I moved here and it's just as good as H-town Beck's Prime.

Silas texted when we first sat down with our snackage: What's new? and I sent him a shake and fries pic with Hungry artist works for food and he wrote back, Ah, Shake Shack: notorious artist hangout. G grabbed my phone and texted him, Potatoes for Poets and Painters! and I told him that was Grace. He's heard about her.

Si texted, Whatever, Webster Girls and she wrote back You mean Webster Women, and now it's time to eat. Byeeee.

9/3 7:45 pm

Sketching in the garden because it's cooler than my room. A bunch of girls are out here tonight and Yoga Girl is helping someone practice a headstand. The other girl, she's bald with a bunch of piercings, isn't very strong yet, but she's gone upside down once or twice and I have to admit it looks fun. I haven't done a headstand in forever.

Going to talk to them—

Back! Yoga Girl is Jasmine and she's in teacher training and the other girl is Carmen and she said she'd be happy to give me some lessons if I was interested!

Maria jangled her way over to us, shaking out her wrists to show her new additions that she just got at the Brooklyn Flea.

"I like seeing everyone use the garden while it's still warm out."

Jasmine said she needed the green space and I said same here, I've been stuck in the studio and the buses and the birds are a good soundtrack.

"You're getting the hang of it, girls. It's all about the placing and the pacing." She chucked my shoulder and moved on.

"It's all about the placing and pacing." —Maria, the Webster Wisdom Goddess

I feel like I got here yesterday—and like I've been here forever at the same time. Time is so weird. My HOME is now NYC. Crazy!

Speaking of home, Mom called. Her message: "Hi, Piper. My time is all mixed up right now because I'm on Baby Savannah time. She is so. DANG. CUTE. And Marli and Ronnie are really taking to parenting, you know, as well as they can, it's hard, there's a steep learning curve without a lotta sleep, but I'm sure you're thinking about them, maybe you want to give your sister a call." Not exactly, but at least I didn't have to have the convo with her right at that minute. She yawned and said, "Anyway, so I don't know what time it is here, let alone there. But I do know your show is coming up this month. I am so proud of you, my baby, and I love you so much! And break a leg! Is that what you say at a fashion show? Break a high heel? Oh—" I heard the phone kind of clatter down and then the message ended.

She actually remembered Carlyle's show coming up. Miracle of miracles! A boost of good Mom energy is pure magic. I feel filled up.

Okay, tomorrow I put final touches and polish on the pieces. I got this. And following up again on my appointment with Helen because I haven't heard back yet and that scares me.

I texted Si: I wish they would just email or call me. Is it that hard? Do you have problems with them?

Welcome to CFA he texted back.

That's not funny I wrote. How do you deal?

The ". . ." hung out there for a while.

Si?

Oh yeah, I don't do FA. But Mo does. He could help.

So, Silas doesn't need Financial Aid? Is he like mega rich or something?

K Thx I wrote.

Then that weirdo sent me a bunch of devil face and money bag emojis. He is so weird weird weird but I actually miss his weirdness. I'm ready to hang out again.

9/5 7:57 pm

All of Carlyle's pieces are ready! I put the fans on them one more time, to dry last-minute wet spots. My paintbrushes are washed and the leftover muslin is wrapped and extra canvases are stacked and I put the lids and caps back on the jars and tubes of paint. I've cleaned up the best I can.

My hands are cramping and my shoulder hurts, but I'm relieved. I'm happy, just not crazy-happy, not lightning-bolts-and-glitter happy. Not surprised-happy, the way I felt after I finished my senior project.

I followed through and did my job. This was the hardest thing I've ever had to do—is that right? Yes, I think that's right— and secretly I'm glad it's over but I feel guilty for feeling that way. And I am super-duper uber-excited about going to Fashion Week and seeing how a show works and everything. That's like the cherry on top.

All I wanted to do was make art as a working artist—and that wish has come true. But it's sort of like what they mean when they say be careful what you wish for. I should have made a more specific wish. It doesn't feel the way I thought it would. Making art for someone else, for a job, is different. So much harder when it's not just for me or my vision or my time and space. I need my own space. I know that for sure now.

And now I need a new wish.

I don't know what I'm doing next for Carlyle, but I'll talk to Kennedy as soon as the show is over so I can start ASAP. For now, here are two life goals I'm adding and checking off at the same time. My to-dos just became my ta-das!

Make art in New York City. ✔

Live as an artist in New York City. ✔

Now I have to figure out how to make my own art in this city. Find my own place, my own way. Like Maria said, placing and pacing is everything.

I wouldn't be here without my original heart.

It's okay that Carlyle owns all the hearts now.

Like Grace said, they don't belong to me anymore.

And that means I don't belong to them anymore either.

Grace got me out of the Web to get me out of my head. I'm so worried about the show but it's literally out of my hands now, Kennedy said the pieces were picked up last night—so we ran along the West Side Highway. It's got a path with lanes for bikers and walkers and there are benches along the way. This ridic guy was there. He was dressed as the Statue of Liberty, smoking a cigarette and drinking from a bottle in a brown paper bag. He told us we could take a picture with him for ten bucks. Uh, no thanks. Instead I borrowed his pencil and a piece of his newspaper—"Not the crossword page! Not the crossword page!" —and sketched a quick drawing of him in the corner of it, and gave it back to him. Like this:

#NYSeen

I posted it with Liberty is looking rough! for Kit and Enzo. E wrote, Wow, you've really changed your look. Ha ha. Smartass. Also, there are like 100s of likes on other posts. It's crazy. People are digging my sketches, people who don't know me or know that I'm one the creating them! The comments that aren't spam are usually really smart and/or funny. I hate the spammers.

During our run, Grace asked me what I'm doing when Fashion Week is over.

"The money I'm making doesn't give me really anything to save. As long as Carlyle wants to keep me on, I keep working with him, that's our agreement. But my money is going fast. I've been spending $20s like they're $5s. And as soon as our contract is done, I'm outta work." She was nodding and breathing hard. "This city is killing me. A lovable killer! So I have to get more work pronto or I'm gonna be back home before school even starts."

"Like be a Gallery Girl or something? God, I hate running."

"Ideally, yeah! If I could get a gig at a gallery or a museum, that would be amazing. Do you think they're hard to get?"

"Uh, they're insanely competitive," she panted.

"Well, I'll still try. And if not, I waitressed before I came here, so maybe I can find a good gig doing that. Or some cool boutique. Just something that PAYS! I'm not that picky as long as I can find something that will give me enough time and money to paint."

Dad would be so proud that I was showing initiative, I just know it. Hello, I get it so much more now. I'm freaked out but it's kind of the best. Finding a way to afford to live here is now my life and that's fine. I deferred school for one semester, but I'll be damned if I put it off for another. I got in, I'm going.

When we stopped for water again, I was still thinking about it. "I have to make my own stuff, too," I told her. I was still breathing fast and it was partly from our run and partly I think because I'm just running kinda hot these days, everything feels INTENSE INTENSE INTENSE. "I'm dreaming about those damn pieces. I feel surrounded. I have to start my own projects for me."

She squirted me with the water bottle. "Well, you're doing those funny little drawings, right? Like the one you gave that guy. That seems like a good way to keep making stuff."

I shrugged. "Those are just quick one-offs, y'know? Like practice sketches, almost. I've been posting them online and people like them. So maybe."

Grace shoulder-checked me gently. "It's okay to be nervous."

"Thank god," I laughed, "because I'm like really good at it. Maybe I should get my degree in Being Stressed Out!"

We ran until we hit a neighborhood called Battery Park. We reached the lower tip of the island, and I could see the real Statue of Liberty! On our slow jog back the Statue of Liberty Guy was gone.

I hadn't really thought about #NYSeen as a "project" in a bigger way, but maybe G was right. I wrote again to that commenter who wanted me to do a drawing of her cat, but she still hasn't responded. Crossing fingers that maybe that could be some extra $$$.

9/6 9:30 pm

I just texted Kennedy to see if he needed any last-minute touch-ups on the pieces, if there were any problems with the delivery, if there was anything I should be doing.

We're good for tonight. Thx for checking in.

I'm free.

It's just me, myself, and I.

What to do, what to do . . .

9/7 2 am The Cats beau parlor. Meow.

I tried to paint on the roof, but it was too dark. Days are getting shorter.

I came here and laid down a few newspapers I got from the recycle bin in the lobby. I'll find a better place but this was okay for tonight. Oscar saw me but he promised he wouldn't tell Maria. I'm not supposed to be painting in here.

Streaks of gold-yellow like the cabs and the 2 pm sun and the subway platform safety lines. The streaks are speedy but not fast enough. They need to be breakneck and if I really work that way, I'm going to get paint all over the parlor. The gold-yellow should be electric. This looks too constrained, too tight, too "following the rules"—even though I'm breaking them by painting in here. What an outlaw.

But my blood is rushing anyway. I'll find a real space for me and my work. If I can get my blood rushing in the Cats parlor, I can make it work anywhere. ME-OUT.

I woke up from another paint-mouth nightmare to a call from the front desk so I went downstairs in my pjs. Maria handed me a little black shopping bag and said, "Special Delivery for Miss Piper Perish."

I told her I didn't order anything. "Well, it's got your name on it, old-timer."

There was a note attached:

Hi Piper!
Kennedy told me you're staying at the Webster, my old haunt. Such a time warp! I saw these earrings and thought they would look great with your hair. They're the perfect length and color for C's show. See you there.
                                        X, Rashida

She did this for me??? So incredible!

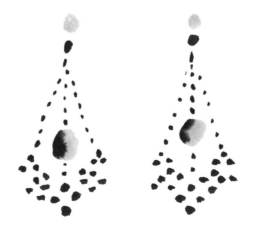

104

It's finally not a million degrees in my room and there is actual wind. Niiice.

The nightmare I was having this time was that my pieces weren't at the MoMA tomorrow.

I was at the museum right before the show was about to start. Fog from a fog machine was everywhere, and I heard people coughing and milling around, but I couldn't see them. Occasionally, a flash would happen, like a camera flash. I kept feeling the walls to find my art, and I was touching these historical masterpieces, but my stuff was nowhere to be found. I could hear Carlyle's voice repeating, "They aren't here, they'll never be here." I kept searching, then crawling on the ground, thinking if I couldn't see my work, I could find them by touch. I remember trying to lift myself up, using the paintings like a climbing wall, and then the runway started to move away. Then I woke up.

I should have been there when the moving guys arrived at the studio, and just lived in the trucks for a few days. What if the screws and safety hinges I added fall out? How do I know the rando moving guys can be trusted to handle eight hearts and not have one of them break? My heart has LITERALLY broken before.

No. My pieces will be there and it's not my fault what happens to them outside of C's studio. I keep telling myself this.

Grace and I are hanging after she's done transcribing Eileen's latest talk and she's going to help me style an outfit around the earrings Rashida sent—I want to look perfect. I think Grace is almost as excited about C's show and my outfit possibilities as I am. I really wish she could come. Maybe I could still sneak her in once I know the layout.

I sent Si a text, since he clearly hadn't remembered: Tomorrow is the big day. Wish me luck. Can we please hang SOON?

Si: What's luck? You've got this.

I texted back: Want to come to the after-party? I can try and get you and Grace in.

Silas didn't write back.

I wrote: Can I take that as a yeeessss?

Si: I'll see you the day after. I'll take you to breakfast.

Me: What about class?

Si: I'll skip.

Me: No, you won't.

Si: I can skip ONE class. Not every day I get to eat waffles with a NYFW star.

Me: But my outfit's going to be rad!

Si: You'll put the Fashion in Fashion Week, no doubt.

Me: You're going to miss it if you don't meet me at the after-partaaay!

Si: Not a partaaay person. Sorry.

Of course he's not a partaaay person. ☹

9/8 11:45 pm

I went shopping with Grace. I didn't think she would have time today but she is definitely as excited as I am, plus Evan is driving her crazy and never sympathetic to her crazy schedule, telling her she's choosing politics and a career over love and she's like it hasn't even been a month, calm down. She says she's still happy to be engaged but I'm thinking thank god I'm not. She's so cool—how can she be with a guy who thinks like that? Didn't he know she was a poet? Or did he just think it was all like fun and games or something?

Found a black jumpsuit at the Goodwill in Chelsea, and it was too long and baggy, so I bought a travel sewing kit at Duane Reade and Grace helped me hem it and take it in. She is a queen with pinning and tucking—she could be a tailor. She said she wasn't crafty, but she's got skills. She's really handy overall, come to think of it. To tie in with the earrings, I'm borrowing a gold arm cuff from her. Also, I got this red scarf with a subtle leaf pattern at Goodwill and I wasn't sure I was going to use it, but we wrapped it around my head like an old-school Hollywood turban and we both were like duh, it makes the outfit. G fixed my hair so just a bit was showing, kind of flapper, kind of boho. My hair hits the bottom of my earlobes now, growing out. It looks choppy and I don't hate it. The earrings make the whole look come together.

Sent a selfie to Kit.

Who dat? she wrote.

Me!

Obvi. You look AMAZING! Next to you!

Grace! Outfit? New scarf? Approve?

10+! Maximus Gorgeousness!

ILU!!!

ILU2!!! Good luck!

Girlfriends > boyfriends any day.

Kit makes everything better and Grace makes everything better.
I wish Kit lived here and was doing this with us now. It's a
no-brainer that G&K would love each other because they are
both total style bosses, though in totally different ways. Kit's
funk-punk and Grace is city-hippie.

Okay, outfit is ready. Now it's all about tomorrow tomorrow
tomorrow.

Tomorrow, my art shows at New York Fashion Week.

Everything has to go right, or or or . . .

I won't think negative thoughts.

I need to breathe. Going to the roof.

9/9 5 am

Haven't slept. Tonight's the night. Already sent Kennedy a
bunch of texts. Only heard back: Busy. Nerves. So many nerves.
Everybody I know is asleep.

How do I even explain the last two days?

~~~~~~~~~~~~~~~~~~~~~~~~~~~~

Yesterday:

I got to the MoMA super early. My pieces were in a room called Holding. After my last nightmare I really needed to see my pieces and make sure they were safe.

All good!

Kennedy had a headset on and a clipboard in his hands and was running through the crowd like a fabulous chicken without a head.

🍂 black jeans

🍂 white button-down perfectly fitted shirt

🍁 red bow tie

🍁 super cute red glasses that I haven't seen him wear before

🍂 black Converse

He came over and touched one of my earrings and said, "Rashida was right. These are HOT on you. Huh."

"Thanks? I'm so nervous. I look okay? You look great!"

"Be cool, Piper. Exhale." I did and shook out my shoulders. He looked over my outfit. "Nice." Then he heard something in his headset and he said, "Be right there." He steered me over to a side door and nodded to it, like go in.

As I opened the door, someone from inside yelled, "Shut the door!" and I scooted in and did. It was like backstage at a school play x 100. There were makeup artists and hair stylists and makeshift vanity tables and dressing areas everywhere. Everyone and everything was moving in a perfect dance and I kept accidentally getting in the way.

I spotted Carlyle standing in a corner with his eyes closed and rubbing his temples and went over.

Me: Headache? I have aspirin.

He held his hand out and I dug in my bag. Felt like Mom, always having what everybody needed in her bag.

Me: I saw our pieces in the holding area. I think they look good.

C: Yes.

He swallowed the aspirin without water.

I don't know how people do that.

Me: Are you happy? With them?

C: Piper—his voice was tense—yes. If you don't need anything else right now, I need to focus. We'll talk after the show.

Poor Carlyle. I felt bad for the "old man." If I was nervous, he must have been 10x worse.

I left him and found a vacant standing mirror. I fixed my hair how Grace and I had planned, and touched up my makeup, which at this point was total raccoon eyes thanks to humidity and sweat. I wanted to redo my sharp cat's-eyes that we had perfected back in the Web after watching tutorials, but now my hands were jittery and my legs were lightning bolts. Texted Grace: So jumpy. Wish you were here.

She texted back: Me too, girl. ☺ Take all the pictures!

I tried to roll my shoulders and focus like Carlyle, exhale like Kennedy said, but I was wobbly and not because of my platforms, so I decided I needed some food and headed outside the museum, where—I ♥ NY—there was of course a pretzel cart with a nice pretzel man. Whew.

I shoved the pretzel into my mouth and took a selfie with my phone, giving a dumb what-the-hell-am-I-doing-just-freaking-out face to send to Grace before devouring it. I looked v. cute in it actually, so I texted the pic and BEFORE THE BIG SHOW to Grace and Si and Mom and Dad and Kit and Enzo, too.

On the way back in my phone chirped.

Knock 'em dead, Piper.
And don't choke on that pretzel.
Love, Your Dad Hank.

Sweet Dad.

Everyone who came to the show looked A-MAAAAZ-ING: over-the-top huge orange suede boots paired with a copper lamé minidress, an expertly cut women's violet tuxedo with no shirt underneath, a Chanel jacket with the sickest tweed cargo leggings and white platform kicks. Beyond fashion. Even the all-black ensembles were super individual and so intentional and well done, and I had a flash of wishing I had done more with my own outfit.

But—nobody was looking at me, just like Kennedy had said.

A few women were photographed in front of the MoMA's special artists' entrance and they looked super familiar. Maybe they were actresses? They were holding hands and posing in these super-casual flirty poses, hanging on like that's how they hung out all the time and it made me think of how me and Kit used to laugh at magazines that always showed barely dressed women hanging all over each other, like that's what best friends do, just wrap their legs around each other. I snuck a quick pic and sent her: BFFS HANGING ALL OVER EACH OTHER IN THE WILDS OF NYC. Kit texted back OMG THEY LIVE!!!

"There you are," Kennedy said, appearing next to me. "Carlyle needs you backstage. You'll be stationed there. We don't have a seat for you, but stand by the monitors and you'll see the show. That's better anyway. Cool? Cool." I nodded and he glided us through the growing crowd on the sidewalk in front of MoMA and into the special entrance.

"Here she is," Kennedy said, giving me a gentle shove in front of Carlyle. People were calling for Carlyle to approve certain looks and he snapped, "Come" over his shoulder to Kennedy and me, and we ran behind him to watch him brush, straighten, and help him make quick changes to models who were lining up in his dresses. I thought the dresses would have more oomph to them when they were all together, but nope. I definitely wasn't feeling some over-the-top, pee-my-pants reaction to his work, which made me think maybe there was something wrong with my taste. They looked like flicks of fire but with no warmth. There was nothing that made them look collectively . . . powerful. Maybe that's how my art really did come into play?

Was he saying something about uniformity? Conformity? We all have the same blood? But we don't. There are different blood types. Maybe it was brilliance and I wasn't smart enough to understand it, but I didn't think so. I wasn't sad about not getting one of the dresses. Hard pass.

I tried to keep my face neutral and be glad my art would at least make his line feel more alive, and then music started booming from the other room. I watched the rows fill up on the monitor. André Leon Talley and Anna Wintour were easy to spot, they were right in the front row, and who could miss them? And a guy I'm pretty sure was Zac Posen, too, and then a whole mess of press and bloggers in another section. Man Repeller's peeps were even there! I was panicked and excited. The show depended on my art (and Carlyle's dresses obvi) but no one knew I existed. I was public and invisible at the same time. Weirdly, I kind of liked that feeling. If it failed, it wasn't me. If it succeeded, I stayed employed.

Anyway, all the seats were filled and everyone was talking, excited, and then Carlyle stepped onto the dark runway—too dark to see anything other than him, in a spotlight. He had changed from the jeans and T-shirt he was wearing backstage, and was now wearing a dark, olive-green suit with an almost blood-red-black T-shirt underneath, black belt, and wingtips. Total Freddy Krueger colors. I can't believe I'm writing this, he kind of looked like old-man hot. Or, handsome. He looked handsome. The silver in his hair complemented the green on his suit. Pretty sure that was planned.

"Hello, friends and journeymen. Tonight, I take my first small walk (he took a few steps like a model, laughter, applause, he seemed to know exactly what the audience wanted) into this astonishing, celestial world we call Fashion. Thank you for letting this humble outsider (oh please) take his first small step into the giant leap, into THE INSIDE. I hope you will join me in our travels into the new landscape of the body, mind, and spirit. Welcome to THE INSIDE COLLECTION!"

The spotlight turned red and then dropped to blackout before it lit up again, back in white light. My work lined the runway, like rocks on the moon. Jutting up and scattered. The music was banging.

I was brain-awake and body-numb. Here, where it wasn't mine, my art was something new, all its own, living in its perfect, pristine space and light.

The models moved down the catwalk, a line of soldiers in black stilettos. Straight-lipped, no expression in their eyes. The red in their dresses was energized when the light hit the fabric and they were in motion, and they looked better than they had backstage. Carlyle's collection was definitely not lacking in tension. I tried to see how Enzo might see it—he could always pinpoint what worked best about a fashion line. They were well made, the tailoring was impeccable, no doubt. I asked myself what Silas would notice about it, what kind of statement it was making. Something about the restriction of our bodies, of women in particular? Of anger, with the red? And I tried to figure out if I actually liked them at all. If they made me feel anything. As hot as they were, they just left me cold. Gut instinct, no. But they worked more than I thought they would on the runway.

The audience was into it. People shooting pics and writing stuff down. They were excited, I could tell. The models finished their walks and returned to the back of the stage. They never even touched my pieces, just walked around them. All of my friggin' extra stress over making them weight-bearing! Why in the hell did Carlyle tell me that? Or did something happen in a rehearsal? God, I hoped it wasn't my fault.

Carlyle escorted the models offstage, taking one final bow, and I looked over at Kennedy. He had tears sliding down his nose, and took off his glasses and wiped his cheeks, clapping,

laughing. He looked relieved. I started to ask him about why my pieces weren't used as anything more than speed bumps, but the applause was still going strong and Carlyle ran back out— an encore bow! A good sign! I chilled and kept my panic in my head.

Then backstage, the models immediately began to change with the help of the wardrobe assistants. One said she had to get to Marc Jacobs ASAP and she became a priority, all the wardrobe peeps swarmed around her like she was the Queen Bee.

I looked at my phone. The whole show had taken eight minutes. Eight minutes. All that for eight minutes. So much time. So much prep. Worrying about those damn weights. And only eight minutes.

Everyone from the front couple of rows was now backstage, buzzing around, and I trailed Kennedy. On the monitor I saw the moving guys taking my pieces, rough, stacking them like they were folding chairs, then up on a dolly, and away.

"Hey," I said to Kennedy. "Where are they moving my work?"

He put his hand on my back and said, "They have to set up for the next show. The art will be back in Carlyle's office before you are."

He was missing the point! They could ruin the pieces the way they were transporting them, and then they wouldn't be good for anything. Each piece needed its own moving blanket.

"But—"

"Piper." He sucked in his teeth, smiling. "Not now, doll."

I looked at the monitor. My pieces were already gone. Now other peeps were adjusting lights and sweeping the runway.

Rashida showed up, thank goodness, and led me around. She is sooo nice. She identified Carlyle's VIPs: friends, his brother, artists, designers, one of the Olsen sisters—I had no idea whether it was MK or Ashley!—and his favorite models, Mercedes and Abril.

"Ra-sheed-ah!" An older woman walked up on us.

Rashida air-kissed the woman, who had short frizzyish brown hair and was wearing all black including a lacquer skull ring almost the whole size of her hand. OMG, Kit would covet it like crazy. Supersized gold hoops drooped from her ears and they reminded me of drippy Dali watches.

"Glenda, this is Piper," Rashida said. "Piper, meet Glenda Frankel."

"Hi," I said, and Glenda grabbed my hand in both of hers and pulled me close, almost tipping over her wineglass, and said, "Where were you sitting?"

"I watched the show from back here."

"Those rocks on the floor—yours?"

I must have looked confused because she said, "A little Rashida bird told me" before I could answer her.

I nodded, hating "rocks." Why not just call them lumps? "I've spent the last month getting them ready for the show. Now I can finally sleep!"

"Oh, you're funny! There is no sleep this week, young one. Here's a hint—if you're looking for rest, take a car. You can catch a quick ten minutes of shut-eye in this traffic," she said, lifting her glass to me in cheers and sharing a look with Rashida.

"Well done."

I couldn't exactly tell what her look meant but I'm pretty sure it was code for something.

Carlyle, Kennedy, and another guy who was all stomach came up.

"Maxwell Silas," Rashida whispered in my ear, at least I thought that's what she said. Silas? The same Silas? Maybe I wasn't hearing her right. I tried to think if Silas had told me his dad's name.

"Who?" I mouthed but it was too late and the music was super loud.

"There you are, Glenny dear," he said, giving drunk Glenda a peck on the cheek.

I needed to grill Rashida right away. This couldn't be! I looked at Maxwell and Glenda. Glenda had almost the same green eyes as Si, but hers were a touch more mossy than emerald.

"What a thought-provoking show," she said to Maxwell, but hugging Carlyle. "How are we feeling?"

They all chuckled in a very insider-y way.

"I'm humbled," Carlyle said, touching his heart. He had his beads in his hand.

"Who are you kidding?" Kennedy said. "If there was anyone who was going to shake up Fashion Week, it's you. Heeeeey!" He threw a wave to someone walking by.

"Edgy," Rashida agreed. "Razor-sharp."

As everyone talked around Carlyle, I watched his eyes. He was listening but his eye was on the room. Nervous, like bad news was around the corner. Our eyes met, and I felt for him. I had been judged before, and it was weird just in Houston, even if I had received a good review. Up here, for him as a FAMOUS ARTIST, it's the real real-deal. Carlyle had to make money off this, had to sell out his line, not just a piece or two. For me the night was over—my pieces didn't break and no one screamed out in the middle of the show that the art sucked. Thank goodness! But this was only the beginning for this part of Carlyle's life and work, and he'd only know tomorrow, after the reviews, if he (a.k.a. if I) had done a good job.

I heard Carlyle mutter to himself "anxiety is an alien" as he twisted his little bracelet in his hand, touching each wooden bead. He saw me and then slipped it back in his pocket. Carlyle's show, Fashion Week—all of it had to work on so many levels. To the outside world, all of this looks so glamorous, but it's also so much work. All these people working their boots off, then doing it again and again for dozens of shows this week and like no sleep and barely any money. All with major stakes in the game: these shows aren't just their art, it's their work. Their job. I had never been around so much contained stress in my life.

I was dying to ask Carlyle about my pieces and why the hell we didn't use them the way he'd planned but even I knew this wasn't the moment.

A waitress brought champagne over and before she was done handing everyone a glass I snuck in a goofy selfie with my bubs and hit send to Grace and Kit:

AFTER: From pretzels to champy!

Then Maxwell took over and said "To Carlyle Campbell and his Inside Collection!" and everyone copied him and said "To Carlyle!"

When everyone went back to chatting Glenda reached over me and grabbed Maxwell Silas's arm and said, "Maxi-baby, this is Piper. What did you say your last name was? Paris?"

"Perish." I was trying not to shout into her ear. "Like die."

"Piper Paris is a fabulous name," she said. But it's not mine, I wanted to say. She whispered in Maxi-baby's ear and his eyes narrowed at me.

"You're responsible for those runway rocks?"

I nodded. Carlyle's whole body stiffened and his mouth pinched, like he had just eaten Sour Patch Kids. Then Maxwell wagged his finger between Carlyle and me. "So you collab'd?"

"Well," I started and then Kennedy interrupted. "It's a long story. You do not have time for all the details now, I promise. Carlyle took little Piper pigeon under his wing. She's doing contract work for us, that's all."

Would it kill him to introduce me as an actual artist? My heels were digging into my shoes.

"Your pieces elevated the entire aesthetic experience," Glenda added, sipping her bubbles. "They are signature Carlyle, with a perfect spontaneous touch. What synchronicity!"

Rashida whispered, "Come with me, I need you." As we walked away, she whispered, "So Carlyle. Always worried about brand control."

"Isn't his brand pretty strong? Like everyone knows him, right?"

She flipped her wrist back and forth, made the so-so hand. "He could be bigger. There's always bigger. That's what he aspires to be. That's the whole point of all"—she flung her hand around us—"this. To be as big as you can get without bursting."

120

"Did you know about him before Fashion Week? I mean, besides through Kennedy?"

"Oh sure. We run in the same circles, and the circles are small. Parties and such." She touched her fingers to her thumbs, making a little circle with each hand, then interlocked them with each other. "I'm a stylist, and he knows work I've done for other shows, so he brought me in for accessories. The silver chokers the models were wearing? Me. Sunglasses? Me."

"Wow. Those were my favorite part! They're so intense."

"Well, so was his collection. He's not a man of subtle taste." She winked and I laughed.

I stopped, suddenly remembering the most important thing ever. "Oh yeah, what did you say that guy's name was? Glenda's husband? Maxwell something."

"Yeah, Silas."

"Do they have a son?"

"I think they have two. You know them?"

"I think one of them goes to my school," I said. Before I could explain, we were by the models but my brain was doing somersaults. I couldn't wait to talk to Si about this.

"Brava, ladies! Benz, Abril, this is Piper. Say hello, biotches." Rashida is so cool. She immediately made it feel like we were already a group of friends.

Benz was touching up her lips and said, "Ay, babe" and Abril lifted her drink and said, "Salud!"

Rashida leaned her shoulder against mine and pulled me to her side. "Baby's first show," she said to the group. "She's working with Carlyle."

"What fun," Benz said. She popped her lips together, perfecting her matte, and rolled her eyes. "Is he working you to the bone the way he does poor Kennedy?" She had a cool British accent. "It's like a leash-and-collar situation between those two." Rashida laughed, but I couldn't tell which way she meant, between me and Carlyle or Kennedy and Carlyle, and who had the leash.

"It's not that bad," I said. Even though it's been stressful I don't feel worked to the bone.

"You're a good one," Benz said, and she winked. "So, we're going uptown for one more show"—she checked her oversized gold watch—"now! We're already late. Merde. See you at the after-party, darlings! Midnight-ish?" She quick-kissed Rashida on both cheeks.

"Natch," Rashida said, and Benz and Abril were out.

Then Rashida hustled us back to Kennedy.

"We had to be out of here like ten minutes ago," he said. "Let's move!"

A guy was hanging Carlyle's dresses in their bags, Kennedy hovering over him, and Rashida started gathering the chokers and sunglasses and slipping them into their velvet pouches. She had me count and stack the shoeboxes.

Outside, an SUV was waiting and they climbed in after we loaded it up.

"See you Monday!" Kennedy called.

"Oh, okay." No after-party for pigeons? I turned to walk away so they couldn't see my WTF face.

"Piper, he's joking. Come on!" Rashida pulled me in. Phew.

The party was fun and glam and bizarro. I wished Grace was there but at least Rashida was cool and there were some GREAT outfits!

Every person I bumped into was more major than the previous one (feathers, leather, and animal prints everywhere) and at one point I got tangled in some woman's face jewelry! She was wearing a huge silver star, half face mask thing that was attached to a head-band and was very Robocop. She let me snap a shot and I sketched it back at the Web—#FaceWear #NYSeen—because how could I not? OMG, people are loving my Fashion Week drawings. #NYSeen totally exploding with #NYFW.

Also, more time with supermodels, because this is my life now I guess. So weird! More on that later. Oh, one last thing about today—no breakfast with Silas. SURPRISE, SURPRISE. Called it.

9/11 8:45 pm

Took the 3 train with Grace to a 9/11 tribute at One World Trade Center early this morning before we both had work. There were firefighters and police and flowers everywhere. The whole time we were there, I felt like I would cry if I spoke—we didn't talk much. Grace wrote in her notebook. I left a note in a pile of photos and posters outside the fence of the Trinity Church. It was the best I could offer in the moment. Every time I started to try and draw it, my hand didn't know what to do. I used a phrase I saw on most of the posters and cards: "We will never forget you." Then I signed it, "Love, a Texan in New York." Saying more felt wrong. I just wanted to be quiet.

I was almost two when it happened, and Mom and Dad still talk about it every year and to be honest I'm glad I didn't see it happen in real time. How do you see something like that, or live through it, and keep going? New Yorkers are tough.

I have to get some water.

Okay, I'm back. So, rest of the day. I had to get my shit together and go to Carlyle's. I've had a blur of emotions today. But, here's me at Carlyle's office:

- black headband

- gold hoops (inspired by Glenda)

- boyfriend jeans

- black tank

- Adidas

- new red lipstick (in honor of the show but also because I wanted a treat and popped into Ricky's on the way there; super-fun makeup drugstore)

Kennedy looked up from his phone and saw me and waved me in. Carlyle rose from behind his desk, balancing himself on his fingers like they were tripods. "Piper! Welcome to the debriefing."

"Hi!" I waved. I was suddenly gossipy like after a party and I wanted to hear how he thought everything went and just dish. Also, we needed to discuss my pieces. He opened his arms again and this time I knew not to go for a hug. His beaded bracelet was on his desk. I threw down my backpack and took a seat.

"Hi!" I said. "Soooo, how's everything? Wasn't it so great? Did you love it? What's next, boss man? What do we do?"

He laughed, surprised. His face was a lot less tense than I'd ever seen it. I can't explain it, but I was 100x more calm around him, since the big show was now over. I'm excited to get started on something totally new—something not mine but totally fresh and real and here. Something that doesn't feel like it's from the old me. He was chill, too.

"We made quite an impression."

"I know!" I said. "I mean, I saw some stuff online." I didn't mention how much time I've spent googling the show. I checked Instagram and saw a few posts there, too. There weren't any great photos of my stuff—more of Carlyle's clothes than my art—but I still saved any that I found. MY pieces were called "grounded," "a latch to reality," and "a welcomed splash of camp, the red road-bumps cartoon foibles to the fascism of the fashion industry"—which I'm not sure I get. How can something be grounded and campy? The words sounded like compliments . . . and attempts at snark. I dunno. I have to decipher with Grace and Si.

"But uh." I tried to play this real casual-like and not get upset right away. "I noticed the models didn't sit on or 'connect' to my pieces."

"Yes, it didn't work out exactly as designed. When we rehearsed their walks in the actual garments, we realized they couldn't bend gracefully down and then rise quickly to move. Your work was too close to the ground."

". . . or your dresses were too tight?"

He cleared his throat and raised an eyebrow at me. "My dresses fit exactly as planned."

What that told me was that I did my homework and calculations and was prepared, but he didn't do his. All that time I wasted and he had no idea, or didn't care about how scared I had been. I was furious but tried to look neutral. I knew he was wrong and he did, too, but neither of us said it, and I knew I better not say anything more. Finally Carlyle tapped his pen against the bulletin board behind him.

I hadn't seen all the clippings they had tacked up to the board. There was stuff fresh from the New York Times, the Post, some other papers I didn't recognize, and a bunch of printouts from bloggers and websites. I drifted over, starting to read, trying to distract myself from my total rage feelings. I didn't catch all of the reviews there but I'm looking up everything again tonight anyway.

One New York Times quote stood out because it was in bold-face and I kept looking up at the board and seeing it: *"Carlyle Campbell's charge is to equip modern women for war, with wide metal chokers as shields, 1980s sunglasses as helmets, and Tibetan silk sheaths as armor—a nod to the working woman. He calls*

his introductory collection THE INSIDE, but truly it is a look at
women's fashion as current-day protection."

Whoa.

"Please have a seat." Carlyle pointed to the brown leather bucket chair in front of his desk.

I sat on my hands. It seemed like he was happy, but I still felt like I was in the principal's office.

"To say that our show was a success would be putting it mildly. The passion has erupted for more product and we don't have as many people in place as we initially imagined we needed. I'll be hiring, managing, and overseeing more in the next few weeks. Of course, we were expecting success, but let's just say, well, our expectations were exceeded."

"Yay!" I said.

"Yay indeed."

He gave his tiny tight smile. I think he likes me, whether he knows it or not.

"Piper, I will need you to stay on contract. You have the option to leave after my next show, my gallery show in October, as you know, but I would appreciate it if you would stay a bit longer, at least through the end of the spring. I will need to attend to more of the fashion and textile buildout of our company and Kennedy will be stepping up into a role of curator."

My stomach was dropping. I thought I was going to get a little more of a break. This wasn't even a little break—this was no break.

"We'll need more pieces, for which you'll need to completely UNDERSTAND my aesthetic. I will direct and you will produce pieces for the gallery line."

"So this is a gallery show, an art show. Do you have pieces for it I could see to start UNDERSTANDING this specific aesthetic, to have something to go off?" I tried to use his words.

He winced but covered it with a creamy smile.

"The art world is moving as fast as the fashion world these days. We'll need you to work quickly."

Okaayyy, not really an answer. He smiled again and the butterflies in my stomach turned into cheetahs.

"How many pieces?"

"One. See? You'll be living the luxe life now."

"I guess. But I still don't have a lot of time to figure out what you want."

He cleared his throat and I heard Kennedy stifle a laugh. "You'll come out more with us now, not just squirrel away in the studio, so that will be fun for you. It's time you absorb the full Carlyle Campbell lifestyle into your pores. You need to understand all of me, to keep our creations at my taste level. You'll do your studio work in the daytime. Do you understand what I'm asking?"

Taste level? No, I didn't (and don't) know what that is. But I nodded again. I can only imagine what Carlyle's idea of fun for me is. Absorbing him into my pores makes me feel like I'm going to break out.

"You can start by taking notes today."

So I did. So many notes. The important ones for me:

C's next gallery show: 10/30.

He's feeling a "New York nights" vibe; next gallery will show his gratitude and appreciation for the "outer life." If his fashion line was THE INSIDE, his art show is THE OUTSIDE. It's up to me, working with Kennedy, to pitch ideas to C.

I said, "Do you want paintings, sculptures, chalk drawings? When I think of outside New York, I think of litter and scaffolding and graffiti and brick walls and glass buildings and sirens," and he said, "What I see is you making pieces that represent all five boroughs. This is an opportunity for me to give thanks to the city that's given me so much. The energy, the passion, THE CHAOS! Your mind knows what I want. Play! Be free! If THE INSIDE was elegance, THE OUTSIDE is pandemonium. Think disarray. Think turmoil. Think outside the box, but like me." He smiled when he said that.

"So . . . messy?"

"If that's what it means to you. But still polished, of course."

"Of course."

"Think sociology, not psychology," he said.

"We see where you're going with it," Kennedy said to Carlyle, to cut me off, but I was just silent. When I didn't say anything, he snapped, "Piper!" as if I wasn't listening.

"It's just, it's your brain." How was I supposed to know exactly what his brain wanted?

He cracked his neck slowly and looked at Kennedy, who looked at me. "I look forward to the options," Carlyle said.

Great.

As for C's next fashion show, spring next year, he's already thinking "New Mexico new-age crystal spiritualism." He also wants to consider more fashion pop-up opportunities, which could be mini shows, mini stores, a combo. There are lots of possibilities, according to him.

I'm half-super complimented that he wants me to work on this and tempted to stay, half-feeling no way. I didn't come to New York to work on New Mexico.

Still, trying to be in the moment and feel happy he wants me to stay. All is good. I'm going to keep working for Carlyle, which means I still have a place to live and $. Now to find another gig so I can afford to stay in NY no matter what I decide about spring, save some $ for school, and more importantly, find another studio (not the beau parlors!) so I can make my own stuff! If I don't find my own studio and I keep working for Carlyle up through school starting in January, I have guaranteed income, but I don't get to work on any of my own stuff because he has first rights to my work made there. So it's not a question. I must get my own studio so he can't claim anything I make for me.

9/11 11:25 pm

Doing laundry and just got off the phone with Kit! We had some real-deal screen time.

"So you're telling me all that weight-bearing nonsense was . . . nonsense?" She shook her head. "Unbelievable!"

"Right? I feel that way too. But I guess, fine, whatever. I learned how to do it. And I guess not everything gets to be used, maybe that's the lesson. It's not like it was <u>MY</u> show. It was his. And I'm working for him."

"Next project, you need to trust your instincts and make a bigger stink. Don't let that guy scare you."

"That guy," I laughed, "is my boss, Kit Kat. And now I'm just trying to think of it in the context of all the times I worked on something and it wasn't right and I had to scrap it. It didn't mean the work wasn't worth anything, it just didn't get to be seen by anyone else. It was like . . . practice."

She wasn't having it and I totally got it, I was still a little bit pissed too, but the more I thought about it, the more I had to let it go. What was I gonna do? Sit there and dwell on something I couldn't change?

"Well, I think he's power hungry and just wanted to see you sweat. Hashtag PowerTrippin'. Now tell me something good or I'm gonna lose my mind." She wanted to know everything about the show and the after-party at the Odeon.

Kit: So like, is the Odeon still cool? I remember reading about that place forever ago. It's still a thing?

Me: It seems to be!

I didn't mention that I spent half my time there bumping into people and the other half drawing on paper cocktail napkins—a girl standing alone, people laughing, a waiter feeling totally out of place.

Everyone there was too cool for Sunday School. I should have just been like whatever and casually popped into a convo but I felt small-town and trying too hard and my brain couldn't stop circling the news about Si. Why were his parents there, or his mom and his adopted dad he'd had his whole life, and who were his parents, anyway?

"You loved it, didn't you?" Kit sighed into the camera. She looked supermodel starstruck.

I wished I had, just so I could tell her yes. "I kind of just wished you were there, or Enzo. But Rashida was really nice and everyone was very cool."

"Yes! Become besties with her and send some cool jewels back to Tejas! My jewelry box needs a refresh and everything I'm making these days is dullsville. I don't have my inspiration here with me!"

"Awwww. Just come here! I'm broke, we can be broke together!" Even though she's never broke.

I went to the rooftop and held my phone up so she could see the breath-stealing Tribute in Light art installation, the beams of blue light that shoot into the sky in tribute to the twin towers that Grace and I learned more about this morning, and Kit said they were faint and I said if you were here, you would see how strong they really are.

What a weird day.

I miss her so much it hurts.

9/12 8:15 pm Rooftop

We went to Shake Shack for lunch so I could finally catch Grace up on the show, the party, etc.

I got a frozen custard called Brooklyn Pie Oh My and cheese fries because they're vegetarian.

"So, you didn't meet the Olsens?"

"I wish. Only one of them was there and I don't know which one."

She said, "I wish you would have just gone up to her and asked 'Which one are you, my friend needs to know'!"

"Can you imagine?" We were dying.

"And what was everyone wearing?"

"Best look at the party: Rashida, hands-down. She is like the most stylish person I've ever met in real life. But everyone there was just so . . . so . . . pretty. Like in all kinds of ways, everyone here is just kind of gorgeous and amazing and stunning."

"Well, it was a Fashion Week party!"

"Yeah, but like even the waiters and the normals like me? HOT."

"Did you just call yourself hot?"

Again, dying of laughter. She's the best.

"I have something for you!" she said.

Even more proof:

A fake NY State ID with my photo on it. THE FAKEST. SO BAD.

I put my hand over my mouth.

"What? How? It's so phony-baloney."

"It's from our night on the rooftop. I blurred the background."

"It's horrible. And wonderful."

"Perfect for a DMV photo!" Both of us were laughing. She was so proud and I felt weirdly honored to have been thought of by my first real NYC friend, enough to commit a crime for. Ha!

I decided to give it a run back at the counter and ordered two beers. My first legit beer in NYC and I couldn't even finish it because I was stuffed on custard and fries.

Finally, Grace and I had some real talk about Evan. She said she thought she couldn't get any more depressed about him, "but I was wrong," she said, finishing my beer in a long slug. "Every day now there's at least a text, an email, or a call about me putting my life before our relationship."

"He needs to chill."

"We're supposed to be honest with each other, communicate," she said. "But then, I guess I'm not being honest with him. He wants me to feel regretful, not grateful, about this trip, about studying with Eileen June. Mostly about leaving him."

"Do you?"

"Maybe? But only because I'm hurting him. He could have come with me. He had the option. And he didn't take it. He had a choice also and he didn't choose me."

"Look," I said, feeling like I actually had something to offer her, "are you happy? Because I don't think his unhappiness should take away from you following your dreams and your happiness. What's that saying, you have to follow your bliss? You have to follow your bliss and he needs to get on the USS Bliss ship!"

"Dropping a little Joseph Campbell on me?" She raised an eyebrow. "Nice. You're right. More than ever, I am so happy when I'm working with EJ, or just working on my own writing, or whatever, just being in this city. Being away from Salt Lake!

It's making me revaluate everything I do and DON'T want. Eileen June's research means something to me. My help means something to her. What do Evan and I mean to the world?" She shrugged. "We're just another couple taking up space at this point."

"Right. So the only question you have to answer is, is he worth it? Is he worth you?"

"Hello, Dr. Phil! You are bringing the realness." She laughed again. "I want him to be happy, but I need to be happy, too. And I feel happiest when I'm making a difference in people's lives. Do you know what I've worked on with EJ just this week?"

I shook my head.

"Today we applied for a grant that helps immigrant kids with their writing and communication skills. She's going to get it again, she's won it like three times already. Yesterday we worked on a lesson plan for her poetry course with incarcerated high schoolers at Rikers. And tomorrow she teaches at Pace and I get to audit her class, which is one of my favorite parts of my week with her. She's just amazing. She makes doing good look, I don't know, cool. Like life."

She was practically preaching. I didn't feel this way about Carlyle at all.

I shook my head again, not "no" this time but "wow."

"I'm helping her with all of that. That's important. I feel like I'm making a difference."

"No kidding."

"And so, Ev? How am I making a difference by being with him?"

"Maybe you give him a sense of . . . purpose?"

135

"But he doesn't give me one."

"You're going to break up."

"Ugh. Don't say that."

Frozen custard and Real Talk and Girl Power and the best lunch date ever. Maybe I'm a secret Dr. Phil and she's a secret Oprah and we're gonna fix. this. world!

Oh and also a little shopping stop after and Grace got a purple fitted midi dress that she's going to wear at her reading.

I got:

✻ Steve Madden gold gladiator with ½ inch wedge

✤ two black sheath dresses that Grace talked me into buying, one short, one long, calling them classics. "Black never goes out of style in NY," she said. Truth.

Also, we passed twins who were dressed the same carrying the same prissy parasols even though it wasn't rainy. I know they'll probably show up in my weird-ass nightmares! I sketched and posted quickly.

Okay, now I've gotta cut myself off from shopping until I find out about school loans—the financial aid office still hasn't set a date for me to talk with Helen so I'm going in—and figure out how I'm going to make more dough 'cause Carlyle's checks aren't going to cut it for the next few months. Adulting is such joy. I gotta get real.

9/13 3:45 pm

Si showed me around the rest of the school, besides the photo lab, since he'd cancelled my Very Important Post-Fashion Show

Celebration Breakfast, and since he only had a half day of classes (guessing that's the bigger reason). I told him I needed to meet Helen Mundy and deal with financial aid.

After Carlyle's show, I have to admit, school seems a little less like a big deal, especially knowing Carlyle needs me for his spring New Mexico thing. I DID just premiere my work at Fashion Week (at MoMA!!!) and I already have another show to work on. But I was trying not to think that way too much. Don't want to be a diva. I keep flip-flopping but when I'm visiting CFA, everything feels really right, not just kinda right.

Me: I knew you wouldn't skip class for breakfast!

Si [looking uncomfortable]: If there hadn't been a test . . .

Me: Uh-huh. Sure.

Si: All right, Rebel without a Cause.

He likes that I give him shit. He tries not to smile but I see it.

All it took was his tour of the main building and like that, it made me want school again. I could smell the art in the air. What was there was NOT on the runway. This place is art top to bottom, not just tops and bottoms. Ha! I can't wait until I'm officially a student.

So, Helen Mundy. Silas was not surprised that seeing her was at the top of my school to-do list since I've been worrying about financial aid. Mom and I talked to Helen so much when I was accepted that I felt like I already knew her and besides, I wanted to make sure I had all the most up-to-date scholarship and financial aid forms. Anyway, she was in a meeting, but the office assistant, wearing bright blue glasses that matched her hair, made an appointment for me.

It's official: Meeting with Helen Mundy, 9/16, 10 am! FINALLY! I wrote it on my hand.

I said I liked the girl's glasses and Silas said her name was Carly Fishman and she was a senior. "Is she good?" I asked him and he said "She only works with neon," which is so him. Never a good or bad, but always SO JUDGY. Anyway, I want to see her stuff.

Then we walked to another building, all red and glassy and shiny-looking, and I got to peek into some of the studios. I started to take pictures even though Si winced like I was a twerp but I don't care because I'm not trying to impress him like a girlfriend anymore. Whatever. It was exciting! There was one lecture hall where a teacher was pointing to a slide of a furry teacup, saucer, and spoon and I cracked open the door to hear her.

"So, why do we think Méret Oppenheim would object to her aptly named OBJECT being called surreal? What isn't surreal about taking a porcelain or ceramic object and wrapping it in fur? Is it that we expect these objects to be smooth, and she subverts and softens our expectations at the same time? Or does she? Is the obvious answer necessarily the correct one?" She called on a guy raising his hand.

"Maybe it's surreal that she insists it isn't surreal?" the student asked. "Some kind of meta-metaphor?"

His classmates giggled and he looked around at them. He had short brown curly hair and a killer smile, even from where we were standing.

"Go on." The professor leaned on her pulpit, as if there was no one in the room but the two of them.

Si pulled my arm and I followed him out the door.

"Wait," I whispered.

"Why?"

His eyes creased toward each other.

"What?"

"It's dumb. Never mind." Silas sighed. "It was that guy."

"The one who said meta-metaphor?"

"That's Joe Gillman."

It took me a sec.

"Oh. Oh!!! Joe the conceptualist? Joe, god's gift to the art world?" I started giggling.

"That's him."

"Oh, please," I said. "I was excited about the teacher. Not that dork." I didn't mention that I had ONE HUNDRED PERCENT noticed Joe Gillman's billion-kilowatt smile.

He kept walking, faster, and I tapped his elbow.

"Si! I didn't know that was him. Who cares if he's funny?"

He looked at me then shook his head. "Well, that's really it anyway," he said, ending the tour. "There's not much else." He had fallen into a bitchy mood just because of Joe. I tried to pull him out.

"Okay," I said. "Well, thanks. Now that you've shown me the school, I get to show you something, okay? I'm going to a poetry reading that Grace is doing at the Café Angelou tomorrow and I want you to come with me. I don't want to sit alone." I had just thought of inviting him in that moment. "And besides, you have a thing for words. It might be fun. Even good." I wiggled my eyebrows.

His dimple was back. "I'll try."

"You should try just a yes or a no sometime." I nudged him.

"I don't love poetry, though," he said.

You're cryptic enough, I told him, and things were semi-OK again.

Then we were stopped in front of the lobby glass doors.

"Jamie."

"Hey," Silas said, kind of abruptly, though it always sounds like his words are slamming into walls.

I couldn't help staring. Robbins McCoy was eye to eye with us. He raised an eyebrow.

The sharp chin and diamond green/copper eyes from the pictures I had seen of him were real.

Skinny. Sharp. Devilish. Familiar. I guess just because I had seen him online so much.

Robbins McCoy was one of the main reasons I wanted to come to CFA. His paintings are scary and intense and alive and I love them. One of the most AWAKENED moments I've ever had with art was when his first collection was visiting Houston: hyper color Italian horror posters, bizarro and twisted and somehow commercial. No wonder Warhol loved him.

"Just leaving for the day?"

"We were, yeah." Silas cleared his throat, then tried to sound more put together. "This is Piper. She's a first year next semester. I was just giving her an early tour."

"Piper Perish?"

I nodded in disbelief. He knew my name???

"I was on the admissions review board and one of your most vocal supporters," he said. "Why aren't you attending this semester?"

"She got a job!" Silas said at the same time I answered, "I couldn't afford it."

He looked at both of us.

"Financial aid wasn't enough," I said. "I'm still coming, but I'm working with Carlyle Campbell, just for now." I was trying to convince myself, too.

"An apprenticeship," Silas said.

"I'm a contractor." I thought that sounded more professional, but Robbins made a huffy noise. "Well, good luck with that. And we'll see you when you're ready to join us."

"Oh, I'm ready now," I said, desperate and a little clingy. I didn't want him to think I didn't care. But he just started to move past us, when I had a sudden spaz attack and said, "I'm a big fan of your work. I saw the exhibit at the Menil Collection. In Houston."

He lifted his chin.

"I'm not trying to put off school," I told him, in case he thought less of me for taking a gap semester or whatever this was. "I'm just trying to make enough money so I can study here. And I start in January, so."

He looked me right in the eyes and I was like, YIKES, this guy is intense. Not that I thought he wouldn't be but . . . jeez.

"I really liked your portfolio. Don't lose yourself between now and then. You stood out." Then he nodded at the security guards and passed through the gate into the school.

Don't lose yourself between now and then. Easy for Robbins to say, I thought.

Si tapped me on the arm to stop me from staring at Robbins as he walked away.

"Is he always such an ice king?"

"That was Robbins being nice, Piper. He's a hard-ass. He breaks you down to build you back up. All the faculty does it. Don't take it personally. Especially coming from Robbins."

"Easy for you to say. He likes you."

"I wouldn't say that." He huffed, just like Robbins. Copycat. "C'mon, let's get lunch."

9/14 2:45 am After the Café Angelou

Grace KILLED IT tonight. She's a hugely mind-blowing writer. She's raw onstage and her poetry is political—not a surprise— and some of it rhymed but it was mostly free verse and it just flowed so fast I could barely keep up with it. It was like going out dancing, when I don't even notice I'm sweating until the end. Or when I'm really painting and I'm in the zone and hours have passed and I had no idea. She made me want to paint right then and there. I told her that and she said, That's how I felt after I saw your pieces for Carlyle's show.

Oh, sure!!!

Her words are worth a thousand of my pieces. More!

I introduced Si and her. He couldn't keep his eyes off her the whole time, onstage and off.

"So you're the Silas I've heard so much about!" She gave him a classic Grace hug and even though he's so non-huggy-awkward, he let her. He and I were both fan-girling Grace, but his vibe was different. "I'm really glad I got to meet you tonight," she said. Grace is so charm central, everybody just connects with her on sight.

"Your poems are really, really . . . good." He laughed, nervous. Hand in his hair. "Not good. Better than that. I guess I'm not the poet."

"Thank you! I was nervous, but I think The Flying Lesson came out well."

"I loved that one," he said. "Was that a sestina?"

"You know what a sestina is?" Her smile took over the whole room.

"Yeah." He shrugged like it was nothing but the two of them were clearly vibing each other.

"Me too!" I said, but neither noticed me. Hi, I'm super dumb. Seriously, I need school. WTF is a sestina?

She headed off to meet more of her fans and I turned toward Silas.

"So you don't like poetry, huh?"

He blushed.

"What?"

"Silas! What's a sestina?" He was blushing even harder. So busted.

Grace interrupted. "Sorry, guys. I gotta head to Eileen June's and I think it's no friends tonight. No offense."

"It's all good," I said, relieved. I didn't really want to witness Silas falling for Grace up close, which was so obviously happening. It would be so stupid to force something between us that clearly doesn't work, but still, I don't need to have a front-row seat to their love connection. But good for him/them. Si and I share art and that's what we have and I'll take that over a lukewarm love any day. I can't wait to talk to Grace about everything at breakfast.

I drew on some bathroom paper towels and left them tucked into the café mirror. "Grace, the poet" with a ☺. The lighting in there sucks.

Oh and also, this is big—Si and I met the Angelou manager, Lita. She was wearing a red chef's smock with Café Angelou mono-grammed on the pocket and a blue bandana holding back her huge curly gray hair. We asked her what else happened in the café. She handed me a calendar of events and asked me if I was a poet, too. Nope. Artist.

"Oh yeah? What's your poison?"

"I'm a painter."

"Walls, houses?"

"No, I mean"—(possible career option???)—"fine art."

"I'm busting your balls, Pippin."

"It's Piper."

She just cackled.

"Well . . . do you need your walls painted? They don't look bad or anything, but I am looking for some extra work."

She tilted her head. "You've got some chutzpah. What's your price?"

She made me want to have chutzpah! What a great word!

"I could do the whole place for"—I looked around—"$300? You pay for the paint and pick the color."

"Oh, I get that honor, do I?"

"And I'll even"—idea alert!—"hang one of my pieces here."

"Way to hustle, Pippin. I like you. I hope your work's got as much punch." I liked her too. She reminded me of an old hippie grandma crossed with Tony Soprano.

"You get these walls in good shape and you might be able to hang a few of your beauties, as long as me and Mort like 'em. And you repair any holes after you take your work down. Never leave a mess in somebody else's home, first rule of business."

"Of course."

"Mort has to like them, too."

"Got it." Got it the first time she said it, too. Mort must be the other owner or something.

I agreed to email her a pic of my work. She has a Hotmail account—I'm praying she knows how to open an attachment.

"Never leave a mess in somebody else's home." —Lita

I showed up exactly on time. I made sure to leave early enough, even if my train—a red one, the 1—was late and it was.

"Come in," said Carly, the girl with the cool glasses, sitting at the desk. I wanted to ask her about her neon work but decided to be chill since she seemed chill. There would be time to talk later.

"You're Piper? Ten am appointment?"

"I am, hi," I said.

The door opened and I heard, "In here, Piper."

I crossed my fingers at Carly, for luck.

Helen was sitting behind her desk, removing her reading glasses. A silver necklace with a moon was dangling down her black turtleneck. There were no overhead lights on, just a small lamp turned on at her desk. Kind of exactly how I pictured admissions in art school. Even though it was morning, it felt like night.

"Hello, Ms. Mundy!" I said, reaching my hand over to shake hers.

"Helen—" she said at the same time I said, "Helen," because it was just then I remembered she told me to call her Helen. I was just too excited and it felt too real, like I was finally meeting my fairy godmother. She shook my hand and gestured for me to sit and I tried to get calm but my legs were shaking a little.

"Tea?" she asked.

There were photos of cats and a dog and a big, bright bird. Her desk was cluttered and her bookshelves were stuffed with knickknacks. She definitely liked <u>stuff</u>.

146

"I'm okay, thanks." I picked up a stack of books off the chair so I could sit down and put them on the carpet next to a messy pile of her shoes.

"Wonderful." She poured hot water into her cup and I caught a whiff of lavender.

"Thanks for seeing me today," I said.

She was so calm, and I was trying to appear relaxed too, but it was hard because I was so hyped just to be there, to feel it all coming true. This meeting just made NY and school one level more legit.

"So, welcome to New York. How have you been spending your days? What do you think of our little city?" She slipped open a file and looked at her notes.

"Well, um, I participated in my first Fashion Week show, working for Carlyle Campbell, the artist, and it went really well. There were some good reviews, but I'm not mentioned by name, but the artwork was mine, so, that's cool. But it was his premiere clothing line, THE INSIDE? Maybe you read about it in the New York Times?"

She gave me a Mona Lisa smile. "You worked with Carlyle Campbell? That must have been a valuable learning experience."

"It was! Is! I've learned a lot."

"Like?"

Like? Oh god, I wasn't ready to talk about him outside of Kennedy or Rashida or Grace. I knew I had to make him and my experience sound good. I sat up straight and planted my feet.

"Like, um, deadlines? Like meeting deadlines and being very organized? And where to buy art supplies. He likes Soho Art

147

Materials." I laughed nervously and waited for her to ask another question, but she sat quietly.

"And I've gone to poetry readings and explored my neighborhood and tried to find my way around the subways and the city, you know, just figure it all out. And I finally started running although I still haven't made it across the Brooklyn Bridge. Or to the Bronx. Is that what you mean? I've only been here a month."

She was mid-sip of her tea, so I kept going. Mom would say I was having a very Chatty Cathy moment.

"And I got another job!" I remembered in the moment all of a sudden. "Outside of working for Carlyle. I'm painting . . . free-lance. Like a contractor gig." I was trying to make myself sound professional, like I actually knew what I was doing with my life instead of winging so much of it, but maybe that's what it was like to live here, kind of always winging it.

"I'm very impressed, Piper. You're very enterprising. We like to see that in our students. So, you're still on course to attend the winter semester beginning in January?" She was so much more abrupt than I expected. I don't know why I thought she'd be all warm and fuzzy.

"Yes, of course."

She blew on her tea. "Even though you're having this very productive life outside of school—working for a newly emerging designer who's also an established artist, AND working as a painter?"

"Yes, but . . ." She didn't know how much I needed this place, needed to belong here, and needed to improve my skills. "I'm ready to be here."

"So has your financial situation changed?"

Gulp. "Um, not exactly. That's why I'm here. I definitely need to apply for grants and scholarships. And I'm willing to take out loans if possible, in my own name."

"What about once you're enrolled full-time—do you think you'll stay committed to your employment and be able to focus on your school assignments? CFA is a full-time job itself."

"If I have to, yes. I'll make it all work."

"All right, then. Your paperwork is due back to our offices on October first."

"That's soon!" She shot me a look and I said, "Yes, ma'am, I'll have them in on time."

"I feel confident that you're going to make this work, Piper." She gave me a little squeeze on the arm and even though she apparently wasn't the hugging type like Ms. Adams or Grace, I think she liked me enough.

As I left, a guy walked in with his parents. "We're here to see Mrs. Helen Mundy," the dad announced. I was a little jealous and had a little ping of missing Dad, but also, hey, I did this on my own.

I'm going to C's studio now to paint. He won't know I'm there and if he does, I'll just say I'm staying warmed up for his October project. But really, I need to work on something fresh to show Lita for the Angelou. I didn't hear back from her yet and I hope that she just doesn't know how to reply or something, not that she hated the photos of my high school art I emailed her. I just need to get messy with some paint or I'm gonna go crazy.

9/16 8 pm Hiding out in the Barnes & Noble Union Square

I left the studio and ducked right away into Hamid's to buy an umbrella. I'm soaked because I also trip-slipped over a bag of garbage on the curb right into a huge puddle and cut my cheek on something. Bleck. This storm is insane.

"You stay here! Freddy will be on shift at ten!" He put a Band-Aid on my cheek and gave me a cup of tea on the house.

"No, thanks, Hamid. I'm not waiting around for two hours."

"Love is worth waiting for."

OH PLEEEEEEASE. Also, Freddy is 40. If he's like H, I'm sure he's super nice, but c'mon, not trying to marry anyone right now.

9/17 Morning in the Web caf

Coffee and burnt English muffins—dumb toaster—and Grace, who looked like she was going to cry when I sat down.

"What's up?"

"I have to get going, I'm going to be late," she said. "I'll tell you about it tonight, but—just Evan being Evan and first-world engagement problems." She wiped at her eyes, then put her face in her coffee mug and took a last gulp.

"You sure?"

She pulled her MetroCard out. "I have to catch the train to Queens and then get a bus to Rikers to meet Eileen June and I don't know what the hell I'm doing and I'm definitely about to break up with him. I'm not okay. But, I'm fine."

"I'm sorry. Text me when you're on the way back and I'll be here!"

"Later, babers."

She gave me a quick side hug that got my neck wet.

9/17 3 pm-ish In cab

Running errands—not art errands—all day for Carlyle. Writing later. Dude has a lot of dry cleaning and likes good cheese. Good = $$$!!! His groceries come from five different places, he likes to cook. I've already spent like $300 on his cards and not half done.

9/18 4:45 am Back from party

Si and I met at 9. Took the L to Williamsburg, which is in Brooklyn! Finally made it to Brooklyn!

We could hear the party from the street even though it was seven flights up on the building rooftop—omigod they need an elevator in that building—and when we finally opened the door, it was an explosion of people and music. Mo was already there and screamed, "THE BLAST!"—the band name—"just went on! KILLING IT!"

Somebody put beers in our hands and we cheers'd.

"I thought you wouldn't go to paaaaartays," I shout-said into Si's ear.

"I like these guys, the drummer went to CFA." He was bobbing. I think that's how he dances. ☺

"To the Blast!" We touched red cups and threw 'em back.

I was dancing, and it felt so good to dance, it had been too long, when a girl in a ratty fur jacket and jacked-up black hair walked over and flung her arm around Silas. She turned to me. Very screwed up/drunk/stoned/something.

"You okay?" I said to Drunk Girl.

"It's a free country, right? Or wait, is it!" She came over and linked her arm in mine and looked up at me, resting her head on my shoulder. Such a hot mess just waiting to be my next #NYSeen. She had no idea.

"Right." I kind of laughed, looking to Silas for a clue about what the hell was going on.

Silas looked super uncomfortable and excused himself, saying, "Let me refill you" and then he ditched us. He swerved around a bunch of party peeps to the garbage-can punch and started madly ladling cups, leaving me with Drunk Girl.

"So, what's up?" I asked and she just laughed and danced away into the crowd. Okayyy. I watched her move, she kind of seemed fun, and then my view was blocked.

"Hi there."

"Hi," I said to the most ridiculously charming smile connected to the clearest honey-brown skin, the deepest brown eyes, and the curliest/waviest brown hair I had ever seen in my whole life. It was like Bruno Mars and Rami Malek were mashed together, and the most perfect human in the world was swaying in front of me.

I actually lost my balance, and not because of the beer. He didn't seem surprised I was gawking at him.

"I'm Joe."

We did a hello wave thing, not shaking hands, which was good because I didn't want him to feel my sweaty palms.

Then, whoops: "Seriously?" Si said, stepping to him. He went from wiry to puffed up, trying to tower over Joe. It made him look very dumb and very boy.

"I was just meeting your friend," Joe said, still with that amazing grin on his face. "I didn't get your name—"

"Piper—"

"Move it along, Gillman," Silas said.

Of all people, that's who he was!?!? Of course, I should have remembered the smile. He had bounced around in my head a couple of times after I visited the school, but I tried to put him out of it. Silas hates him so it's not like I want to start more shit between them.

But seriously, everybody knows everybody here. I didn't expect NY to feel this small.

"Okay, tough guy." Joe shook his head, laughing. "Don't worry, my man, I got my hands full." He gave a half-wave goodbye and then made his way to Drunk Girl, but not before he shot one more look at me.

"See ya, Piper." GOD.

Just then Mo showed up, leaning on me tipsy-style. "Piper plus Joe plus Astrid equals Stay! Away!" He drunk-wagged a finger at me. "You should. She's a pain in the ass. She screwed up my boy here something good."

"No, she didn't, he's drunk." Silas shook Mo off and went down-stairs into the apartment so he could pee and I asked Mo for the

411. He yelled, "Mo already told you everything!" and made the zip-up-the-mouth motion over the music.

Obviously he didn't. Duh! I'll find out everything when those guys aren't drunk as skunks. But I assume Drunk Girl is Astrid.

Dancing was the best. While Silas was gone I got in my zone, dancing, drinking, totally into this band, and, what do you know, it wasn't long before Joe and I locked eyes again. It wasn't hard because I hadn't stopped tracking him and hoping he would turn back to me! He did and we were locked in. It was like he had been hoping too. We couldn't stop looking at each other, even as Astrid hung off him and the peeps in front of us kept backing into Mo and me. He looked calm. In control. I knew he was supposed to be an untalented jerk and that there was no reason in the world I should have been looking at him.

But.

If Mo wasn't there.

If Astrid wasn't there.

Mostly, if Silas wasn't there.

I don't know. Oh I know.

"Hey, Tex!" Mo said, snapping his fingers in front of my eyes. He saw me looking at Joe and I tried to refocus. Mo gave me a hard stare. He must have seen me and Joe and the apparently not invisible line between our eyes, the line that was bold and vibrating and electrifying like us, like the potential of us. The chemistry of us. I'd had moments on dance floors before. But not like this. I didn't understand my reaction to Joe. It was beyond physical.

Of course, Si came back. "What did I miss?"

"Nothing, bro," Mo said, thumping his chest. "Mo said dance! Mo said feel the music!" He started dancing when the Blast started playing again. He didn't say anything about Joe and me, not that there was really anything to say anyway. But I couldn't stop thinking about all of it:

Mo & Silas &

Silas & Astrid? &

Silas & Not-Me &

Silas & Grace? &

Silas & Joe &

Joe Joe Joe.

We were all dancing around each other in my brain.

#ThatPartyLife #NYSeen

I left a copy of this sketch on a paper towel on the roof inside of a red plastic cup. Sure someone tossed it but whatevs. At least I have a pic of it on my phone. Proof that I actually go to cool parties in THE CITY! And people are loving #NYSeen so much! So surprising to see what people react to! Loving all my likes! Somebody asked me if they could "live my life for a day!" Omigod.

9/18 11:15 am

I can't get out of bed. I'll go to the studio later.

After the party, Si and I grabbed snacks in Chinatown, which is much bigger and busier than the one in Houston. It's like an entirely different city down there. I had my first NY dim sum and I tried chicken feet for the first time! The texture was bigger than the taste. Super crunchy!

At the dim sum place, I asked Si about Astrid, a.k.a. Drunk Girl.

He shook his head. "There's nothing to say."

Me: Uhhhh, there's everything to say! You could barely look at her. Or Joe.

Si: What do you want me to say?

Me: We're friends, right? So just tell me, and I won't tell your new crush Grace that you liiiiiiike her!

He blushed and twirled a chopstick in his hand and stared at his plate.

"Omigod, are you giving me the SILAS treatment?"

He tried to hide his smile. He took the pen from behind his ear and started drawing on his paper place mat, the word "Yes."

156

"Why?" I said.

Si (on the place mat): "It's better when I draw. Or write."

Me (out loud): Okay. We'll both draw.

He drew a King Kong holding a little Astrid. I drew a smiley face looking shocked with a speech bubble that said OH NO!

"Sorry," he wrote, and then said, "I'm over Astrid."

"It's okay if you're not," I said, thinking of Enzo and how long it took me to get over him. Even when I was legit happy for him and his boyfriend, I still had flashes of missing the old us. People are so complicated.

"I just wish I didn't see her and Joe everywhere. I'm over her but he makes me feel . . . so out of control. Like I've lost my mind."

Well, that stopped any idea of me and Joe together. "Is he really that bad? Is it so awful they're together?"

"He is categorically the worst. He's just beloved, like he's the second coming, at school."

I sighed.

"You're fixated on him."

"Piper, Joe just . . . sucks."

I laughed but he was serious.

"Yeah, right, and meanwhile Robbins, Robbins's approval of him is . . . it's just, Robbins and me—"

"Yeah?"

He kept his eyes on a series of linked 3-D boxes he was drawing. "We're this."

"Connected? Interlinked? Square?"

He was drawing tenser, his hand gripped around the pen. I could tell he was getting weird but I didn't know what he was trying to say or what I should say.

"Robbins isn't just a teacher to me. I mean he is, but we have a very . . . difficult . . . relationship."

"Because he's like, your guru? I love him, too!"

"Because he's my real dad, Piper." He kind of spit and laughed at the same time, like he couldn't believe he had just said it out loud. He gulped his water and I stared at him over his glass.

"Your dad?" Oh my god. "No. No! Are you for real? You're not for real. How do you know?"

"Well, my mom told me, obviously."

I shot him a look and he mumbled, "Sorry. Of course you don't know. Hell, I didn't know all my life. Mom and Robbins met at some retreat in the Hamptons, where apparently everyone was hooking up all night. My dad, Max, my mom's husband, was off in Berlin working out some deal for an opera house. So, Mom and Robbins were a thing at the retreat and after, once they were back in the city. Until she found out she was pregnant. Robbins wanted her to leave 'my dad'"—he made air quotes around "my dad"—"but she wouldn't. I don't know why, it's not like staying with him made any of them happier."

"Wow." I let go of the napkin I had twisted into a paper snake.

"Yeah. You can't say anything, Piper."

"I won't. I wouldn't. Never." The whole restaurant was busy around us, noisy customers and waiters calling out orders and breaking dishes, and there was so much quiet at our table now, both of us just watching each other.

"So, you're the son of Robbins McCoy."

He bowed his head, and said, "The one and only . . ." and I couldn't tell if he was ashamed or what. No wonder he hated Robbins complimenting Joe and not him. No wonder he hated Joe, even though Joe doesn't know. It's still not Joe's fault, but no wonder Si was so weirded out about him and everything.

"That's why your mom told you last year? Because he was going to be your professor?"

"Before I started school, yeah. She felt she had to."

"Okay." I said. "Okay okay okay. It's okay." I was stroking his hand like he was a little kid.

We both drank our green teas. We didn't know what else to do. I was vibrating, I had so many questions. He wiped off his eyes and had stopped tearing up. I held his hand.

"Si, now is the time to tell you something weird."

He exhaled and kind of laughed at the same time. "Why not?"

"Um, I've been meaning to tell you this, or ask you this, actually, but I wanted to ask in person. Is your mom named Glenda by chance?"

His head popped up. "How do you—"

"I think I met her, and your dad, at Carlyle's show."

"What? How?"

"They came backstage."

"Well, that makes sense. They run in the same circles. I can't believe you met Mom."

"And Maxwell is your . . ." I guessed the right word was dad but I didn't want to call him "his dad" right after what he told me about Robbins.

"Yep, he's the one I call Dad. Let me guess: he was drunk."

"He was something." I kind of laughed.

"Then you met him," and then he kind of laughed too and relaxed a little.

"Si, I really like you. And your work. And about relationship stuff, I promise I'm not judging you about Joe or Robbins. And between you and me, my money's on Grace breaking up with her fiancé. They're NOT good together. So . . . I think you like her and I think she might like you, and I want you to know that it's good by me. What you and I have is different. We're like . . . like . . . Warhol and Basquiat. We're Van Gogh and—"

"Gauguin?"

"Yes! Yes, exactly!"

He gave me a sad grin and asked, "So, are you my life mentor or something?" and I laughed and said, "Oh god, you'd really be messed up. Nobody wants that!"

Inside I was like, OMG, I'm having another Dr. Phil moment.

We split the bill and Si picked up the place mat I had been sketching on. "Don't forget your masterpiece." I rolled my eyes but laughed. "No thanks. It's not for me. It's for them." I nodded toward the waiters and busboys busy near the kitchen and wrote quickly #NYSeen #Chinatown #ChickenFeet before I took a pic with my phone.

I was so happy to be back in my cozy apartment, my hideout from the world. The world is loud and sad and strange and scary and I wanted to be alone and home after Chinatown with Si. My head can't stop thinking about him and Robbins. My body can't stop thinking about seeing Joe at that party. And my soul feels extra guilty thinking about him when I know how much it would hurt Si now to do anything with Joe. ☹ I guess I just can't. I shouldn't even think about it. I probably won't see him again until January so what does it matter?

9/18 10 pm-ish? The studio

Painting—avoiding gold-yellows and grays, those are MY NY colors, so trying purples, greens, and browns for Carlyle—and sketching and tinkering and brainstorming all day trying to come up with ideas for him. Maybe something with the subway lines? I really want to work on something about the graffiti I saw on this brick wall on 9th Ave—it was obviously done by a company, it wasn't spontaneous and didn't look like it was from an actual graffiti artist at all, and I kind of want to mess around with maybe graffiti and typography and trying to look like advertisements? I dunno. Would that be Carlyle? Or is that just me? I've been scrolling through my pics and all the #NYSeens, which I don't want to use for him, but I'm trying to figure out what his inspiration looks like . . . and it's hard not to see through my own eyes. DUH. It's hard pretending to think, be, feel, and attempt to MAKE ART as someone else. But there's also this teeny-weeny part of me that likes the challenge. If I can BE CARLYLE, it's gonna be epic.

Grace just buzzed from downstairs. We're going to grab late din and some intense midnight movie she wants to see at Angelika Film Center. Maybe some inspo there? Byeee.

9/19 7 pm

This afternoon was the best, maybe the best since I got here. I worked on Lita and Mort's small office in the basement, but the space was so homey and Lita is so perfectly New York (or the way she says it, NU YAWK), I could have stayed there forever.

Lita only wants me to do a little work at a time so I'm going to work Tues. and Thurs. afternoons with her. I told her it might be easier for me to do it all in one weekend, but she said she couldn't afford to stay closed all weekend. Because I'm not just painting the café, I'm doing her office, the bathroom, and a room/studio above the place that she rents out. (She just lost her current tenants.) But that works out since I gotta kick it up a notch for Carlyle's next show.

"How long have you lived in New York?" I asked her.

"In this life? All 65 years."

I asked her about hanging my art, hoping she liked the pics I had emailed her, and she said, "Let's just keep it plain for a bit," and I looked at the floor, embarrassed, and she said, "Your stuff is good, but I don't know what I want yet. I have to see what the paint looks like! Nothin' personal. Okay, Pippin, what do you think of these?"

She held up three color samples.

"Whoa! I love them!"

"Thought I might add a little spice to the joint. Can't look at the beige anymore. That was Mort's choice. It's time for Turmeric Gold, Golden State, or Yellow Submarine. But I can't make up my mind."

Man, New-York-cab-yellow really is everywhere.

"Turmeric Gold," I told her. "That's the one. But doesn't Mort want to see it before I start?"

Lita looked up in the air, shook her head, then shrugged. "Mort says he doesn't care."

"Um . . ."

"From the other side, Pipps."

Lita's the sweetest kind of weird.

Okay, off to meet Si.

9/20 1:30 am

Met Si and Mo at Veselka before they had to go back to school for a film screening. I asked if they could sneak me in and they couldn't. Yay for them but bummer for me.

Veselka is cool and cheap.

Mo made sure to tell us that the food at Veselka is Ukrainian (Silas knew this), and then the history of Ukraine (Silas was aware), and which Ukrainian artists he really liked. Mark Khaisman is his top pick and I want to see his stuff.

I asked him, "How's school going?" like no big deal, and he stared at me and said "It is what it is don't worry about it." I wonder if that means things are getting better or worse for him probation-wise, but I don't want to be pushy. I'll find out from Si.

Oh, also Si asked me why I didn't bring Grace and he tried to play it off casually but he so wanted her with us! That boy is in luv-luv-luv!

We paid the bill and squeezed past a woman with swinging silver hair coming in the door and Mo's mood changed and he mumbled, "Look, look."

"Oh shit," Si said.

She looked familiar, but I couldn't place her.

"That's Patti Smith," Si said, gritting his teeth.

"The Patti Smith!?"

Mo said, "Shhhh, don't freak" but I was like, "Should we say something to her?"

And both the guys shook their heads and pulled me to the curb, saying, "Nooooooooo."

"Dude!" Mo said.

"Don't," Silas said.

"But she's the coolest," I said, like a doof.

And Silas said, "Yeah, so be normal. This is her neighborhood place. Get it?"

I agreed but like holy shit, this was a very New York celeb moment in a very New York City place! All the biggies at

Fashion Week were awesome, but she is old-school cool. The only celebrities I ever saw in Houston were the other Channel 2 weather forecasters Dad was friends with at work.

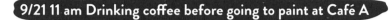

9/21 11 am Drinking coffee before going to paint at Café A

This is me.

Not journaling much because SO MANY FORMS. I <u>must</u> get all this financial stuff just right. No wonder Mom and Dad always look so stressed over money. It's another language.

I haven't seen anyone except Maria when I went to check mail and Grace in the elevator where she was on her phone, finger up and mouthing "Eileen June" at me.

My room is messy. No clean clothes. I don't have time to care.

Sometimes my place is so small it's perfect and cozy and sometimes I feel like I'm going to be swallowed in it. I wish I was better with money. I wish Mom or Dad had taught me how to do any of this stuff.

9/22 3 am Back at the Web after a "Carlyle Immersive" night out with Carlyle & Co.!

I'm supposed to be absorbing Carlyle's world but have mostly been in his studio, so I actually got to go out with C and Kennedy tonight and it was strange and weird and I took a lot of Carlyle-related notes. One of the perky-perks of the job!

I met the guys on Mulberry Street last night, in front of a pastry shop with the most fantastic-looking, fancy treats. They totally put me and Dad's fave TX donuts and kolaches to shame.

Kennedy was wearing a bolo tie, this cool print tunic, a black blazer, and fitted, faded blue jeans. I wore my black dress and gold gladiators and headscarf. Basically just rotating different outfits with the same five pieces now.

"Look at all the yummies," I said to Kennedy when they came up and he said, "Little Italy's best," and I asked, "Little Italy?" and he rolled his eyes, and said, "Look around." All the restaurants had Italian names and the souvenir shops were draped with Italian flags. OK fine, duh.

"Hi, Carlyle!" I said.

He does cool-casual better than any adult I've ever seen, like he has 24/7 access to Kanye's closet.

He cleared his throat. "Shall we?"

Shall we go to an event in a pastry shop? No-brainer. I nodded and he said, "Remember, take mental notes of everything you see for the show. You never know what we'll use. I'm still generating up here." He tapped his head. "I'm sure you are, too."

"Of course." I've been in the studio and playing but have nothing I'm ready to show him yet, because I can't figure out what he wants and obviously he doesn't know exactly either. No reason to panic except every reason to panic. And everything else I've been generating has had to do with financial aid forms.

We went through the pastry shop then through the kitchen to a door near the standing mixers. He knocked twice, the door opened, and then we followed a woman up a very steep stairwell covered with old-time photos in old-time frames. She opened another door into this gallery/studio/space that was decorated like an old-fashioned western bar. Kennedy called it "a modern-day speakeasy," now being used for an artist who didn't want a traditional showing, but needed an "immersive experience." There was janky cowboy saloon music playing but no piano around, just an iPad in the corner.

People recognized Carlyle, some of them said they loved his show, some of them asked what's next, I saw a few girls just whispering when he walked by, and eventually we got to the artist, a guy named Mikhail Lenin. He had a thick red beard and a bun on top of his head and he was wearing chaps and a western shirt with pearl buttons, the kind Ronnie, my sister's boyfriend, wears not ironically, and looked super-dumb, trying-way-too-hard. In my head, I could hear Enzo calling him out.

Mikhail's deal: he had manipulated some of his Instagram photos with filters so they would look like they were from the American West in the 1910s and '20s and contrasted them with some original, old photos he had also hung to play with our sense of "perceived mythology and legend." On some of them, he had also painted outlines around the scenery and the people in blinding fluorescent colors. Carlyle was saying things like "rustic tribute" and "outlaw photography, breaking the bounds of time and history." Maybe this was a trend, the old and new mixing, whatever that was, but this version of it didn't feel special.

Mikhail's work made Silas's work look downright groundbreaking in comparison. I thought of Silas's project at school, inspired by old Weegee pictures. But he was using his own art and concept, not some app technology. Si was making stories with his words and photos, and would allow the changing of the original stories by his viewers, instead of just throwing on filters and calling it outlaw. Si's art is almost collaborative, where Mikhail's is presentational.

Maybe Carlyle is just too old to understand how filters work so he thought Mikhail was reinventing film or something. I play around with filters on my phone, too. That's not what makes me an artist.

Carlyle pushed me forward.

"Young Piper, she's from Texas. I knew she would find your work a gas."

A gas as in ha-ha-funny, yes.

Mikhail put his hands in front of his heart and gave me a little bow. His nails were buffed.

I wasn't sure if I was supposed to, but I did it back. Kit would be laughing her ass off.

"Oh, that's lovely," he said. I didn't know what he meant, my bow or the fact that I was from Texas, and I couldn't tell what he was going for. The cowboy thing kind of conflicted with the whole Zen thing he had going on with his outfit, and it seemed like he was trying to sound Australian or something. "What do you think?" he asked. "As a Southerner."

"It's, well, it's," I said. I'm not going to tell another artist at his own show that he's reductive, that great Adams word. But I also didn't want to lie.

"It's STUN NING," Kennedy cut in, thank god. "I'm obsessed. AND please tell me where I can find those chaps!" Luckily then some other people came up who wanted to talk to Mikhail, so we went to the bar that was serving something called the Gold Rush—it had a lot of wine and fruit and gold flakes in it—and it was free!

"You think the work is stunning?" I asked Kennedy.

"Stunning isn't necessarily good." He winked at me. "You can be stunned by something because it's so. god. awful."

We both covered our mouths, giggling. "Why are we here?" I whispered. "If the work isn't . . ."

"Mikhail is H-O-T HOT right now," Kennedy said. "You saw that huge piece on him in the Times Arts section this weekend, right? And the upcoming show at the Guggenheim etc. . . . etc. . . . So, one does what one must."

"The Guggenheim! HE gets to be in there?"

"Shush! We all applaud him for that, don't we?" He raised an eyebrow as he sipped off the tiny drink stirrer.

I have to start reading more important NYC art reviews. God, I have so much to learn—how do people keep up with so much? Maybe I need to read art news every morning or something because I'm just supposed to know a LOT more than I do.

Also . . . couldn't help thinking, if he could get a show, I could get a show. Or just make one. Maybe after the gallery show. I wonder how he got that space, and how much it costs to rent it and how much I would have to save to do it (plus of course make stuff). Once I start making my own art again . . . hmmm. Since when had I decided to be a painter of café walls? Ugh, I need to focus on myself and my work.

Kennedy was still talking.

"It's good business for Carlyle to be here. He's showing Michael support AND he's showing you off."

"You mean Mikhail."

"Oh." He laughed. "I know him by his actual name. Michael Johnson."

I rolled my eyes. "And why does he need to show me off?"

"You're darling. You're his little protégée. And he can take credit for bringing you into this world. You're one of his now."

I thought about how the whole reason I'd ever heard about Robbins McCoy in the first place was because he was a protégé of Warhol. Was Carlyle as good/important as Warhol? I didn't really want to belong to somebody just because I'd worked with him, no matter how popular they were. "Are you one of his?" I said, taking a sip.

He got a funny look on his face. "I play the long game. I'm not in a hurry."

"Well, maybe I'm playing the long game, too," I said, but I didn't even know what I meant, or Kennedy. Did he mean he was going to work for Carlyle forever? Would even Carlyle be H-O-T forever?

We found Carlyle with his hand on Mikhail's back, laughing as if Mikhail had just told the best joke, surrounded by a whole group of smart-looking people, almost everyone wearing black with a dash of color here and there, all the faces concentrating and focusing and trying too hard. Just then I felt a tug on my dress.

"Hey, Piper!"

It was Benz, the model from Carlyle's fashion show, wearing this fabulous painted lady ensemble with a band in her hair and a big white feather sticking out of it.

"Hi!" I said. "You look incredible!"

She leaned in and gave me a big hug like she really remembered me!

"How do you know Mikhail? Isn't his show SO GREAT?"

"I just met him through Carlyle."

"Love Mikhail," she said. She whipped out her phone and grabbed Kennedy and me close to her. "It would be like LITERALLY WRONG to NOT take a selfie here, am I right? Like a crime?" Um, no, I thought, but her phone was already out. "Is Sheed here, Kenns?" These people used so many abbreviations it was sometimes hard to tell what the words even were. She snapped the three of us and he said, "No. Home sick."

Benz pouted. "That is like, literally, the saddest thing I've ever heard. Tell her to put some crystals on her chest." She got over the saddest thing she'd ever heard in three seconds on her way back to the bar, dragging me behind her. I asked if she knew Mikhail through Carlyle.

"Omigod, you're so adorable, no. He's my fuckbuddy," she said. "But we still hang."

I AM SO GLAD I didn't say anything about how mediocre his work was.

"So, is Abril here, too?"

"Mikhail and I are probably hooking up tonight and the odds are higher if she isn't here." She shrugged and stirred her drink. "It's all up to him now. If he's not being a total shithead, he might get some of this." She popped her butt toward me, and I laughed.

"You're fun," she said and then got my number. I don't know if she'll ever text but I was glad she thought I was fun considering I barely said anything. Kit is going to lose it when I tell her about more crazy NYC model encounters.

Carlyle caught my eye and tilted his head, like come over, so I walked through the crowd, feeling a bit spinny from the drink and wacko Benz.

What I remember of what he said: "This girl right here, fresh from the fields of Texas (what fields?), is my muse. Everything I do, I do for her, because of her. She's a throwback. She's an inspiration. She's a Joan Crawford in a Twiggy body. She's high-brow-lowbrow. She's garnets and garbage. She's art. She's my latest and greatest, she's my Piper Perish." Everyone laughed and a few people clapped and I didn't know what the hell he was talking about. Muse? Throwback? GARBAGE? And how did I inspire him? I didn't! I made his art for him!

The crowd circled around us was nodding and smiling. "And you just showed up out of nowhere?" one of the people asked. "Classic New York story!" someone else said, and they all laughed.

"No, I—"

"Yes," Carlyle said. "Can you believe it? This angel fell right into my line of vision."

"No, I—" I didn't just miraculously arrive here, I wanted to say. I bought a ticket on Southwest with my waitressing money.

"I don't know how Texas was so lucky to have Piper for so long, but she's all ours now and you have me to thank for it," Carlyle pinched my cheek lightly, laughed, and lifted his champagne flute.

It was the second time that night that I'd been told I "was" someone else's, and the third time I'd felt WEIRD.

I don't want to be here because someone else decided they need me here.

I came here. I made it happen. I'm not some angel falling.

9/23 11 am

Still in bed and I woke up dreaming about money. I have $88.00 until I get paid again. I need my $300 from Lita. I'm going to work on my loans and grant applications today, and I'm painting for Lita, then more serious Carlyle studio time, trying to come up with more stuff to show him. Even if he hasn't come up with any of his own ideas yet, I can't keep playing because I'm going to have to present options to him soon. Maybe something about Little Italy, which is more touristy than real? I don't know, need to space out and think.

Kennedy left a message and wanted to know how I was feeling and if I could stop by the office today. My brain is all NOPE but my fingers typed him sure. I'm hoping for an early paycheck.

My plan is to walk everywhere and eat all my meals at the Web. If I'm really careful, I'll be okay.

9/23 4:45 pm My little room at the Web. Cozy! Cool weather today!

At the office, K said: You mentioned getting paid last night, if you remember. (I didn't. Thanks, multiple Gold Rushes.) K tapped a plain envelope that was on the reception desk. Then he said, "Please don't discuss money in public anymore. You know it makes Carlyle upset." I do? I didn't know.

Another $800. The good thing about checks is knowing more money is coming and the hard thing is making the moola last between each check.

"Oh, by the way," I said as I was leaving for the studio, "did I do okay for Carlyle last night? Like is that what he wanted? I tried to pick up his vibe, and see how people reacted to him, and what he liked last night, where he was gravitating . . . I'm just supposed to go out to parties with him and be his like . . ." I didn't know how to finish it, other than some terms I didn't want to use—his highbrow-lowbrow token Texan.

"His muse? Yes."

"Yeah, muse is better than LOW-BROW GARBAGE. You heard that, right?"

"Oh, that's just him. Don't let it bother you. It's all branding and relevance."

"Carlyle is relevant. His show was like, a second ago!"

"New York moves fast, Piper. You'd be surprised how relative relevance is." He jumped on a call and I told him I would see him at the studio later.

Anyway, the plan for today at Lita's was: paint the bathrooms. But I got there and it was this:

L: Sorry, kid. No bathrooms today. It smells like a mouse died in the wall.

I said, "That's so gross" and she said, "That's life" and I said, "Actually, that's death" and then she said, "You got a quick mind, Pipps" and laughed.

"So, should I come back tomorrow, then?" I REALLY didn't want to possibly deal with a stinky dead mouse wall.

But she just said I should work on the second-floor apartment instead, and she took me up the stairs (dirty, cracked marble) in the back of the café and she unlocked the door.

And then there was light. SO. MUCH. GODDAMN LIGHT. I felt . . . everything.

- sunlight flooding the entire studio
- wood floors
- white, cracking plaster walls

- a fireplace

- one wall all bricks

- BYOK—bring your own kitchen. You have to put in your
  own fridge if you want one? There's a tiny sink and pantry,
  but that's it. No oven or stove!

- another bathroom-down-the-hall situation

Spent some time in there just looking at the view out the huge
window—across from me were rooftop gardens with expensive-
looking flowers and plants and if I looked down I could see
jacked-up backyards with overgrown weeds and then if I
squinted past the other rooftops, I could see into other people's
apartments. So much blue sky. It was like being on the Web roof,
only inside.

That place is definitely bigger than my room here and my
bedroom back home. New York can feel so small and tight on
certain streets, especially downtown or in Times Square, but so
big inside places like that studio. It's like the city is shrunken
outside, but once I'm in a pastry shop or the Web lobby or the
café, space feels normal-size again. Houston big and New York
big are not the same; they take up space in totally unique ways.

"Lita . . ." It was hard to talk with my jaw dropped.

"Spit it out. You don't want to do this? Too much for you?"

"No, not that. What's the rent here?"

She popped her two fingers up like rabbit ears, and said, "Two
thousand for Floor 2. Bargain, right?"

Not exactly what I was thinking. I was calculating in my brain:
$2K was three to four months of working at my old waitressing
job at the diner if I saved everything I made and didn't touch a

penny. Not possible with any kind of waitressing job or retail I was going to be able to swing here.

"I wish I had $2K."

I hoped she would just say "It's yours!" but instead she cracked her knuckles and said, "That's a great price, Pippin."

"I'll do a good job in here. I promise." I wanted to just for the sake of the room. It needed someone to want to take the time and show it some love.

"I have no doubt." She started back to the café. "Take your time. Do it right."

She said EXACTLY what I had just been thinking. That room . . . oh man, I want that space. I NEED that space. Floor 2 was everything I was missing in Carlyle's studio. I was charged-up there, not desperate. I could really work on Floor 2.

Now I'm back home after a few hours there, slowly, very slowly patching the holes in the walls and feeling all the vibes of that place. Those vibes are my vibes. I belong there. I know it.

I know I just got paid but I want to try and put some of that $800 toward $2K. I know that's just a month but it would be worth it to live there for a month. How do people ever get rich here? If I can barely afford life now, how the hell am I going to do it when I'm actually in school? Helen made it sound like it was almost impossible to keep a full-time gig and go to school.

I saw Grace and told her all about Floor 2 and she's going to go with me next time and write while I paint, since she has to have new material for her reading and needs a change of atmosphere to write. She says every place she's been writing—her room, library, all the Starbucks, Eileen June's—is now too charged with Evan and they're so unstable right now that she can't focus with feelings about him all around her. I remember when I was painting and trying to get over Enzo. I tried to avoid how much it hurt, but he was in everything and everywhere in my life, even in the way I painted. I'd see his face in certain strokes, hear his voice when I put on certain music. Switching to watercolors and ink didn't make me forget our relationship, but it made my brain focus on something besides just him. Sometimes you just have to change it up to give your brain a break. Anyway, she's psyched to have clean space for her brain. Now I just have to take as much time as possible to paint that room, so I can stay there forever.

9/24 2:30 pm Still in bed. Desperate for coffee.

Last night was a mess.

#NYSeen like this:

Grace and I met over at her new hangout, FC's, this cool bar playing a lot of old-school hip-hop on Washington Place. The security guard gave my ID a suspicious look at the door, but let me slide in. After seeing F2 yesterday and feeling super inspired but poor, I just wanted a Coke anyway.

G was drinking whiskey and I couldn't stop talking about her poetry night.

"I can't wait until the next one."

"Well, it was the highlight of my month, that's for sure," she said. "My writing's only gotten worse since then. You should bring Silas again to the next one."

"Oh, I will. He's so into you, as if you didn't know."

"Oh, please." She blushed, fluttering her eyelashes and leaning into me. "He just liked my rhymes. And if there's any chance for you two to work out your biz . . ."

I watched her eyes. I'm not wrong, I know it. He and I didn't have this blushing stuff. She and Si have a connection, the way Joe and I did. I've been trying not to spend every idle minute wishing we would run into each other. Do I really have to wait until January to see him again? I couldn't ask Si for help on this one.

"There's nothing between us," I promised her. "Silas and I are just friends. We just got a little mixed-up on each other this summer. But we're good, so you and he can be . . . whatever you want. You know, when you're available, fiancée."

She threw her credit card down for the tab and said, "Thanks, lady. You deserve a real drink."

"I'm good," I said, putting my hand over the top of my Coke. Just then my phone buzzed in my lap and a picture popped up. Benz blowing me a kiss! Abril was photobombing her.

Hi! I texted.

Girl, we out. You coming?

Where?

Derelict and Duty. Come over.

With a friend. On our way.

☺

"Hey Grace," I said, thinking she would dig a night out with fashionistas, "want to go hang with my new model friends?"

Ack! Getting too windy! Going back to room, more in a min!

9/24 9:28 pm

Grace was super nervous and honestly I was a little, too. I was no pro at hanging with models, but I didn't want to psych myself out either. Still, I secretly prayed Rashida would be there.

"We should change, right? I can't wear this!"

"You're killin' it."

Grace was wearing this cute fitted navy T-shirt dress and my gold gladiator sandals.

With a name like Derelict and Duty, I thought it was going to be more of a dive, but instead, it was a 3-story super-girly bar. It had old-school burlesque glamour feels with a punk edge, like if Blondie or Kesha owned a restaurant. The chandeliers gave off this girly pink light that should have clashed but instead looked totally glam against the really trashed-out black leather walls and torn black leather candle-holders. It was so New York.

I texted Benz We're here and we headed over to the bar where there were three gorgeous bartenders. One guy, one girl, one I wasn't sure, but all gorgeous, all hardcore ballerina types.

Grace's drink: The Mojo Mojito, $18.00

My drink: The Cotton Candy Express, $17.00 (That was the least expensive one.)

GREAT, there goes my cheap night. I could hear the windows in my Floor 2 apartment dreams banging shut.

We made our way over to an oversized booth where Benz (black dress and silver moto jacket) and Abril (high-rise black palazzo pants and a sick red tube top) were sitting.

They were snapping their fingers at the waitstaff to bring over more chairs and I was embarrassed. If someone had snapped at me like that at the diner, I would have avoided the table altogether.

"We're regulars, don't worry," B said, patting the booth for me to sit down. "They want to make us happy. It's like LITERALLY their goal in life. So, what's your name, Piper's friend?"

Abril was slumped down smack-dab in the middle of the booth but pulled herself up when Grace said "Grace" and put on a super-sweet, super-drunky smile, like a very happy leopard.

"You were amazing in the DVF show," Grace said to Benz. I swear she can charm anyone.

"You were there?" she asked, tracing her finger around the rim of her glass.

"I wish," Grace said. "I watched the live-stream. You stole the whole show. That green wrap dress?"

"Right?" Benz said and she tipped her drink for cheers toward Grace's drink, but tapped it a little too hard. "Oopsies!" About $12 of drink sloshed over the table, and Benz dabbed the table with her napkin, but it pushed the spill even more to the edge of the table and onto Grace's dress.

"Can someone fix this please?" Benz shouted toward the middle of the restaurant, and two busboys ran to her fast, like the wet table was a NASCAR event. Grace widened her eyes at me like what the hell while she was patting herself dry and apologizing to the busboys.

"You know what that means," Benz slurred, pointing at Grace. "'Nother drinky-drink."

"I'm good," G said. "We're not staying long."

Between the night at Mikhail's gallery and this mess in front of me, I was itching to get away from all of it, too. In theory, it was fun and it was exciting and everyone looked cool. In reality, I didn't want to be with any of these girls except Grace. I'm not being a hypocrite, I've been drunk before. But they were capital R rude and I didn't like the way they were acting. I had an angry I-call-bullshit flash of: what are we doing here going out with girls spending $15 per tablespoon of drink and acting like money is nothing? These girls probably have $2K in their clutches. These aren't artists! Maybe Andy Warhol surrounded himself with peeps like this and liked it, and maybe I'm really just not that fun. Or maybe it was my PMS or whatever. I was so irritated by them and the way the whole night was turning out.

I wanted to leave so I could draw the whole table and use the weirdness of the night, so I told the girls that we had to go, we were just stopping in to say hi and Grace shot me a look like THANK GOD and Mercedes said "Whyyyy," like a pouty little kid and we were out pronto.

We took the sidewalk home.

I exploded right away. "They're so spoiled!!! It must be nice to have that model life, but no thanks! I don't want to turn out that way working with Carlyle."

"They didn't seem so awful at first. They just seemed . . ." G paused and I could tell she was considering her word choice carefully.

"Awful."

Both shaking our heads.

She said her dress was ruined and I said I was sorry and would pay for it if she wanted, since I dragged here there in the first place, but she waved off the offer.

We waited at the light while a bunch of cars were stuck behind a garbage truck and honking their asses off. It felt like the whole city was blaring at us. I looked up at the building across the street and saw a woman in her robe standing in her apt. window, bouncing her baby on her hip, staring down at the cabs and then up at the sky, like she was praying and cursing at the same time. I looked up too, to see what she was looking at in the dark, and there were lights, lights everywhere. She pulled her blinds shut when she saw me looking back at her.

"So?" Grace broke my stare. "Earth to Piper. Why would you end up like them? It's not like you're living that model life."

"I dunno. What if it's that easy to just fall into all of it? What if it sucks you in because it looks so glamorous."

"Well, are you being sucked in? With Carlyle? The fame and fortune, or misfortunes, of the art world . . ."

"No. No! But before I got here, it all looked so . . . special. Like there's some magical invitation into the cool-kids club, and I basically have this golden ticket with access to all this coolness through Carlyle, and I don't think I want it. Wow."

"What?"

"I never thought I would say that."

We walked on. My mind was going a million miles a minute.

"Eileen June makes sure that I'm getting practical experience and talking about how things can play in my career and life. It sounds like Carlyle keeps you, like, locked away making stuff and presenting you as his pretty assistant when it's convenient for him."

"Ew. No. No!"

Maybe it is a little like that, maybe more than I want to admit, but I didn't want Grace calling me out like that.

"That's not at all how this works. Carlyle just isn't like, a social activist."

She tripped but caught herself, laughing, on my shoulder. "And you think that's a good thing?"

"No, no. I mean, yes."

I couldn't remember the point I had been trying to make.

"I just . . . Carlyle makes the art he wants to see in the world, and I am helping him do that right now."

Grace said, "Okay, well think about what you just said because what I just heard was LAME-O. Doesn't he want his art to be useful? Does he not see what's actually going on in the exact world he's trying to make art reflect? And how is he going to do any of that if he's not actually making any art himself?" She tilted her head toward a homeless woman asleep against a fence, using black garbage bags as blankets. I thought of Carlyle's THE OUTSIDE vibe and felt a little sick. He sees the world as fast and messy and CHAOS, and it's all that, but it's also this. Slow. Silent. Still. Sad.

"Carlyle isn't about useful," I told her, "so much as about . . . about . . . feelings. He wants the emotions he feels to be felt, and that's useful, right? He wants his stories to be told. To connect people that way."

"So, let me get this straight. His art is his emotions?"

"Right!"

"But you're making his art for him?"

"Well, yeah."

"So, his art is actually your emotions. He's paying you for your views and feelings and reactions and passing them off as his own, only then deeming them important or worthwhile. Well, that's the patriarchy for you, I guess."

I felt dumb and confused and cheap and embarrassed all at once. She nudged me with her elbow, I guess trying to take back some of the seriousness, but I felt it anyway.

"I'm not trying to help the patriarchy. It's my job." But it was really more than that to me. Art—not "useful art" but art that did exactly that, capture my emotions and try and communicate them—had saved me every time I needed it.

"I know you're not ON PURPOSE," she said. "Look, this isn't an attack on you, Pipes. It's just that if you're lucky enough to make art, then make it matter. That's the real reason behind all of it, right? I think YOUR art will matter. But Carlyle? C'mon. He's doing it for his own relevance. Isn't that what that Kennedy guy said? He's using you."

I didn't know what to say. I never thought about anyone when I was making my art, outside of my family or friends or me, maybe Andy Warhol, and I didn't want to admit that to her because then I would have to admit how small-minded I was. And sometimes I really do think as an artist you have to be that way to find your voice, close yourself off to everything but your own vision, your own feelings. But walking in the middle of the night in NYC, taking in the world around me and not just making stuff in my high school art studio, being challenged by someone who actually was DOING SOMETHING with her art, was making me see things in a different, bigger, better, scarier way. My whole brain and body and soul felt like I was in a weird weather pattern, like snowing and sunny and windy and rainy at once. What would Dad call it? Like one of his weather disturbances, a pulse of energy, except mine were all over the place.

"I didn't mean to come at you," she said. "I'll shut up."

"No, it's okay." I was relieved and thoughtful and confused. My brain was just trying to put all the pieces together. "I like talking about this stuff."

I couldn't stop thinking about what she had just said.

Her phone chirped. "Evan-it's-late." She said it sharply, but then tried to be softer with him. I overheard some of it, but was caught in my own thoughts, watching the city around us pop and glow and sparkle, even in the humidity. The last thing I heard was "Well, that's a choice you're making, not me." Then to me, "Sorry about that."

"You okay?" I asked.

"Oh yeah. I'm fine. But it's time he gets a life and stops trying to make my decisions his excuses. That was his nightly call to remind me that I'm breaking his heart. There's that belief, y'know, that if you're a writer or an artist, you can't hang on to a relationship? I used to hate that stereotype. But maybe there's something to it. Maybe we're too selfish."

"Maybe," I said. "Or maybe you two just weren't the right fit."

- Enzo, who I now know is gay but didn't at the time

- CJ, who was sexy as all get-out but dumb as nails and oh yeah, had a girlfriend the whole time!!!

- Silas, great by email but in real life we're just better off as art buds

None of my boyfriends matched me perfectly, even though we seemed like matches in flashes and fits. Maybe we connected too fast and had so much energy that we just blew each other's fuses.

When we got home, I dropped Grace at her room and made sure she got into bed. I put a glass of water within reaching distance, on the floor.

I crawled into my own sheets, relieved the heat had finally broken and wind was coming in through my window. It smelled like rain.

I crashed out thinking of Grace. Of "making it matter."

9/26 6 am In my room

My sleeping is all off from all these weird-ass nights. I'm awake now. I've gotta finish loan applications. Heading to the roof to do them with the sunrise, after a little more bed time.

9/26 4 pm The Reading Room at the NYPL

I bagged up my CFA paperwork and walked here for a break from the Web. Jasmine was up on the roof earlier and she taught me a couple of "restorative" poses and I tried them up there and it was fun though a little boring, or I was just too nervous to be calm or something.

Anyway, on my way here, a family from Toledo stopped me by the Empire State Building and asked me for directions to Grand Central and I told them how to get there. It was a Real New Yorker moment! Then another two people interrupted—I thought Texans were proud, but the New Yorker pride thing is so real, everybody here knows "the best way" to do things. Anyway the family handed me a phone and asked me to take a picture, and I did and then I drew a quick pic of them in front of the ESB and signed it #NYSeen. They asked what #NYSeen means, and I said, "It means you've been seen here as part of the New York City scene. Follow the tag online!" They of course loved it.

So now I'm here.

This library is majestic. I don't think I've been to my Houston library branch since junior year, and it wasn't this. NYPL is like something out of Harry Potter. It's got me thinking about size and painting and light. My freak-show brain is bouncing around all of this:

- double-checking and turning in the forms and praying I will receive some loans and scholarships OR ELSE

- Carlyle's next show—need to get feedback ASAP on everything I'm planning.

- Spent all day in F2 yesterday, caulking the walls and thinking deep on Grace and my convo. Couldn't really even draw or write, so lost in thought. Working on the scratched up wall just felt . . . right. My brain was bouncing everywhere.

- Floor 2, Floor 2, Floor 2

- Everything Grace said. Am I a selfish artist? Am I a selfish person? These two questions have been in my head ever since our stumble home.

God, I love journaling and walking so I can think this all out.

Calling Mom on my walk home. I miss her.

9/29 9 am & making a plan! Starting fresh thanks to Mom!

Today:

- laundry—first load already going

- going to Carlyle's to work for a few hours (I WILL make something besides a mess today and tell him he must see it)

- drop off applications with Admissions

- catch up on painting at Café A and patching Floor 2—I'm a little behind and it's a lot more work than I thought

Mom's right—making a to-do list and checking things off feels so good.

9/29 10:47 am In the laundry room

Overheard just now:

"Oh, it's $50 every time I step outside. That's the Manhattan door tax."

Laughing and wanting to cry because it's so true. Between finishing up this loan and scholarship stuff all day, and hoping and praying for a paycheck by Thursday, I am desperate for cash. Been keeping decent track, but I lost a couple of bucks along the way and who the hell knows where but it doesn't matter anyway because I don't have it.

9/30 11:30 pm Union Square

Turned in my forms! I'm praying praying praying that at least one scholarship will come through.

But right now, OMG, this: I was walking around the school before I met up with Silas in the photo lab and then turned the corner—right into Joe Gillman!!!!, who was wiping his mouth from the water fountain, looking all off-duty rock star, with his backpack casually clipped across his chest and his skinny jeans the perfect faded gray.

"Heyyy!" He held his hands out to me for some kind of 2-hands handshake. Across the fingers and thumbs, between his knuckles and his hands I read his tattoos: N-E-V-E-R-S-A-Y-N-O.

"Never . . . say . . . no?"

"And I never do. Do you?" He had a drop of water on his bottom lip and I tried not to stare.

"Huh." I had a chance to play it cool but yeah, blew it.

"What's up? Piper, right? You okay?"

"Oh, I, um, yeah! I'm great!"

"You go to school here?"

"I start in January. I was just dropping some paperwork off. Sorry, I thought the photo lab was around here. I'm a little turned around."

"Nope, that's downstairs." His smile for days. "On 6. Want me to show you? I'm happy to help out a new student."

"It's okay. You probably have stuff to do, and I'm . . . kind of meeting Silas there, and—"

He nodded. "I got it." I grinned like a big dummy and we stood there, not saying anything for a second. Then finally, "No matter what he says, I'm not enemy number one. We could be friends. But that's up to him."

"Well, I mean—" I wanted to say you wouldn't understand at all, you have no idea what he's been through, but I couldn't tell him about Robbins.

"I didn't take Astrid from him. She's her own person. I help her with some stuff. And she helps me."

"Oh, it's not just that—"

His eyebrows perked and I told him I had to go before I leaked any more information. He called out, "All right, then. See you around, Piper," and I hightailed it out of there as fast as I could, jumping down two stairs at a time to the sixth floor, and found Silas in the lab.

I felt nervous talking to Joe because it's betrayal. But what had Joe done to me (besides something major to my heart—still beating fast just thinking about him!)? But again, I know friends can't talk to their friends' sworn enemies. I'm not a dummy.

Si was pacing beside one of the big tables in the photo lab when I walked in and that gave me a second to get my shit together.

"What's going on?"

He pointed to some slips of paper next to a set of photos. He picked up a photo of a girl—Astrid—about to bite into an apple, and held a piece of posterboard next to the photo, then above it.

"Here." He put my hands on the paper and photo he was holding, then he let go and backed away from them, looking at them, tilting his head left and right. He rubbed his hands together.

"They're going to have speech bubbles! That's what these are missing!"

"Like in comic books? You're not going to use the headlines from earlier? I liked those!"

"I do too, but they give too much direction. I want the audience to have more input, come up with their own language. Why should I tell them how to think? I want the words to scroll across digital message boards, you know, like the kind you would see in storefronts or the lottery signage at a bodega. I saw a huge one at Madison Square Garden and that's where I got the idea. Except I'll use ones that are appropriate for the size of each photo. And I want people to be able to type in their messages right there as they're looking at the piece, straight from their phones, so the words could change daily, constantly, while the photos stay the same, like 24-hour revolving captions. Think about how they could feed off each other! The words would be dependent on the day, the news, the weather, whoever was looking at them. The context to the art will evolve as fast as whatever is happening in the world! The piece won't just be made by me, but whoever is looking at it."

"Interactive!"

"Exactly," he said. "A collaboration between artist and viewer." Silas was electrified, bouncing around the room. "Yes!" I'd never seen him so happy.

He was in full connection mode and the whole room felt sparky and alive. I wanted to absorb it and race to the studio. Work breeding work, energy making energy!

I told Si I had to go and I raced to F2. I painted until a couple of hours ago, lost in the streaks of grays, black swipes, gold-yellow stripes. Lost in possibilities.

I am full of ideas, probably mistakes.

Going to the TV room to see if anyone's awake.

Need to distract myself from making a potentially fun, potentially very messy move. Do I risk losing my first pre-NYC/NYC friendship with Silas? Or can Si be open and not hate who I date? Oh, I rhymed. Si would like that, at least.

Joe & I just texted on and off for like an hour.

Me: How did you get my digits?

Joe: From Admissions.

Me: Aren't those files confidential? Isn't that breaking the law?

Joe: Your file was on the Financial Aid desk in plain sight. I can't help if I saw it.

I started to type and then deleted and typed Really? but then deleted the question mark, just let the ellipses sit there while I thought what I wanted to say. Then he texted again.

Joe: You there?

Me: That was kind of a creep move.

He was looking at my personal information.

Joe: It wasn't like that. I just wanted to get your number. My bad.

Me: Why didn't you just ask me for it?

Joe: Really?

Me: Yeah, really!!!

Joe: Because you're into Silas and do whatever he says!

Me: I do NOT!

Joe: But you think I'm a bad dude because of him?

Me: You did get my number off my PRIVATE forms.

His ". . ." hovered again for a while.

Joe: You're right. I'm sorry. I should have asked.

Me: It's okay.

I waited for a zinger or like his last word or something, but neither one of us made a move.

Finally I typed, Going to bed and he wrote back, Last word!

Funny.

Three guesses who I'm gonna dream about?

10/2 11 am Floor 2 BEST NEWS EVER

But first, Houston time. I called Mom and Dad walking to Café Angelou yesterday and told them I filled out all my scholarship and loan forms for school and when I said loans, I swear I could hear Mom zip air through her teeth.

"And I know, I just know, that you will become a big-time artist and the first thing you'll do is pay those off."

"Yes, Mom."

Dad of course contributed the Dad-est things ever, like "You're really doing it, kid. We're so proud of you."

I'm feeling the Perish fam vibes and missing them a lot more than I thought, especially when it comes to doing the school stuff. I don't know if I made mistakes. I wish I had someone here who could double-check my work and tell me it was all going to be okay. If I don't get enough financial aid, I don't go. It's that simple and that complicated. I wish I could teleport Mom and Dad here and show them my New York and we could have dinner together and just everything.

That was my homesick part of the day.

But my happy part was with Lita just a little bit ago. I had to go over the walls first with grit paper because the Floor 2 walls, even though they look pretty in the sun, are janky and weirdly sticky. What happened in there? I don't want to think about it.

So I was gearing up in a square of sunshine coming through the window and then Lita let me know we have a little more time until someone moves in. "Our potential tenant just fell through."

"What happened?

"Didn't pass my background check. Their politics were way off." She slashed the air with her hand, like chop-chop.

"Seriously?" I wondered what that meant or what the tenants had done to tip her off.

"I don't kid about politics, kid." She winked. "Look, I could rent this out today if I wanted, people will take any apartment these days, especially at such a steal, but truthfully it looks like there's more work to do. A coat of primer ain't gonna cut it."

"Right, right." I eyed her. "Soooo . . . what would you say if we made a deal? I'll keep painting everything I said I would paint, and do the maintenance if I know how to do it, and in return, I get to use the studio. Just for painting and drawing. I promise I won't make a mess. I'll lay paper down. I need a studio and you need a painter, so . . ."

"What we talkin' about here? Like a couple of canvases or some-thin'? And I'M still gonna pay YOU to do this?"

"Well, yeah!" I was biased, but it seemed fair enough to me. "I'm increasing your rental value, right? And the second you find a tenant, I'm out." I was feeling like such a bad-ass hustler and I know if Dad could hear me he would be high-fiving me so hard.

"I'll do you one better," she said. "You can use it until November first. You don't have to do all the maintenance, but I do need—"

"Yes! Of course!" I was excited.

She gave me a look. "You don't even know what I'm going to say yet."

"Anything."

"I need a dishwasher for the café. My regular dishwasher, Dev, broke his leg, and it looks like he'll be off it for a while."

All I could think about was "steady source of income." Wash some dishes? Easy-peasy. "Every day?"

"From 5pm to 8pm, and not on Mondays or Tuesdays. But that's $45 a day guaranteed. Yours if you want it—and Floor 2 is included."

"I'll be paid for dishwashing and painting AND all this?" I was doing the $$$ math quickly in my head.

- $300 for the painting.

- $225 a week until Thanksgiving, plus a free studio until Nov first.

- $800 every two weeks from Carlyle until Jan first.

That's enough!

"Of course. Like you said, I need a handywoman and you need space," she laughed. "And Mort likes that you'll respect it. You will respect it, won't you?"

"Oh yeah!" I looked up at the ceiling/sky/heaven. "Anything to stay on Mort's good side," I said, shaking her hand. "Deal."

Now I'm alone in Lita's Floor 2—my temporary studio—my glorious, sun-filled studio.

Today's TA-DA list is BIG:

GOT A JOB ON MY OWN! ✔

A STUDIO OF MY OWN (even if it's temporary)! ✔

I'm going to put a show on here. I can just feel it in my bones. One day it's going to happen.

Wait until Grace finds out I have F2 for another month! I guess I was feeling cocky or something because I texted Joe, just to say hi, and maybe tell him about having my own studio, I dunno, but he didn't text back, so whatever, I don't care anyway.

I've gotta head over to Carlyle's now. He wants to do a Think Meet Vision Check to see if we're all on the same page about his work, the work I haven't even really officially started yet, GREAT, and I'm supposed to spend the day with him. Just need to be back at Lita's by 4:45. Maybe I will love dishwashing and be the best dishwasher Lita has ever had and she'll say Pippin, you're so good at this job I'll just let you live up there. If nothing else, that big sink and the sudsy water will give me time to think about all my possibilities.

10/2 9:45 pm The Webster library

Got back to Café A five minutes late and it was packed and Lita was scribbling orders.

"Get to it, kid. It's a mess in there and I needed you ten minutes ago." I wasn't thinking of how much time this is all going to take, getting around the city. Might be getting in more running than I expected.

The big double sink that Lita calls Mom and Pop leaks and my boots got all wet. Okay, then. The warm water felt good at first, but after a while it was too gray and gooey. My fingers are pruny. Maybe I will like this job more when it's colder outside.

Joe finally wrote back tonight.

Him: Hiiii!

Me: Hi! Whatcha doing?

Him: Study break. Cramming like crazy.

Me: Oooh, fun. What class?

Him: History of Video Art I, 1965-1985.

Me: So you're watching films?!?

Him: Not exactly. Have to read 3 more chapters.

Me: That's a lot.

Him: Yeah. You texted me earlier?

Me: Oh, yeah. I just wanted to . . .

I had to think about how to answer without sounding like a super nerd.

. . . say hi.

Him: So, I'm off your creep list?

Me: For now. ;)

Him: Okay then. ☺ How about I text you tomorrow? I gotta keep at it.

Me: Okay. Go get smarter. Byeeee.

I don't want to bother him but I really wish we were still texting. I hope he doesn't think I'm a dork now. Maybe I shouldn't have texted him earlier.

Yesterday we had our Think Meet Vision Check, which was basically me pitching my ideas to C and K, and it wasn't 100% awful. Carlyle likes/kind of likes one of the ideas I've been twirling around in my head and already started playing with in his studio. The good thing is I only have to make one original this time, not eight of the same thing, so I think I can actually do a good job and not totally freak.

I told him my New York color story idea: the lilac-oranges in the sunsets and all the squares and stripes of gold-yellow, all the gray and brick-red apartments, and the white-blue building lights that go on and dot the city, little suburban stars that the city turns on and off at will. There is also the early-morning dark, the only time it's really quiet here. Dark grays, dark silvers, blacks.

Squares. Connected. Like a quilt. A city on a grid, duh.

He said I could keep the colors, but lose the squares/grid. "Where's the chaos? The pandemonium?"

Right.

He did not like idea #2 either. 36 silkscreens of the subway map, kind of like Andy Warhol. The subway is iconic, Andy Warhol is iconic, New York is iconic. I mentioned seeing the Ethels at the Whitney and how much I would love to do something like Andy. Elegant, but chaotic. And that the subway links us all, an equalizer and a connector, the best, most organized "chaos"— trying to use his word—in THE OUTSIDE world.

Carlyle said, "Well, that's an idea, isn't it, but that's not me at all," and that I need to find "our own take on that" if I'm going to pursue it. He doesn't want anything "derivative," which he says makes that idea a nonstarter.

Idea #3: A few weeks ago I was leaving Hamid's and tripped over a bag of garbage on the corner. I got this idea of collecting broken bottles, litter, and scraps, paying tribute to the leftovers of the city, but also the perfectly good stuff people leave out on the street when they don't want it anymore. I've picked up two lamps and a picture frame and I found a great chair that was too heavy to bring to Carlyle's studio by myself. I can't believe people just leave their stuff for other people to find. Grace said in EJ's neighborhood in Brooklyn there are always "stoop sales." SO NY!!! Anyway, I want to tackle how and why we discard things, how we reuse them, and how we forget about them. I thought this would work with his OUTSIDE theme. He got this immediately and said, "The infinity of the discarded."

"Okay," I said. "So I'll just focus on the discarded."

"I like that. Let's use that title for your piece," Carlyle said. "Yes. That's very me." To Kennedy, he said, "We were so smart to keep her on board, weren't we?"

Kennedy nodded like his head was going to fall off.

Everything I did, Carlyle found a way to make about him. My piece was him, he was smart to keep me around, everything came back to Carlyle. I was right there in the office with him but he treated me as if I was some mysterious fairy that appeared in his daydreams, only to serve his whims.

"Are you actually going to come to the studio? To see the work before then? Maybe you should see it in person as it develops? So that you know it's 'really you'?" I was chomping for feedback.

I'm already planning to bring in Silas and Grace, but I need to know if what I made feels "like Carlyle" and the deadline is really really close, and he said he would be there but didn't say when, so great, now I get to worry like crazy that he'll just drop in unannounced. It's his studio, but jeez.

So now I'm in the studio doing more brainstorming and obvi journaling. Silas and Mo are coming over so I can interview them about their take on "their" New Yorks. Want to hear what Grace thinks, too. How to make this piece matter more, even if it's not totally mine. Thinking.

10/4 9:47 am The Web

I blasted tunes and painted at Carlyle's until the sun came up, around 7 am, when my nose finally needed some fresher air than what I was breathing in the studio. Spent a lot of time glazing discarded deli coffee cups and epoxying stirrers to each other, making little pinwheels. Walked home deep-thinking about everything Silas and Mo had said and trying to see the city through their eyes, since I can't fully grasp whatever Carlyle's vision is yet. But I think I'm on to something.

Not surprisingly, Mo sees the city decaying: cavernous potholes, empty storefronts, overflowing trash cans and garbage bags left on the sidewalks. So true. You haven't really lived until you've tripped over one. He said we can't live in a place with this many people without living in our by-products, which is nasty but true.

Before Si even began to talk, I tried to guess what he would say, thinking back on all his emails to me before we met IRL, from our night out at Studio 54. But he still managed to surprise me.

"You can't capture New York, you know. It's slippery, and everyone's got a different view of it. For me it's home, but for somebody else, it's just an airport stop or a weekend visit or a dream. Like for you, right?"

I nodded.

"I've never dreamt of it because I've always lived it. So I'm never going to see it like you. I'm a little jealous of that, actually."

"And I wish I grew up here."

"Yeah, but then you wouldn't be you and this city wouldn't mean the same thing to you."

I loved when he talked to me like this. Si had a certain way of making me feel like I was the only person in the room he cared about. Not romantic—he was definitely bummed that Grace had to cancel last-minute for some errand for Eileen June—but just that spark, that he-is-so-my-person feeling I used to get from our emails.

Adams used to say just walking down the street could be a cultural event, and I have been doing a lot of walking and running. But I'm creating for Carlyle, not me, trying to think about how he would see things. But, but, he should like my ideas exactly, because they're mine, because that's why he orig-inally liked me—for my ideas when I didn't even know him. Maybe I should just stop trying to think like him and just create like me. BOOM. Why did it take me so long to figure this out? It's always been ME.

When I walked into the lobby—fingers, nails, and clothes stained deep gray—Maria told me it looked like I got in a fight with a cement mixer and I said you should have seen the other guy and she asked, Where ya been? and I told her at my boss's studio and she said, I love you artistic types, but don't touch anything in the lobby until your hands are cleaned.

I promised her no paint would rub off and she interlaced her fingers, covered in a zillion rings, and prayed aloud, "God help us all."

10/4 4 pm

I wanted a hot shower and to fall dead asleep for a few hours and that's what I did. I woke up to my phone chirping: I told you I'd text today. My word is bond.

Joe. Joe Joe Joe. Now that's a nice way to wake up. I texted him back but he's in class.

So, I found Grace in the library and dragged her running with me to Central Park. So many people cozied up in sweaters and scarves. Weird to live in a place that isn't still 90 degrees out in October. August sucked, but this is a-okay.

We stumbled into the Strawberry Fields section, a couple of acres in the park that are dedicated to John Lennon. Tourists were taking pictures and leaving flowers on top of a black-and-white "Imagine" mosaic in the middle of it. I want to be that kind of artist. I want to make things that mean something to other people, like Grace does. I made a quiet promise to myself. That's my now and always and forever goal.

I asked G, "How do you know what you make makes a difference? Like, what proof do you really get?" And she said, "You don't. But just existing isn't enough. I have to try to better the world in the way I can. If we're blessed enough to be artists, then we have to use our tools. I think small—not small as in closed-minded, but specific. Local. I find the most apt word, and that's how I nail a tiny moment, and that's when I hope readers relate and feel something bigger, more. I try to write local to be global." She laughed and went AHHHHHHH. "I sound so pretentious, omigod. But starting small gives me a strong foundation and I know what I'm doing if I think about a very small, very specific audience or point I want to make. If I think my audience is going to be 'the whole world' I end up making something that means nothing special to anyone. So maybe you could do that with Carlyle's project too. Go small to go big?"

"No pressure," I said, wiping my neck with the back of my shirt. We stopped in front of a huge fountain while she stretched out her calves.

"The only pressure is to do what you're good at, infuse it with meaning—or better, bring it from meaning."

Even though I was wrung out from the run, I could feel myself filling up. She's better than Gatorade, she's Graceaid.

"Right. Right! I want to do that, exactly that! I feel like I'm not bringing anything from real meaning yet. I don't want to be Carlyle's robot. Robot, come up with ideas. Robot, Robot, figure out my point of view for me. I feel like Siri."

"Don't be Siri," she laughed.

Then in her best or worst Siri voice, she added, "Pipe-er, be the An-ti Si-ri. Nav-i-gate your own life."

"Navigate your own life." —The genius called Grace

We just got back to the Web and my heart and brain feel like they are going to explode. Grace pumped me UP!

I checked my phone and there was a message from Kennedy:

Doll, we'll be at Jazz at Lincoln Center tonight for an 8 pm program. You'll be sitting with us. Please meet us at 7:45 pm in the lobby. Wear something high-end but "Piper." Please confirm.

Texted back: CONFIRMED.

Holy shit. I'm exhausted. Have to run to Angelou's, do the dishes, and see if I can bust out at 7:30—maybe Lita will understand 'cause I have to make this happen, maybe she'll just pay me $35 for this shift? That's fine, that's fair—bring clothes and clean up there. I need a portable washing machine/dryer. And a shower! ACK!

10/5 11 am

Jazz at Lincoln Center is right by Central Park, right where G & I had been all day, which meant I had to go all the way down to Café A and the Web and then turn around to go all the way up to the Upper West Side again. I'm living on the trains. I know some of them go aboveground, so you can see outside, but I haven't been on one of those yet. Thank goodness I spent the day in the park so I had some sky time. Being underground feels like a trap sometimes, even though I do kind of like it when the trains are on time and not too crowded.

Jazz is at Columbus Circle, inside the Time Warner Center, which is basically a giant fancy mall. The closest thing we have to it in Houston is probably the Galleria? I wore:

♣ the earrings Rashida had given me for Fashion Week

♣ a black sheath that was splattered with paint (at first an accident, then I just added more until it worked)

❋ an oversized deep-purple leather obi wrap-belt I found in the Webster's lost and found

❋ black stilettos also from lost and found. A size too tight, but they worked

Unfortunately, I was 15 minutes late. I tried, but the C train and running in heels don't mix well. Luckily the show started late, too.

Carlyle and Kennedy were both in tuxedos!!! They both looked so handsome, like two very different James Bonds. K, checking out my dress, said, "That looks familiar."

Whatever, it's what I have.

When we stepped out of the elevator, the lobby was filled with adult-adults. This was a benefit and I was supposed to blend— Kennedy's word.

"Should I really be here? Everybody looks very . . . polished," I said, leaning into his shoulder. I felt like I was sticking out, and everyone would know I didn't belong there. That imposter syndrome thing is real.

"Believe it and be it, doll. This is the jazz event of the year."

As soon as the music started, I knew he was 100% right. I got totally lost in all of it, in the best kind of way. I stopped worrying about what I was making in Carlyle's studio or at F2 and just let ideas float in and out of my head like the melodies we were listening to. I didn't think about scholarships and loans. I didn't even think about Joe. I just. Stopped. Thinking.

I saved my Playbill—my very first concert in New York!

When it was over, we went back to the lobby. Carlyle was stopped by someone named Jimmy and they chatted, name-dropping Esperanza and Wynton, two of the musicians we just saw, and then Jimmy asked, "Quick one of you three?" and before I knew it, Kennedy was on my right, Carlyle on my left, and we were having pictures taken by Jimmy, a bunch of clicks all at once. Don't nerd out, I told myself, and I rolled my shoulders back and smiled. It was fun. It felt special, like we were on the red carpet.

We got into the black car waiting outside of the Time Warner Center. Kennedy told the driver, "Next stop, Bryant Park, library, north side."

"We're going to the library?"

"It's after-party time, doll."

Tonight's music just made me want to paint. See, this is why I need to be in school, around artists, around my people. Grace's poetry, this music, Silas's new idea for his project—that whole creativity-breeds-creativity thing is real. The last thing I wanted to do was make small talk and pretend I was from some field in Texas. I like the painting part of this job so much more than the public part. I tried to get my head in the game, though, and figured the inspiration would be with me later, too. And besides, I knew I had to shadow Carlyle and watch his "lifestyle."

The library was packed and it was hard to move around. A bunch of glammy types were calling Carlyle's name and Kennedy pushed me after him to join a group on the patio. My toes were hurting.

Carlyle didn't introduce us to anyone, and Kennedy either shook hands or smiled. I was trying to catch names, a Laurie here, a Neil there, and just watched Kennedy be so calm. Everyone here seemed to know how New York worked. I thought I would just come here and be a New Yorker. But I am still trying to figure it out. Unless this is how New Yorkers feel all the time, too.

A waiter offered me a sparkling water with lime and I took it, wishing for a shot to make me feel as calm as Kennedy looked. Then someone tapped my shoulder and I turned back, thinking it was the waiter again.

"Why, hello there!"

Robbins McCoy!!!!

"You're here?" I said, trying not to totally freak out. My hero. Silas's dad. But my hero! But Silas's bully, in a way! But Warhol's friend! And he was saying hi to me!

"Where else would I be?" he asked. His hand was wrapped around his martini—I think it was a martini, it had an olive—and he lifted it up. "Cheers."

"Cheers," I said, clinking his glass.

"So, what do you think of all of this?"

"The music was sooo good. I don't know the right word for it, I've never experienced anything like it." I snapped my fingers. "It really hit me. I felt it, like, in my collarbones." Oh god, why did I say that? I laughed nervously and hoped he couldn't see my hand shaking. "What about you?"

"They really blew it out this year." He whistled. "It really got these bones moving!" He thumped his chest with one hand and danced around in a circle with his martini, laughing. (Not what I was expecting! It was fun to see him like that!) "I'll tell ya, they're doing what the art world isn't: they're letting some air in! Some movement, yeah? Some room for the spontaneous! It's ALIVE art!" He took my hand and twirled me around, and

I couldn't believe what was happening and I was just laughing and spinning with him—ROBBINS EFFIN' McCOY! I wish he could show Silas this side of himself! Our drinks were half on the floor and half on us and I forgot I was at a "work event" and it felt great.

"It gave you that buzz too?" he asked.

"It did, it really did! Especially that one song, about the potholes—"

"'The Pothole Prance'?" he said, and shuffled his feet. "That song is a goddamn anthem! YES!"

"I wanted to download it to my brain and go to the studio and paint!"

"What are you waiting for?"

"I'm working for Carlyle tonight, so I can't. Different part of the job," I straightened up while he sipped his drink. "So, what are you working on? Besides dancing?"

Maybe I was fitting in to New York!

He swallowed-coughed-laughed and smiled at me really nicely but said, "I don't usually share what I'm working on with my students."

"Well, I'm not exactly a student yet."

He smiled, like I'd caught him in a clever trap, and there it was. A dimple. Just like Silas's. But he didn't answer. "And what are you working on?"

I tried to be jokey back with him. "I don't usually share what I'm working on with my teachers."

"Touché." He did a little fake bow with his head, like he was taking his hat off, and smirked at me. "I respect your process and your integrity. I'll see your work this January."

Right then Carlyle walked over and looped his arm under mine, and said you won't mind if I steal my Piper back, will you? And Robbins said she's all yours.

No no no, I'm not all Carlyle's! I wanted to stay and talk to Robbins forever.

But whatever, I held my own with Robbins McCoy! I still can't believe it. He danced in front of me! I wanted to tell Silas but what was I thinking? Of course I couldn't! But I told Grace.

I stood next to Carlyle for the rest of the night, listening to his story of how he had discovered me, had plucked me from the fields, how one of the perks of being a cultural tastemaker was recognizing untapped potential.

Nodded? ✔

Smiled? ✔

Laughed? ✔

Listened? ✔

I did my job. I didn't create anything, except a new version of myself: The Pretty, Young, Relevant Girl, the one to help Carlyle keep—find?—reinvent?—his cool factor. I paid attention and my mind wandered at the same time. I was in environment overload. So much in my brain.

I tried to pull an Adams and Be Now. Which meant having a genuinely great time. And once I was Now and relaxed into it, I didn't hate it. Once I just gave in and stopped fighting the public part of my gig, it was fine. I could see doing more of these events next to Carlyle, especially if I don't get my loans or grants. Coming up with enough for one semester alone seems impossible at this point. But last night, all I really had to do was laugh and have a drink and listen to cool people talk about how cool they were or what they were making or why Carlyle was the best thing to ever happen to me. It was fine. It was fun and easy and that's when I had to be real with myself: this party was great and my ten seconds with Robbins were amazing but what did the party really mean? Do easy and fun and fine equal art? No. Well, maybe sometimes. Art isn't all work. But easy and fun and fine equal a night off, which is fine, but fine isn't what Grace and I talked about.

I didn't come to NY to just be fine. Fine isn't good enough. I don't want to be someone who can't express herself publicly. I want to be legit on the inside and out. I won't get to be that when I'm out with Carlyle. Texted Grace, Wish you were here and she wrote Me too. Have a fancy time for me, Fancy Pants.

Before leaving, I kissed my lips on a paper towel in the bathroom, and smeared the print into a smudgy heart. "#NYSeen: This is my job."

I finally got home and dropped the way-too-tight shoes back in the lost and found box and tore off my dress. I jumped into my pjs, grabbed my lucky brushes, acrylics, and a canvas I had swiped from the studio, and went to the rooftop. Painted more gold-yellows—I can't stay away, what can I say—and added oranges and purples, too. Those were the colors in my brain from the night, so much orange and purple, and I howled at the moon, like a lunatic. Nobody was up there and I needed it and my soul needed it and I don't care how silly I looked or sounded, it was GREAT!

I danced, too.

The roof was a mess when I was done but I cleaned up. I can't have Maria start hating on us "artistic types." So far, she hasn't said anything. Whew.

10/5 3:45 pm in Union Square Park, picking up Greenmarket stuff for Carlyle's office

Overheard: "Our pickles save lives! Fermentation Nation!"

I drew the peeps manning their pickle barrel stand and they gave me some samples! Woo-hoo, they're spicy! I hope these are the ones Carlyle wanted.

10/6 9 am

Was at Carlyle's yesterday except for my shift at Angelou's. Kind of broke up the momentum and Carlyle did NOT like that, but I didn't know it was going to be a whole-day thing, and I told him "a girl's gotta eat" and that kind of shut him up because if he didn't want me to take another job, I'm pretty sure he could pay me more. He did buy me lunch, though.

We talked about how our ideas could or could not work together, about Carlyle's more specific plans for his show—just a few weeks away. Carlyle wants our pieces earlier than I thought—10/26.

Good to be loose. Less control = more discovery?

Kennedy had ordered salads and iced coffees, even though it was cold out, but hey, free lunch. Hamid himself brought the food and when he saw me in Carlyle's office, he gave me a hug.

"My friend!"

"Hamid! Hiii!"

"This is your big office? I knew Freddy should marry you!"

"No," I giggled. "This is my boss's. I work at his studio on the corner."

Hamid smiled and tipped his head to Carlyle, who gave him a nice warm smile. I was relieved—and surprised he wasn't a jerk.

When he left, Carlyle said, "See? Everybody just loves Piper Perish. You've got that pull."

I shrugged. Didn't know what to do with that.

After lunch, Carlyle pulled up a photo on his computer. In the pic, Carlyle was holding two white rectangular containers in his hands, maybe pottery, standing in front of a bunch of kilns.

"What are they?"

"Milk cartons, such as those beloved by schoolchildren, used to feature the faces of missing and kidnapped children to bring awareness and help find them. I want to bring back the milk carton, call it nostalgia, perhaps, to find the missing ethics of our communities. What are we doing to help people outside of ourselves? What man abides by the Golden Rule? My milk cartons, all in ceramic, will feature the values I believe are missing from today."

Huh. I was impressed. That was kind of outside of himself.

"Why ceramic? What's chaotic about it?"

"The material must be fragile, yet strong. Something long-lasting, but something that can be broken by a child."

"Wow."

"I don't only make things that sell," he said, looking a little shaken, like something was revealed. Not sure what exactly but he was paler than usual.

I called Lita on the way there, and explained why I was getting in a little late and I thought she'd be forgiving but she was pissed. When I got there, she said, "I hired you to be on time, not to come up with excuses. It's a good thing your painting's better than your punctuality."

My heart dropped. I hate being in trouble. But I didn't try to push my luck or get cute, just said I was sorry and went straight to the sinks.

Hector was pouring coffee beans into the grinder when he saw me coming in. "I'm never late," he said.

"Okay."

"You got poor time management."

"Hector! I have two jobs!"

"I got three!" he said, and before I could say Wha—? he turned the loud grinder on, shaking his head like, Catch up.

A bike messenger, dressed all in camo with reflective stripes, came into Angelou's and insisted someone called for a package pickup, but nobody had. He was upset and convinced he had the right address, it was his first day, and Lita took pity on him and gave him some cookies and he said, "Thanks, Mama" and blew some cookie-crumbed kisses. I gave a rough sketch of him to Lita at the end of my shift.

"Just what I always wanted. Mort's gonna be jealous." She tousled my hair and I felt glad she didn't seem too mad still and I was tired and left. Yesterday = long.

Grace did her reading—wow wow wow—at Angelou's and she killed it but that's not the only thing. One of her poems got a standing ovation and people were stomping and chanting "Weeee the Peeeeople" and somebody broke a glass, accident, and I had to clean it up but I didn't care, I was loving it and Lita was loving it and even Mo was loving it, but no one was loving it half as much as Silas.

Afterward, Grace and Si were laughing at the bar, in a corner section I hadn't painted yet. They kept bumping elbows or hips or legs, always touching. I know I shouldn't be jealous, because they both like each other and they are both important to me, but I couldn't totally shake the part of me that at one time thought he was the One for me, but if I'm really honest, when we are in <u>the now</u> together we don't click and I know that and so does he. Besides, I have Joe on the mind like 24/7 and even if I don't really get to see him until January, we haven't made plans or anything, I'm keeping him as my secret prize for being a good sport. I'll suffer the Si-and-me consequences then. I just texted him and he wrote back What's up girl and I said I was at a poetry reading, and I was thinking of him and he wrote Dirty Limericks? (HOT) and I sent him a winky face.

I shoved my phone into my purse like I was getting caught— even though I wasn't doing anything wrong—when Mo asked me, "Your girl Grace is engaged, right?"

"So?"

Mo shrugged and put his hands up, very "It's none of my business." "He's complicated. She's complicated. That's people, man."

217

Thanks, Mo, so profound. I looked over. "Si's just more comfortable, more him with her, isn't he?"

"Yep." Mo had a beatific look on his face.

"What about you?"

He waved his hand like he was wiping off a chalkboard. "Too much trouble. Love dies, baby. It ain't for Mo."

10/8 9:45 am

At breakfast today, G and I played our what if we were millionaires game for the 1,000th time and talked about being broke. "At least we have the Web?" Grace said, scraping her burnt toast.

If she was rich, she'd open a poetry commune and bed-and-breakfast. I'd run my own gallery and we decided proceeds from both would go to local food banks.

She yawned and stretched again. "I'm so tired. I was up all night trying to figure out which poems to submit for a chapbook contest, but two aren't finished yet and they need to be included. I don't know how to end either of them. I'm the worst with endings."

"Speaking of beginnings, I don't know if you even want to think about this right now, but Silas is like falling-down-dumb for you. He's so in luvvvvvv."

She rolled her eyes.

"I would crush him."

"What does that even mean?"

"I know me well enough," she said. "I'm as big a mess as anyone else. It's nice that he likes my work. I like having a fanboy. But I'm not about to date someone who isn't even 21 yet. Besides, how weird would that be if the guy you like—liked . . . whatever—and I were hanging out?"

"I don't like him anymore. I used to want to but I don't. Plus, maybe I would feel less guilty."

"Huh?" she said, wiping the crumbs from her pajamas.

"Well . . . there's this other guy, and he's like Silas's enemy. His major competition at the school."

"Piper, you better be honest with Silas if he's really your friend and you hook up with Non-Silas. Don't hurt the baby's feelings."

She gave me a quick hug before she left to buy groceries and pick up books for Eileen June.

10/8 4pm Bench outside Hamid's

Been sketching all day, trying to channel what it would be like to be Carlyle sketching and drawing and it's not really working and I needed a stretch-my-brain-and-legs break so I got more coffee and Hamid told me that Freddy is seeing someone else, I lost my chance with him.

"That was fast." I smiled.

He wagged his finger at me. "You let a good one get away."

No doubt.

Off for a walk.

Studio again but stopped by Carlyle's office this morning because Kennedy said he urgently needed to see me. I was already in my paint-splattered apron, so Carlyle had to deal with my tragic look.

"This is the exact color I want you to use," he said, showing me a swatch called "Eggshell." "Incorporate it into your work. This is the milk-carton color. It's not traditional white."

"Okay," I said. "You could have had Kennedy send me a photo of it."

"No," he said, "I wanted you to see it unfiltered, not diluted on some stupid smartphone."

Crazy. "Well, it's a perfect choice."

"Of course. It's pure eggshell."

I liked him when he was like this. Then, he said "So, you're in the studio today, yes?" Part question, part statement. And before I could answer, he said, "We're going to St. Ann's tonight. Please don't wear the same dress you've been wearing to every event. It's tired. And not that either."

Snap-crackle, back to Carlyle being Carlyle.

Googled St. Ann's. It's a warehouse. Brooklyn. New clothes, other clothes. Maybe I could borrow something. Texted Grace: Any chance you could meet me at Angelou's around 5 and let me borrow something awesome to wear for a work event tonight? It's at a warehouse?

G: Warehouse? Sounds fun. ;)

I told her I'll probably be in the middle of a pile of dishes, look for the wet rat in the back. Thank Goddess 4 Grace!

10/10 1:30 pm NYPL reading room

Sketching and writing in the library at Bryant Park—the one where the jazz party was. I found out the two lions in the front entrance are called Patience and Fortitude, a.k.a. one thing I don't have and never will, and one thing I want to think I do have!

The good thing about going to parties is that I don't have to pay for anything, except new clothes ($40)! Bought two dresses and one skirt and one tube top and one shrug at Housing Works, which is a super-nice thrift store here that does amazing charity work for helping homeless people and people living with AIDS. New favorite place to shop and I don't have to feel guilty about spending money there, 'cause it's helping! I wonder if they take volunteers. I loved some stuff in there that I can't buy right now so am going back as soon as I have anything to spend and find out if I can help. Also, got a scarf that looks great/smells moldy. Should probably wash everything. Also had to buy a MetroCard so I could get to Brooklyn and back ($6). I'm down to $42 plus a nickel I found in the library just now. Wanted to just borrow stuff from Grace, but none of it fit me right, everything too short, and I need some more clothes anyway, because Mom still hasn't sent me the box of my winter stuff she promised—and she calls me the procrastinator!

So: St. Ann's, wearing the long black skirt and new tube top, hair clipped behind my ears kind of nerdy style like I did back in middle school but now with purpose, and hanging with Rashida, who was wearing a long ruby-colored velvet coat, black capris, and black boots, like a bad-ass cool pirate chick. I like her so much. Kennedy and Carlyle were being very buddy-buddy and kind of ignoring me, even though they were literally paying me to be there. Anyway, the show/performance/what-ever was going on right in the middle of the lobby. Everyone was standing around this "statue," a dancer who had come to life, named David. I whispered in Rashida's ear, "Did we all show up for him?" and she said, "Girl, it's opening night."

Long story short: It was fun-ish, but mostly because of Rashida and me being snarky about outfits. The performance was pretentious and I was trotted around by Carlyle as usual but it was kind of a snorefest. I hoped to see Robbins or the models there but nope.

10/11 4:35 pm-ish Carlyle's studio

Been gluing little pieces of glazed discards to a canvas covered with hefty bags for The Discarded all day. My fingers are red. Today's playlist has been mostly Frank Sinatra and Jay Z and Blondie and the Strokes and anything NY I could find, which is a lot. Heading over to Lita's and can't wait to stick my fingers in the dish sink. I have blisters from hot gluing.

10/12 5:57 am Bed

So, winter is coming and surprise: I have a radiator. I didn't even know what it was until it started banging. I called Maria and told her what was happening—my radiator goes on when-ever it wants and it clang-clang-clanged all morning—and she laughed at me. She gets that call a lot, she said. That's how they work.

222

NY is the coldest it's been since I got here. I don't wanna get out of bed.

#NYSeen #MorningTrain: The A train at 4:15 am.

10/12 2 pm F2

I've been working on my own stuff since noon. Was at Carlyle's from seven until 11, then here. Never thought my entire days would be in studios, but it's great. It's what I wished for back when I was using the art studio in school, and it made me nostalgic for Kit and Sammy Chang, my old art class partner, and Adams, of course. It would be fun to be making stuff and not be alone. When I paint, I don't feel alone but the minute I stop, when I want to get an opinion or just shoot the shit, there is nobody in the room but me, myself, and I.

It's gray and white (not eggshell! WHITE!) and so chilly outside but it feels warm and toasty here in F2. I'm not sure what I'm making yet. I love this great not-knowing. But right now I've got to stop and go work on the café's first-floor accent wall, which is going to be bright blue. I've already painted the primer, which happens to be a really pale blue, very uninspiring. According to Lita, Mort said to her early this morning, "Bring the sky inside."

She handed me the cans of paint and I'm a recharged battery! The color is a fantastic superhero blue. I love it. Need to wash off the oils I was working with in F2. I'm going to play with lilacs, lavenders, deep purples, too. I'm gonna give the blue some tone. Lita will like it, I'm sure. Now if I can just convince Mort.

10/13 9:45 am My room

I had planned on spending last night at Carlyle's studio after Lita's. Instead I spent half of the night with Joe Gillman. YEP.

He texted me when I was painting and said he'd be walking around the Met with a guest pass if anyone I knew was interested in hanging out (wink face), so I decided to "not say no" and went up to the Upper East Side and texted him from the Met steps. He was so cutely shocked when he came down. "I can't believe you came," he said and I said, "I said I would. Let's go!"

I followed him in and this time, I didn't just see the lobby. It's HUGE. We stayed until closing time and I still have so much to see. A lot of the time we were in the Temple of Dendur in the Sackler Wing.

"Who made this temple?" I asked. "I like their work."

"The Egyptians?" he said. "Yeah, they're decent. Amazing style."

"Right? There's this woman where I live, Maria, who wears all these bracelets and rings, and she always reminds me of some modern-day casual Egyptian queen. I want that look."

"You got a great look." He tilted his head at me.

"Ew, shush," I laughed and pushed his shoulder lightly and he said, "Why not" and I said, "Fine, go ahead, if you must." He told me he'd look at me all day if it'd make me smile like that.

"You're corny," I said.

"I'm honest."

We were looking so much at each other that we were forgetting to look at the exhibit, and bumped into people stopped in front of the great temple.

"I mean, what's it really take to build one of those, anyway? A few bricks and a glue gun?"

"Maybe some twine," he said. "And mud. I hear mud's a good adhesive."

"Or just tape," I said. "Take the easy way out, build your temples with double-sided tape." Someone told us to shush and we pulled away from the group that was on a tour.

How could this be normal, I thought. We're talking like we've known each other for a long time, the way I thought I would be talking with Si. But instead, this "enemy" is incredibly chill and cute and I wonder if he knows how alive being with him makes me. And happy, and also nervous, and not just for getting found out by Silas.

And overwhelmed by the entire museum because it's THE MET, duh.

"It's just so weird this is working," I accidentally said out loud, and as if reading my mind, he said, "See? I'm great! Surprise!"

He laughed at my non-poker face. "Your boy Silas holds a grudge, I know. But you could try and figure me out for yourself, by just, I don't know, hanging out with me some. That's how most people get to know each other, right? Here on Earth, we talk to each other and that usually helps. What could you possibly owe Jamie Silas?"

"You wouldn't get it."

"Try me."

"He's my student mentor. I wouldn't be here without him, seriously. He helped me believe I could be here." I looked at Joe. "I never knew if I could be somewhere not Houston. I was really stuck with my family, my life, and he was like . . . like . . . don't laugh, but Silas was like my Statue of Liberty. He made me feel like I could make it out and make it here. I think that's part of why I fell for him over email." If Silas had been there right then, I would have thanked him again. When I said it all out loud, I knew how true it was. Silas had rescued me.

"Well, I wish I would have been your mentor, then." He looped his thumb in his belt loop and eased back, looking at me like it was all over. "I'm gonna let you in on a little secret," said Joe. "You're holding on to something that's not real. You think you don't belong in Manhattan? No one thinks they belong here. Silas helped you. Carlyle helped you. But the fact that you're here? You did this by yourself."

"You honestly believe that?" I asked, shaking my head, and he said, "I do. I really do. You're working, what, two jobs, to go to school next semester? You're hustling, girl. It's not easy and you're doing it."

"Do you work?" It just occurred to me to ask him, to see what another student did.

"I'm full-ride but I also do work-study at the school library and I still babysit and do back-up nanny work sometimes."

"Full-ride?"

"Full-ride scholarship. My first two years are covered and I live at home in Harlem, so—"

"Two full years?"

"Yeah." He smiled. "Full-ride for artistic commitment and promise."

"Wow. I can't even imagine going to CFA for free. It's my dream school."

"Yeah, mine, too." He put his fingers between mine and brushed his thumb softly against my palm. "See? That's another thing we have in common." He took a deep breath. "So, did you and Silas ever hook up?"

"No. I mean, I think we both thought we would, but we didn't really connect that way."

He nodded, looking surprisingly serious.

"We'd need a lot more than double-sided tape." I laughed. "Look, when we talk about art, it's all there. When we talk about anything else, we're just friends. Maybe like you and Astrid?" He whistled when I said that. I know I was throwing a little fire into our convo, but what the hell.

"Astrid's. My. Friend."

"So, Si's mine. Platonic."

"Are you always this annoying?" he asked.

"Oh, this is nothing." I smiled and bumped him with my elbow.

Our laughs echoed through the hall. I like him so much. One of the walls was covered in windows, and Central Park was right outside. People were riding in horse-driven carriages and pushing strollers and walking in business suits and selling hot dogs and I felt like I was in a movie set in New York.

"Just so you know, I'm really not after Silas. He's not even on my radar, except for when I'm with you," he said quietly. "He's had it in his head since Day One that I'm out to ruin him."

"Well, how do you think he got that idea?"

"Honestly? I know exactly when it happened."

"When?"

He shook his head. "Robbins McCoy compared our pieces in a freshman seminar. I didn't know he was going to do it, and there was nothing I could have done about it; he compares pieces all the time. It's called crit, and you gotta get used to it if you're gonna be an art student. He just liked mine more than Silas's, that's all there was to it. And he made it very clear to the entire incoming class which piece he considered 'great' and which piece he considered 'crap.'"

Ouch. Poor Silas. "Robbins didn't have to be a dick and do that, but he did. And that sucks. But that's also art. Everybody's got an opinion. But ever since then Silas has assumed I'm this devil art imposter. And by the way, Robbins has torn my work apart a million-plus times. When he says one of my pieces works, I don't even believe him anymore. He's rough."

But you're not Robbins's son, I wanted to say. You're not being embarrassed by the man who won't even acknowledge you unless it's as a second-rate artist.

I wondered then if maybe Silas would have been happier as an English or creative writing major somewhere else. God, what a mess.

"I'm really going to have to see some of your 'controversial' work one of these days," I hinted.

"Anytime," he said and opened his palms wide. "I want to show you. We could today if you have time. But would it be okay if we didn't talk about school or Robbins anymore? It's kinda ruining the mood." He was smiling the amazing smile.

"What mood?"

"My I-want-to-kiss-you mood."

"We're in public."

"Yeah, Piper." He laughed again. "It's New York, it's all public. Do I have to go somewhere private to kiss you? Because I will. But right now, I really, really want to kiss you here, in front of this temple and the tourists and the security guards and the cameras. APAP. As public as possible."

And it was the perfect kiss. The kiss I had hoped for with Silas. But it was happening with Joe. In THE MET. It was everything.

I finally came to my senses and pulled away and braced myself against the wall behind us. WHOA. I was dizzy.

"What's the NEVER SAY NO about?" I asked, trying to get my head together, reading his fingers' tats, tracing them with my own fingers.

"A tribute to my mama," he said. "She never said no to anything in life. She was a fighter." His eyes crinkled. "I try not to say no to life, too."

Was?

"Your mom—"

Again, his smile. I kept my fingers on his, and he looped them into mine. His mom was diagnosed with ovarian cancer when he was 11, he told me, and her specialist was transferred here from Orlando so they all—him and his parents and his three sisters—moved to a two-bedroom in Harlem so that his mom could get treatment. And then she died, when he was 13.

I was so sad I couldn't say anything because I knew I would lose it. I kept my eyes on the temple and the tourists.

"I'm okay. I mean it's horrible and I think about her every damn day and it's never ever going to feel normal . . . but I'm okay. We're okay. But that's why my family is really important to me."

"What was her name?"

"Joanne. I was named after her. She was always busy, always happy and busy. She was a science teacher. Everyone loved her. She wanted to do everything all the time, always open to goofy experiments, never said no"—he held up his knuck-les—"to anything offered. She used to say she led a big life. Then suddenly she was always lying down. But she had the most energy and the biggest laugh of anyone in our family. She believed all that seize-the-day crap, all those sayings that get printed on magnets. But she, like, really believed them."

I thought of Silas saying Joe had everything handed to him, that he never worked hard for anything. What did he know? Everybody's got shit to handle, like the way I had to handle my

Marli shit. Nobody's life is what it seems.

"She sounds amazing," I said.

"She was," he said. "If there's a heaven, she's up there challenging everyone to tennis and poking fun at the angels losing to her."

We both laughed and he kind of squinted at me.

"It feels good to talk about her. I miss her all the time."

I said, "I'm sorry, Joe. I'm so so sorry," and then we kissed again and this time there wasn't just heat, but a sweetness between us. I didn't want to let him go.

Silas is going to freak that Joe and I are becoming something. I thought I left friendship and love dramas in Texas. Why do I always step right into this shit? Love is so messy.

10/14 8:15 am

Just got off the phone with Mom. She said I sounded happy and I said, I just really wanted to hear your voice and tell you I love you. She asked if everything was okay.

"Definitely definitely."

I told her I made "a friend," and he told me about his mother dying and then Mom said, "Oh, so that's what has to happen to get a call from you!" and I said, "Well, you're always busy anyway" and she said, "I'm just yanking your chain, kiddo. So, no more of this Silas guy?" and I said I was pretty sure we were just meant to be art-bestie buddies. "Well, follow your heart, Piper. Look how far it's already taken you."

She always knows just what to say.

Had to stop by Carlyle's before the studio and get that money, honey. Yay paycheck time!

"Have a seat," Carlyle said. He signaled to a chair and I sat while he stood.

"How are things?"

"Great!" I said. "I've been really excited by the project."

"We know." Carlyle smiled. "Kennedy was just at the studio early this morning."

"Oh. Oh, sorry I didn't clean up last night. I went to the Met and I got inspired and I guess I just lost track. I was tired and ended up staying until late late. I'm going back there now."

"Well, sit for a second, Piper. We're liking what we're seeing develop for this gallery show, and it's time to talk about your future. I think there's a place for growth with us, to stay on until June."

"But . . . I can't. School starts in January, Carlyle. You know that."

"You came to be an artist. I know that. And you are an artist now. Because of me. Because of everything I've done for you."

"Um—" I thought of what Joe had said to me, that it wasn't because of them. I was up here because of me.

"Why would you stop your momentum to go to school? What aren't you learning? We're ushering you into the community. The art community is a community of connections—the names we're linking yours with are going to take you much further in the art world than some degree." He wrinkled his nose. "You'll think about it. You can go on to the studio and work now."

I had a sudden feeling like I was in a scary movie and I was about to find out that if you worked for Carlyle, you were bound to him for life by blood or something.

If I took a break from school, school that I've never even officially started, just to keep working with Carlyle, would I ever find my way back to my education and my art? Everything I would make would be for him, or worse—"by him." How was that being an artist in any way? That may be his idea of being an artist, but that's not mine. Not even close.

I just devoured potato leek soup from Hamid's because it's friggin' cold out and the studio is freezing. I gotta stop journaling and get to work and pray for my student loans to come through. My head is tight with Vampire Carlyle's offer and Silas vs. Joe. So much in my brain.

10/14 8 pm Café A painting and dishes

Joe and I played phone tag all day today while I've been here, mostly texts, but then he left me a voice mail and he was singing—SINGING! He has a really great voice, it's super deep when he sings, I'm kind of surprised. I'm saving his message forever. I want to play it for Grace and Kit. Or not. Oh my god of course I will.

I painted the stairwell from the café to Floor 2 today and felt like I was going to pass out. Not enough air combined with paint fumes and no fan. Lita told me to take breaks whenever I needed, esp. 'cause the café wasn't too full today. She said she's going to hang a new light fixture in there and line the hallway with art or photos. I offered some art and she said we'll see. LITAAAA, just say yes or no. Mort would!

And I just scraped off someone's mac and cheese. How could someone not finish Lita's famous m&c?

Oh, my phone—Joe calling! FINALLY WE CAN TALK!

10/16 4:30 pm

Spent the last two days collaging and painting my ass off. Everything I look at now feels discarded. The more I collage, the clearer I get on how the pieces really work. Instead of just one big Discarded, it's a lot of little ones together. Like a land-fill isn't a big deal with a few pieces of trash in it, but when it becomes a mountain of garbage? It's one entity.

I lost control in a good way (not thinking, just doing, being a part of it) and then the trash knew how to lay itself out and did. After a few hours, everything was finding its place, as if I wasn't there. I now have two big, connecting Discarded pieces. A set.

Okay, off to my dish shift, then coffee with Si. Need to talk about Carlyle with someone who understands. Haven't seen my people, no Grace, no Si in what feels like forever. Total art hermit.

10/17 11 am

Still collaging—Styrofoam chunks, plastic bag turned into a rose, a plastic soda ring cut up into tiny confetti pieces—all last night after Lita's. I was hoping Kennedy (or Carlyle?!) would stop by to see my work again while I was there. I really think they'll like it. I made sure to incorporate Carlyle's eggshell color. Hopefully he'll pick up on me trying to create some cohesion for his show.

I caught my reflection in the Web lobby mirror, after cutting and gluing and painting for hours, when I got back last night. My leggings and tank top were covered in gray and silver and spots of orange and gold and eggshell. My hair's long and getting boring. I need a chop badly and maybe a new color. Maybe this NY yellow that's invaded my life, but then I might look too Big Bird. But Sesame Street happened in NY, right? ☺

I'm starting to like my NY look, though. I look real. I look like I know what's up. Finally.

10/18 9 am

At Carlyle's studio early this morning with a bag of stuff I've collected to add to the Discarded borough piece: a bodega coffee cup from Hamid's; wax paper from a donut or bagel—I think it was a donut, because it's sticky—a pair of broken reading glasses; one dirty, unlaced shoe. Also, big news!!! Grace FIN-A-LLY broke up officially with Evan yesterday. She's a mess, which kind of surprised me, because she's been so over him, but maybe it's different when it's a fiancé. I sent Silas a text that said, A little birdie told me that Grace doesn't have a fiancé anymore.

Si: . . .

Me: Happy?

Si: Yeah. She told me yesterday.

235

Me: SHE DID?!?!?

Oh, wow. So those two are . . . wow. Okay? I have so many questions for G!!!

We're going to Coney Island later today on a trash run.

10/19 2 am

How am I sunburned—or am I windburned? My skin hurts. We bought cheap beer and Grace's voice was breaking ALL DAY no matter what she was saying, except when we were in the Circus Sideshow. We took a pic with a bearded lady, who whispered in my ear that it was fake! (#NYSeen #Beard)

I did buy a CI red ringer T-shirt. It's super cute.

It took us about two hours to get back to the Webster on the train. That's like Houston to Galveston time.

Grace isn't wearing Evan's ring and said she was trying not to talk about him so much, but then she did a whole bunch when we were walking along the ocean. I said, "You're going to get some good poems out of this" and she said, "Not helpful." Grace put her head on my shoulder and sighed.

She's going to be so much happier. She said so herself.

I asked her if she had told anyone else yet. I wasn't quite sure how to tell her that I had texted Si about their breakup.

"Well, my mom for sure. And Evan's sister, who flipped out. And Silas."

"Oh yeah?" I said, acting surprised. "You told Silas?"

"We grabbed a coffee yesterday."

"YOU DID?"

"You said you were working all day at the studio. I didn't want to bother—"

"You wouldn't bother me! I'm here for you, y'know."

"Are you upset?"

"No." I shook my head. "Not at all." She was so on the edge of tears and I didn't want to tip her over or make her feel weird about Si and her. I mean after all, he and I were clear of being anything. But I did feel a little left out thinking of them hanging out without me, I guess. "I'm definitely not upset. I'm glad he could be there for you."

"I shouldn't be crying," she said, wiping her eyes and nose on her sleeve. "I'm the one making this choice. But outside of Eileen June and you, I don't really have anyone else here and, to be honest, I'm lonely. Ev made me feel less alone, even if it was just to have someone to argue with. It would be easier to be with him."

"But it would be wrong."

"Yeah." She wiped her face again. "I didn't think I would be scared to be alone."

"Being alone and being lonely aren't the same, though," I said.

"Dr. Phil, at it again," she said, pushing my shoulder and laughing.

"Maybe you're crying because you're relieved," I said and she said, "Maybe I'm just lucky you're my friend."

And then we were all huggy and tears and walking on the beach like some Hallmark card.

Last thing:

Coney Island is weird. It's like, real-life Twin Peaks and I love it.

Oh, and trash treasures: two beer bottles, one filled with sand, a ticket for a boardwalk ride, I think?, and a MetroCard. We saw some broken glass and pizza crusts and a banana peel. G wanted me to take the food, but that's more Mo's area and I really didn't want to carry stinky food remains on the long train ride home.

10/19 10 am Carlyle's studio

I need rubber gloves or tongs. Picking up trash is gross. I figure if nothing else, the good I'm doing with this project is cleaning up the city, haha. I kept it tied up in plastic bags outside of my door last night because it smelled too bad to keep in my room. Now the Web hallway is kind of nasty.

Luckily, glazing it makes the odor dissipate. I'm testing which works best—glazing, laminating, or a gloss varnish.

10/19 8:45 pm, but feels like midnight! It's cold and dark.

Si met me at Carlyle's studio today. First we met out front, grabbed coffee at Hamid's, and he followed me up.

I opened the door and flicked on the light, walked to the windows to open them for some cold fresh air and daylight—rats be damned. He looked at my trash collages.

"Piper."

"Yeah?" I asked, opening another window.

"You built these?" He was tracing them with his fingertips.

"Don't touch my trash!" I laughed and exhaled. Between the paint and the trash, it was garbage-disposal smelly and the studio felt . . . thick.

"Your patterns, your brain . . ." He took off his hat and was breathing into his hands to warm them up. "The piles look like bulging strands of DNA."

"Do you think it lines up with a signature Carlyle piece? Like it comes from him?"

He didn't say anything.

"I'm going to be adding a bunch soon, so maybe it will disguise some of me and feel more like him." I was nervous talking.

"Carlyle wouldn't puzzle these together, not like this. Your logic isn't his." He walked between the two pieces I had mostly finished, back and forth, looking from one to the other. "He doesn't have your warmth or your connection to the message behind the pieces."

I showed him the gold-yellow and orange panels that I wanted to put behind The Discarded.

"They were supposed to be panoramic at first, more horizontal than vertical. But—"

"But they had their own ideas," he said.

"Yes, exactly!" I said. "I wanted them to feel like they would block out the sunset or sunrise in different parts of the city. And I painted the orange and yellow panels that I'm placing behind them to—"

239

"The skyline behind each one, morning and afternoon! I see it, Piper! Skyscrapers, the garbage, and the sky, the sky—"

He pointed his finger in front of each painting, almost touching them again.

"This is how you see the city?" he said and then he kind of stopped talking and was zoning, so I just got to work.

While I worked, Silas studied for midterms. His Intro to Computing for Creative Processes class is kicking his ass.

"I thought we didn't have to take written tests at a conservatory."

"Did Helen tell you that?"

"No, I just thought our tests would just be, I dunno, more creative."

"Yeah, no."

My fingers were red-raw from constantly unsticking glue from them, and I was covered in paint and trash. I've been ripping up and hacking newspapers into smaller and smaller confetti, mixing it in paint, sticking it to both Discarded pieces.

It's like Seurat with trash pointillism. I'm messing with focus and the contrast feels right—the rough litter and the way we ignore it, so it just becomes fuzz, filler. It blends into the world. It's background. It's softness. Static. I'm feeling my way through this literally. It's not so much about how it looks—it's about the texture, at least at this phase, but then again the texture informs the appearance, so . . . it's like knitting to make a sweater. Right now I'm playing with the yarn, but soon it's all gonna look ready, finished.

I was breathless when I finally turned back to him and said, "I'm starving." He jumped.

It felt like 30 minutes, but when I stopped, I saw it had been four hours. It had been a perfect friendship date. Si never interrupted me and I hadn't bothered him. He took off his headphones and looked at my work.

"If only."

"If only what?" I asked.

He shook his head.

"It's effortless."

"How's that?" I was wiping the sweat off my forehead with a washrag.

"You just . . ." I looked at him like hurry up, and he said, "We better get some food in you."

We walked to Veselka and the fresh air felt good, made me want to run.

"You got your New York legs! Finally walking at the right pace." He laughed. I realized we were walking pretty fast next to each other. I felt like we had also found the right pace of our friendship. I think he did, too.

"Fall in New York is the best. My favorite season by far."

"Suck it, summer." He pumped his fist. Dorky.

Si slipped in a little Grace talk, of course. He was so ready to rave about her. I wonder if he had been holding it in the whole time at the studio!

"You don't think she just wants me as her rebound?" He was so happy-blushy just thinking about her. "Although, well, I guess, who does this to someone they aren't into?" He took my forearm and softly stroked it.

"Stop, weirdo!" I shook out my arm, smiling. "That's between y'all!"

"She also gave me a really tight hug when she was about to leave the last time I saw her." Silas nudged me. He was so pleased with himself. He's just so dorky.

"That's how she hugs. She's a hugger."

"It's okay for you to be jealous." So now teasing was okay? Okay.

"I'm not!"

"Sure!"

"It's cute!" he said and I rolled my eyes.

"I promise you I'm not jealous. If it wasn't for me, you wouldn't have met. I've done my part! Consider me your love Dr. Phil!"

We got to Veselka and I was hoping my bank card would cover it and it did, whew. I could have eaten three more bowls of chili. I should have told him about Joe. But I didn't. We were having too good of a time and I was just happy we were being honest about Grace and him, and him and me. Baby steps.

10/20 8 am C's studio

Couldn't sleep one minute last night. As soon as it was light enough for me not to be freaked out I ran down here. I wanted to see the sunrise and I did, right before I left a sketch of a sun rising over the NYC skyline for Hamid on his front counter while he made a fresh pot of coffee.

He yawned and said sweetly, "You brought the sun!"

Everything I have been making all my life until now has been typical—appropriately sized—and I'm feeling this need to go really really huge, like gigantic. Why the change—all I want to do is get super specific, examine every single speck and smell of NYC. Shrink. So to create big, I need to go small, see what's inside all the small. Crawl around in it. Microscopic. Micro-living. I like how this city is so big and it makes you feel so small and you can't have the big without the small and vice versa. It's all connected. I just want to mess around with size and be a monster.

Stopping writing—work time.

10/20 Almost 5 pm—dish shift

The woman sitting on a foldout chair on the corner of Cornelia St. and Bleecker, right near Café Angelou always asks to tell my fortune for a mere $10! "What's ten dollars?" she always asks. Uh, only my dinner.

Finally asked her if she'd be willing to trade a pic for a reading and she agreed, told me to sketch her good side. My tarot consisted of a death card and a card with cups and a heart card: death of a current relationship (Silas?), something I had to let go of (Carlyle? guilt about Joe?

all of the above?) and money troubles (DUH!) But, yay! my cups would be overflowing with *the stuff of life.* (Well, that's just New York, right?) Great. More stuff of life, please.

It's getting so dark so early now.

By 5:30 I'm losing light. I can still work on the F2 walls after the dishes because there's only one color for them, but not my own work. Too dark.

10/21 11:15 pm BED

At Café A tonight, there were two sisters on guitars. One did slam poetry. Hector told me not to miss the Anabels when I was washing dishes and I stretched at him, said "I'm tired" and he said, "Lean into it, sister. Enjoy the mellow for now. Then sip your energy later."

So I did—they were fine, not GRACE GOOD, though. Then painted, now EXHAUSTED. Need many sleeps.

10/22 4:10 pm TV room

Grace met me at Carlyle's today, insisting we pick through the "rubbish of the ruined" together, though I don't need that much more. I texted Silas to see if he and Mo wanted to join us, even promised that Grace was here and Mo could get into all the trash stuff, maybe show me something with new eyes, but Si said he was with his fam and couldn't get away. ☹ He sent me Mo's number and I texted him about our garbage adventure and he said, No can do, P, working on my own shit today. Peace.

Anyway, I brought more trash, probably the last batch, to the studio for The Discarded. This trash was supposed to literally be that: trash! I wonder if the people who tossed this *stuff of life*—old photos, perfectly good Mason jars without lids, clothes—would ever guess that they're having their 15 minutes of fame. I'm using one Mason jar in the project and Grace and I are keeping the rest for flowers and desk stuff and I'm going to put my spare change in one and at least pretend I'm actually saving money.

"You're doing something really good, here, Piper. You're telling a city's story. You're tracing what didn't make the cut of people's life events, even when the stuff is in great shape. Like these?" She held up one of the Mason jars.

"Well. It's Carlyle's name on it, not mine."

She sighed. "But there's plenty other, more glamorous pieces you could have made him stamp his name on, but you're secretly—or maybe you knew it all along—making him use art for the greater good."

I told her about Carlyle's milk-carton project.

"I guess if he didn't do some stuff just to make money, he wouldn't be where he is today, and he does the stuff that does make money to be able to afford you. Just like Eileen June going on all those morning talk shows to address and defend feminism. People should already be living the F word. But it also means her books sell. It means she can afford an assistant like me, which means I get to write and do more for the greater good. Like Carlyle's milk cartons. It's all part of the same game."

"Game?" I asked, blowing on the cup of hot cocoa I got at Hamid's. I planned to use that as trash, too.

"The game of do what you <u>have</u> to do so you can do what you <u>want</u> to do. You do it with Carlyle. You make his work so you can make your own. You made changes in your own life so you can do the things you want. Be the change you want to see. You know?"

"Gandhi!" Adams would be impressed I remembered one of her favorite quotes!

She nodded. "'Be the change you wish to see in the world.' That's actually a paraphrase from a longer quote, but it works."

"I don't think Gandhi meant playing 'the game' the way you describe it."

"I dunno. I can't speak for the Big G."

I feel out of my league the more we talk. Grace is so full of brains. I'm still not sure I agree 100% with her, but I'm thinking thinking thinking . . . about "the game."

We left the studio and stopped at Nomad Valley and Ricky's. Halloween is for REAL in NYC! Grace got a blonde wig, wings, and a devil's pitchfork and is going as Tinkerhell, Tinkerbell's evil twin sister. She came up with it as we were shopping and we were both like yassssss. I bought fluorescent hot-pink fishnet tights for $1.50 at a costume and prop shop, trying hard not to spend too much. I want to fill that Mason jar, and with school coming up, I have to think about how much I can actually spend on stuff I won't use again. Plus I don't want to generate as much trash anymore. I guess <u>The Discarded</u> is changing me.

Grace suggested I could go as a slutty flamingo but I just liked the tights and wanted an excuse to buy them. Maybe I can go as Broke Piper. Oh wait, that's just me IRL.

Four days until Carlyle's show. I'm also supposed to work my butt off for Lita, who wants to add more hours to my shift and hello, that's horrible timing but I can't say no to more money, not now.

And now back to my work, his work, the city, the garbage.

The Discarded is finished. Kennedy came by today and sent final pics to Carlyle, who apparently had been coming into the studio at night, after I had left, to evaluate my progress. Really glad I didn't know he was dropping in or I would have been a mess, but also, I was leaving the studio really cluttered and stinky and I know he doesn't like that. Also, why couldn't he just stop by when I was there?

"Congratulations," Kennedy said. "Carlyle just signed off."

A deep sigh of relief rolled out of me. "What if he hadn't?"

He chucked my cheek, like, "Isn't that cute of you." He said, "You wouldn't let that happen."

I would love a straight answer from either one of them about anything, but that doesn't matter at the moment. Carlyle likes the two Discarded pieces and how they work together, and the panels/screens that hopefully will be mounted behind them.

"Why didn't Carlyle ever come during the day? I really could have used his brain on these pieces, instead of just guessing everything I was doing."

"Do you assume he has endless free time to devote to you?"

"No, but it's his work going out with his name on it."

"And you did a great job," Kennedy said, handing me my paycheck.

Then he gave me a separate envelope filled with petty cash for cabs and a list of supplies I have to pick up tomorrow and deliver to the gallery for Carlyle's show:

- paper towels, plates, cups—Village Party Store

- prosecco, champagne, seltzer—Astor Wines

- cheese trays, vegetable platters (no olives!)—Murray's Cheese

Easy-peasy.

So my pieces will be picked up tomorrow. Tonight I say goodbye.

Discarded, I'll see you again soon, but not here. You belong to the world now.

It reminds me of that book Mom used to read Marli and me when we were kids, Goodnight Moon, except it's:

Goodnight trash

Goodnight art

Goodnight paints

Goodnight heart.

It took me a bajillion hours to do all the pickups and transport everything to the gallery. The traffic, rain, and sleet were B-A-D, bad and it was almost impossible to get cabs and when I did, the back seats were slick from previous passengers so my butt was wet all day, like I was wearing a soggy diaper. Bleck.

Anyway I finally got everything back to the gallery, Kennedy didn't write down the address so at first I googled the wrong place, then took a cab to the right place from there, so annoying but luckily I'm not paying for the cabs, and of course when I got there the front desk wouldn't let me proceed into the gallery because I was WET. I told her I was working with Carlyle and she went to go get him.

Carlyle came out, a confused smile on his face.

"You're wet."

DUH DUH DUH.

"I know! It's been pouring out but I did manage to get everything on the list!" I put the piles of bags down. A thank-you from him would have been great. "So, can I sneak a peek?"

"Wring yourself out," he said. "Then follow me."

A crew of all dudes in head-to-toe black were adjusting lights, hanging and mounting the pieces, and attaching labels and colored stickers near the pieces.

"What are the stickers for?"

"Price points." He looked at me like that explained everything and I just stared at him and he sighed. "Each colored circle equals a different price. If clients want a piece, they sign up in that notebook over there, where the prices are listed."

"Oh."

I saw a couple of pieces I didn't recognize, I guess they were Carlyle's or Kennedy's originals. Not bad. One painting was of this oversized moon, I think that's what it was, this kind of magical bright orb on a black ink background. The label on the wall said (Men Are from Mars. Moonlight, Staten Island. Carlyle Campbell.) I was squinting, trying to figure out what was at the bottom of the painting, and moved toward it to get a better look. He cleared his throat.

"Gut reaction?"

"It's moody. Strange. Out of this world," I winked at him.

"Of course."

"I love it, actually."

"Go on."

"The details inside of the moon—it's a moon, right? Or Mars? Those little lines." I pointed to the bottom of his painting.

"What do you think they are?"

"Well, they're not literal, I know that. Not people or ants. But I'm not sure."

I looked at him, waiting for his answer.

"They're there to make you uncomfortable," he whispered.

"Anxiety is an alien," I said quietly.

He looked genuinely impressed. Like we connected for real. I wanted to ask more but he put his finger to his lips. He was fidgeting his beaded bracelet with the other hand.

"What about your milk cartons?"

"Ah, they're being unloaded as we speak. They'll be up front."
We walked over to where the movers were taking them out of
their bubble wrap.

"How are you displaying them? Not on the ground, right?"

"Of course not. The stands aren't here yet."

I didn't see The Discarded anywhere.

"Sooooo, where's my —?"

He lifted an eyebrow. "It's not placed yet. It hasn't arrived yet
either, due to the weather. Don't worry," he said. "I wouldn't
discard The Discarded—that would be too on-the-nose." He
winked.

Carlyle walked off quickly and snapped at one of the guys about
a piece that was hung wrong (it was off by a millimeter). He
doesn't want any shadows cast, which makes sense, but still, no
reason to scream at the guy.

Maybe when The Discarded arrives, it's getting major placement, like right at the front of the gallery near the milk cartons
or in a dedicated space, like my heart at my Senior Gallery.
Maybe he'll surprise me.

10/29 2 pm F2, pouring rain all day
again WTF and cold cold cold

I have to wash dishes soon. I feel like crying. I don't know what
to work on, besides F2 and the dishes, and I'm cold and tired.

My throat hurts. I miss Mom and Dad. I wish I was sleeping in my own bed right now, my Houston bed. Texas, you are so far away and I'm dreaming of you.

I texted Joe about the show and he said he wished he could come, but he'd promised his dad he'd watch his youngest sister. I told him he could bring her and he said she's too annoying, but he'll see the show this week. Okay.

10/31 3:35 am

Carlyle's Show Opening
_____

Press, artists, designers, and rando New Yorkers showed up. Even if I should be used to shows now after Fashion Week and Mikhail's show and that David production thing, this all still feels new and exciting to me. I like this part of the public part. It's all about the what-ifs—what if they love it and what if they think it's the best thing they've ever seen and what if this makes Carlyle really, really happy?

Carlyle was wearing a steel-gray leather bomber jacket—how many does he have and why do they all look so perfect on him—and was so comfortable we could have been in his office.

Grace came with me and Si showed up with Mo, of course.

I went to read the description card on the wall next to The Discarded, which had been placed in the back. Carlyle had put the orange and yellow panels behind them, but then he switched their position and placement and to me they didn't work as well. I wanted to say something to him but I knew I had to wait until after the show or back at his office. It was really throwing me off, but I couldn't do anything about it there.

The Discarded: A Red Hook Summer.
Carlyle Campbell, Artist.
(A red sticker.)

"What's a Red Hook?" I wasn't surprised to see Carlyle's name, but Red Hook? Si said it's a neighborhood far out in Brooklyn.

"But the trash didn't come from there. I've never even been there, I think."

"Well, yeah, and Carlyle wasn't the artist," he whispered.

It's weird seeing my work up with his name under it and when I told Grace that, she said, "It's like being a ghostwriter." Si nodded his head, agreeing with Grace. He's been next to her since she arrived. I don't want to be a ghost anything. Mo walked up as we were looking at the next one:

A Bronx Trail, 204th Street.
Carlyle Campbell, Artist.
(A yellow sticker.)

A simple painting of a woman wearing a helmet, riding her bike on a trail against a brick wall, leaves and water to her right. She's relaxed, no anxiety alien landing on her! It didn't feel like Carlyle at all. Somebody else did this one for sure. Had to.

"Guuuurrrrlll."

Rashida, Benz, and Abril were standing behind me, heavy pours of wine in hand.

"You're here?" I wasn't surprised to see Rashida, but the other two?

"We go where the parties go." Abril winked.

Of course they do.

Rashida popped a cheese square in her mouth and made eye contact with me.

"He's quite a miracle, that Carlyle," Rashida said. "I really like this piece he made over there. Who knew he spent time in Red Hook?" I bit my lip, smiling, and Rashida slanted her eyes at Carlyle across the room, shade expertly thrown.

"C'mon," Rashida said. "I'll show you guys another amazing piece he made."

$hop Till You Drop: 5th Avenue.
Carlyle Campbell, Artist.

(A money-green sticker.)

It was a stack of gold spray-painted dollar bills on a Lucite stand. Inside the stand were a bunch of burnt dollar bills, wadded up and torn. I liked it. It might have been super obvious, but whatever. I still liked it. "Did he—"

She whispered in my ear, "Kennedy."

"Oh. OH!"

So that's what he was working on! I was excited and surprised! I wanted to talk to Kennedy immediately, bring him over and make him tell me everything. He was working—and not just his grunt work!!!

We joined Kennedy and Carlyle talking to the crowd about a pile of shattered glass spread across a marble-top table. Grace and Si were into it.

Cracked, The Glass Ceiling
Carlyle Campbell, Artist.

Another green sticker. Another Kennedy?

"When Carlyle was creating Cracked," Kennedy said, "he was channeling the energy of a post-9/11 New York, of a post-politics 2016, the things that have cracked us, as a world, as a community, as a nation." Everyone nodded and whispered and a few clapped.

All the pieces were influenced by the boroughs, and that was the connection, I got what he was doing, but really all art in this city is influenced by it in one way or another. The theme, THE OUTSIDE, is a cheat, I think. And though I saw a fair amount of elegance, the chaos didn't really feel . . . chaotic.

After a few minutes of listening to Kennedy talk about this piece, which I had no idea if Carlyle had really built himself or if Kennedy had made that one too or someone I didn't even know made it, I felt like leaving. Carlyle has his cred, I got it, but I wanted to go. But before I could drag Grace out with me, this happened.

"Friends, fellow New Yorkers. Hello."

Cheers. Applause. Clinking of glasses from everyone packed in the gallery.

"I can't thank you enough for coming to THE OUTSIDE on such a winter's night. What an intrepid bunch you beautiful people are!"

Laughter. More claps. Someone yelled, "Hear, hear!"

"You've been so supportive this year, with my first foray into the fashion world, and then returning to my roots, here in SoHo."

He nodded at the randos who apparently felt their whoops were necessary contributions.

"I must thank not just the gallery for hosting our opening and exhibit, but to my team, too, who have been invaluable to me this year. You know who you are, team!" Kennedy looked kind of sheepish and I was about to raise my hand to say "Thanks!" but Carlyle kept going. "But none of us is anything without all of YOU, without New York City!" Then he stretched his arms out like a sun salute and kind of gave a little thank-you out to the streets, like New York was his cult or something, and everybody died clapping all over themselves.

"Can we go now?" Grace asked. "I've seen enough of him not acknowledging you." But I had to stay until it was over.

We headed to the food and wine table and I stopped at the white podium by the check-in desk. It had the notebook with the prices of the pieces in it. I wanted to see if anyone liked The Discarded.

Someone was buying my Discarded piece—for $4,500!!! I don't even know how to understand that amount.

I showed Grace and her mouth dropped and Silas shrugged.

"This can't be!"

"Yeah, that seems about right," Silas said, like no big D.

"How do you know that?"

"My mom? Remember? She's an art dealer."

"Is she here? I should say hi."

He pointed to the corner where she was talking to Rashida. "Yeah, over there."

But I felt like I couldn't move, thinking about that $$$. I tried to balance myself, catch my breath. Silas poured wine for us. I chugged it. I thought it would be a big deal to put something up at Angelou's, but this was HUGE money. And then, oh yeah, right, I wasn't getting a cut of it.

But if I could start selling on my own, really selling like this, then I can pay for school. I know it. If someone liked <u>The Discarded</u>, then they would like more of it. I can pay for my life here. I can even pay for more than that—I can help the people here. My art can be activism, like Grace said. My art can be a business, like Andy Warhol said. Everything was clicking.

Eventually, everyone left and I didn't get to say hi to Glenda. Kennedy and I had to stay to clean up the space and then we were out.

I drew this on the back of one of the gallery flyers and left it tucked into the window grate:

I came home and when I got in the shower, I cried. Relief, sadness, all of it. My time finally felt like my own again.

The NY Times posted a review a couple of hours ago and it was okay. I think I liked it better when I wasn't compulsively checking art reviews and news. Cracked and The Discarded and The Mighty Buck and some of the pieces near the back of the space—He said, He said and Rockaway Beach, Summer 2000—were highlighted but not exactly loved. There was a photo of Carlyle, Benz, and Mikhail featured, and in the background, Grace laughing with Silas, hand on his shoulder. I can't believe my friends are in the NY Times! They look glamorous! But there was another gallery exhibit that also opened tonight and definitely got a better review. I'm sure Carlyle's not a happy camper. I'm so glad I'm not Kennedy right now. Maybe they haven't read it yet.

But my work was mentioned in the DAMN NY TIMES, my third decent review in my life, and that was awesome!!! Even if the review of the overall show was meh. My name wasn't associated with The Discarded, of course, but I'm still saving this online and buying a newspaper when I wake up.

So happy to have a full day off now, including from Café A. And oh last thing, Lita left me a voice mail. I get another week in F2. New tenants are gonna be late moving in. Yay lucky me!

And now I must Zzzzzz. So tired it hurts.

NOVEMBER

Halloween was rad and weird.

The parade was insane. Best costumes and floats and puppets and drag queens I have ever seen—a ton of political ones—and there were cops everywhere, though we didn't see anything bad go down, just some people getting arrested for being too drunk and two guys for peeing outside. So rude.

G and I met up with Mo and Si, and Mo definitely kept nudging them together, and Grace was super nice to both boys, and she was tipsy and flirty, her super-cute talkative Grace self, but when Si started trying too hard, finding reasons to touch her shoulder pads and her outfit to the point of being annoying, she finally said, "Silas, chill?" And he backed down a bit but then he really avoided me, like he was embarrassed. That kind of made me happy to be honest because I don't want to be their third wheel. G definitely does like him, but she doesn't like clingy guys, even though she's a hugger. She likes to call the shots.

Mo was telling me how Halloween was his favorite holiday because "when else do we celebrate Día de los Muertos? Do you even know what that means?" And I was like, "Duh, I grew up in Texas!" and then he said, "Well, am I right?" Sure. So then Mo whipped out his "secret" flask and he became magically happier and Si relaxed.

We went down to Spring St. and into a huge crowd. After the official parade broke up around 11, we started walking and ended back by the CFA campus near a total ninja crew, a bunch of guys and maybe girls, hard to tell, with face masks like ninjas, and hoodies with skeleton bones. In a Donnie-Darko-type mood they would have creeped me out but I was in James Turrell hot-pink Halloween mode. We were walking down the steps into FC's, that bar Grace loves, 'cause she wanted to meet up with her poetry friends, and as we were getting our IDs checked, my cell started blowing up with texts.

Don't go in there.

Turn around.

I'm right here.

I told them, "I'll be in in a second" and walked back up to street level and looked around and one of the guys wearing a hoodie walked right up to me. He pulled down his face mask.

"Hey!" I said.

"Hey ya, Pipes."

Joe's eyes were sleepy-sexy, pulling a Tyra Banks and smizing at me whether he knew it or not and his mouth was curled into a smile that made me want to curl up against him like a pillow.

"How in the hell did you find me in this mess?"

"To be honest, I saw Silas first. And of course, you're with your boy." He rolled his eyes.

"Joe, don't," I said. I tilted my head like don't even start, trying not to laugh.

He raised his hands and said, "My bad, my bad, though I can't figure out why you're spending the spookiest night of the year with him and not me!" Then he gave me that sexy smile and said, "Look, I'm sorry I missed last night. I really wanted to be there. Were you pissed? Are you mad?"

"It's okay," I said. "Definitely not mad. And I wanted to be with you tonight, but then I promised Grace, and it's a whole thing. I think Si and Grace are hooking up, but then now he's acting like a dork, he gets too nervous around her, I don't know."

"Not like you and me," he said. "You're never nervous around me."

"Why should I be?" I touched his chest and he put his hand over mine, patting it, and said, "You promise you're not pissed?" like he really cared and I said, "Girl Scout promise! And I'll catch you up on everything you missed, which really wasn't that much. At least according to the Times." I raised an eyebrow at him.

"Ouch!"

"Yeah, they didn't love it."

"They're overrated," he said as a bunch of little trick-or-treaters bumped into and ran around us.

"So, you're what? Cotton Candy? I wanna take a bite." He licked his lips and I said, "Oh do you?" and leaned into him again, I couldn't get close enough, and he pretended to bite my neck. But then he kissed it and I turned into a giggle fit because it honestly tickled, but I didn't want him to stop. He's just so hot.

"I'm a James Turrell," I said, turning in a little circle so he could see my full look and he said, "Very clever, little miss Lite Brite. Blindingly bright."

"What about you?"

"We're a skeleton crew, get it?"

"That is so cheesy!" I laughed. "The face mask is creepy, though."

"Jesse was convinced we needed them. They're itchy. Look, P, I've missed you. I've been waiting and waiting for you to text me post-show. I knew you were busy. But what's a guy have to do— take you to a fancy museum or something?"

"Very funny." I'd had a feeling like Joe was nearby all night. Sounds kooky but it's true.

"So . . . do you need to go tend to your unsteady friend?" Joe had tilted his head toward FC's front door, where Silas was vaping on the sidewalk. There were enough people on the streets that he didn't see me, even in my blinding pink, which was good. He looked clumsy and sweet. The vape looked extra big in his hands. I'm sure he was trying to find a way to relax in front of Grace.

"Let's walk," I said to Joe. At the end of the street was Washington Square Park and one million people.

"Are we hiding?" he said, skipping alongside me like an excited kid.

"Don't be a jerk." The more he looked at me, the more I found myself losing my breath. His eyes are downright piercing. He sees my insides. I needed to snap out of it. Si, G, and Mo would be wondering where I was, and I didn't want them to come looking for me. I turned us back toward FC's and picked up the pace.

"Can you do just one thing for me?" he asked. "Before we say goodbye forever?"

"Shut up."

"Kiss me?"

"I knew it," I said. "You're so cheesy, Joe. You're a big old block of Velveeta."

He shrugged. "Come on, PP, it's fucking Halloween and people do crazy shit tonight and all I'm asking you to do is kiss me just once, just for—"

I kissed him so he would stop talking and because I wanted to and because he wanted me to and I didn't regret it. As Public As Possible, just the way he liked it. Me too. He tasted like Milky Ways and there was nothing I wanted more than to keep kissing him straight until Thanksgiving.

AND THEN:

"REALLY?" Silas was standing like a weirdo right in front of Joe and me, watching us kiss.

"Silas, I—"

"Well, secret's out," he said, and then he stormed off and the moment was SO over. Did he really have to interrupt us THEN? Why didn't he just walk away when he saw us?

Joe said, "Well, there goes that."

"Shut up, Joe."

I ran after Silas but he was too fast for me in heels.

I found Grace back in FC's, having some big convo with Mo about all the city pigeons—over tequila shots—and she saw my face and said, "You know if you see a ghost tonight, they aren't real!" She cracked up, leaning on Mo's shoulder and he was laughing too—great, both drunk as skunks, and I told Grace I had to go home and she asked why and I shouted over the music, over all the people running around in their costumes having fun, "Silas just saw me and Joe—together—kissing" and Mo said, "Gillman?" and I said, "Yeah, outside. Silas ran off" and Mo palmed his forehead. "Ughhhhawww man, Piper, why him? Why him, P? Silas hates his guts. Now I gotta deal with this."

"Go be a good roommate, okay? He needs YOU now!"

"Girl, this has your name on it," Grace said, handing me one of her shots.

"What am I going to do?"

"Drink it," Grace said, laughing. "Look, you and Silas are friends. Friends. You don't owe him anything. He should want you to be happy. Hear that, roommate?"

We looked at Mo, who was shaking his head and texting. "I'm gonna go get him."

"What's he saying?" I reached and he covered the screen quickly with his hand. He threw some cash on the bar and said, "Later"

264

and left. Grace handed me another shot and said, "Trick or treat, lady" and we threw them back, the second of many more. I texted Joe and Silas but I didn't hear back from either.

11/1 8 pm

I've texted with Silas for most of the day.

At least he's texting me back when he feels like it. He's trying to be cool, but he's convinced I'm making the world's biggest mistake—and not even because he likes me. He obviously luv-luv-luvs Grace! But he doesn't want Joe to be happy under any circumstances. Fine, okay, but what about me? Joe isn't my enemy, he never was, and the connection I wanted with Silas is what I have with Joe. I can't help that! Argh.

I'm going to keep seeing Joe. Silas needs to get over it.

I waited too long to buy my ticket home for Thanksgiving but I got one for the week after, so I can see the fam and Savannah, my baby niece, finally, and catch a little break from all this d-r-a-m-a. Bye-bye paycheck.

I wonder if I'll ever make enough money that it doesn't just automatically disappear into the ether.

I have to get some real gloves. My fingers are freezing all of the time.

11/2 3 pm City Bakery, last hot cocoa I'll ever have

SHIT SHIT SHIT.

Just left Carlyle's office.

He fired me.

I can't. I can't.

I can barely breathe.

I have to be at Café A in two hours and I want to bury myself.

11/2 9:30 pm

I need Grace to text me back. I don't know how to figure
this out on my own. I don't want to tell Mom or Dad. I'm
embarrassed.

I know I did good work but it's never gonna sound like that to
them. I walked into Carlyle's office this morning, everything
was cool or as cool as it usually is, we started talking about his
show, the Times review—which I was right about, he was definitely NOT pleased—and Kennedy was there, being super quiet,
especially for him.

"So, what's next, boss man?" I said, kind of bouncing over to
him. I was all ready to have another Think Meet about any new
projects and hopefully distract him from the review. What was
I thinking?

He leaned forward on his desk, fingers intertwined, thumbs
rubbing the beaded bracelet between them.

"What a great question."

Kennedy cleared his throat and sat in the chair next to me.

"Piper, we appreciate the work you've done for Carlyle so far.
What do you think of your time with us?" It was the most official, mock-corporate I'd ever heard him.

"It's been pretty great, I think. I've learned so much and just getting to be in the studio, has been you know, really cool." I was thinking they were going to offer me a raise or like a job-job, full-time, and I was going to have to make the case for school again. They both seemed so calm, for them. Maybe that should have tipped me off but I didn't see it coming at all.

"That's nice to hear," Kennedy said. "We're so happy you've had a positive experience. And now"—he paused and I got excited—"we believe it's time to terminate the relationship."

Stomach drop.

Wait, what?

"What?" I looked at Kennedy.

They were both quiet.

"I'm sorry, what?" My whole body was squeezing. I was expecting to be the one to make the decision about whether I stayed. I was the one who had say over what I did, not them. I was tearing up immediately and so mad at myself. Why do I always cry when I try to be strong? I hate that about myself.

"Carlyle? I'm sorry, I don't understand. I thought I was doing everything right."

"Yes." He smiled. "I'm sure you read my reviews. The ones about MY show."

I nodded. "I read the Times. They liked the pieces I made." I knew as I said it I shouldn't be saying that.

He pursed his lips. "We are . . . not happy about the show. Our reviews and reception were lackluster at best. We don't accept lackluster. We never have. We never will."

"It didn't seem lackluster at the opening," I said and accidentally whimpered. So pathetic. "People were clapping for you and
telling you how great everything was! My piece sold. I saw the
book, I saw it."

"It didn't sell," Carlyle said.

"Yes, it did," I said. "I saw the red SOLD stamp."

"That's a sales strategy," Kennedy said. "It didn't sell."

"So you, like, lied?"

"It helped encourage the sale of a few of the other pieces, but no,
doll. Yours. Didn't. Sell."

Goddamn, the punches just kept coming. I was gutted.

"So if you didn't sell it, where is it? Can I have it back?"

"Piper, it's Carlyle's."

"What are you going to do with it?"

"It doesn't really matter, does it? That's our business now."
Kennedy smiled tightly.

I was careful with what I asked next, because I was hoping
they wouldn't answer the way that they already had. "But you
wouldn't throw it out, right? I mean, it's not trash anymore!
It's art, it's my art, I worked on it." I was breathing hard and
starting to lose it and they didn't say anything and I could tell
I was starting to sound pitiful, so I pulled up my bootstraps, as
Mom would say, not literally because I was wearing my Adidas,
but same difference.

"Plus, I can do better than that. But just so you know, I thought
you signed off on The Discarded. I thought you approved it. It's

really challenging to game someone else's life perspective, you know."

Let him sit on that.

"Piper," Kennedy said softly, "the contract said that Carlyle could release you at any time. You've made it through two shows with him—that's longer than most. Now, Carlyle is prepared to pay your rent through this year, as a parting package gift, which is quite generous. And you received your final paycheck at the show." Oh god, my rent. I almost started hyperventilating. I had to start saving every penny now, see if Maria would let me stay after January. My mind was racing. Where was I going to live?

Carlyle cleared his throat, and I tried to focus on him but my heart was beating double speed mon-ey, mon-ey, mon-ey.

"I just bought a ticket with it for Thanksgiving, though," I gulped. I've never been fired. I've never been told my art wasn't good enough. Obviously, it wasn't good enough to save me this time. "Is there anything I can do? I can work harder, be . . . smarter—" I didn't know what I was saying.

"You have school starting soon anyway," Kennedy said. "You were never going to stay on."

I wiped at my nose and Carlyle pushed his Kleenex box to the edge of his desk so I could take one.

"Maybe? Yes? I was hoping," I said. "Carlyle, if you'll just let me make it up to you."

He sighed. "You have too much YOU in you to work for me, at least for now. I think that was coming through in the exhibit. But who knows? Maybe one day down the road, if you make it here a few more years, we'll work together again."

Was that supposed to make me feel better? Because it sure as hell didn't.

"So, okay," I said, "what do I do now?" I was shaky and shivery and cold, like when I have a fever.

"Take out anything that's yours from the studio in the next week, and if you need any help, even just a car to transport your stuff, you just let me know. Oh, and leave the key in the studio when you're done, just lock the door from the inside and we'll get it," Kennedy said. "Your rent is covered in full already. So you can really enjoy this paid vacation now. Perfect timing for the holidays, don't you think? You can have some YOU time!" He wiped a tear from my cheek and I could see his own eyes were welling up the tiniest bit. Or maybe I just wanted them to.

I also wanted to scream at him. How could this be a vacation anything?

"Dear, you'll do wonderful things, especially with this experience behind you."

"I couldn't have done any of this without you, Carlyle. You've been really—"

I tried to shake his hand and he did, limply.

"You're smart and capable. I really do believe that, Piper, or I never would have hired you in the first place. But moving forward, it's not cost-effective to keep you on. So," he said, wiping his hands across his jeans pockets as if he was dusting them off, "you've got your whole future ahead of you. Determine your path and make it so. One day we'll laugh about this."

I nodded but I couldn't imagine what that day would look like.

Kennedy walked me to the elevator.

"I thought we were friends," I whispered. "You didn't give me any warning."

"We are friends. But I'm Carlyle's facilitator first and foremost. Surely you know that by now."

I nodded. I understood it, all right. Kennedy had given up trying to be his own artist. But I hadn't.

"I'll see you around, Piper doll. Be strong."

I saluted him, trying to be funny, because I couldn't say anything else without full-on crying. Maybe I had wanted to be released from Carlyle, but not like this, not feeling like I'd failed him and his show. I know the reviews were merely okay but that wasn't totally my fault.

The door shut and the elevator beeped as it passed each floor.

3, 2 . . . street level.

I left one more drawing in the lobby, a sketch of Carlyle and Kennedy's office. I didn't sign that one, but I stuck it in Carlyle's mailbox. Sent a snap of it to Kit and Enzo with "The jig is up. #NYSeen"

So, no more creating my work in someone else's name.

No more cleaning his studio.

No more being his protégée-of-the-day, his orphan-in-an-oil-field discovery.

My contract is officially done.

And suddenly I'm lost. I don't know what to do.

My imposter syndrome has officially gone from a maybe to a reality. I'm a liability. Why hasn't anyone told me? Grace, Silas, anyone? Have they just been stringing me along to be nice? I'm crying—bed—

11/3 3 am

Nightmare city. I can't really sleep now. Just went downstairs to see if anybody was hanging out and nobody is and I know Grace is asleep. I checked my mail since I haven't in a while and one amazing thing happened: my financial aid package was there! Hell yes, I'll take the good news, thank you very much! Just in time. Whew!

It's not a ton, less than I was hoping for, but two loans and one small scholarship is better than nothing and it will get me in there. Helen wrote on the letter, "Maybe more next time."

So, I can officially enroll for school, which I now want and need more than ever. The loans will go immediately toward winter semester, which starts in Jan. and maybe I can stay on at the Webster, see if I can save enough money to stay there and foot the bill myself. Yikes. Then I reapply for financial aid all over again for the fall. It's so stressful but whatever, that's then. For now, I email them my aid acceptance and they'll send me an email with a link to start choosing classes!

I just have to focus on now. I will finally study with Robbins McCoy and level up and learn how to make better art, more important work. My work will mean something.

I CAN FINALLY GO TO SCHOOL!!!! I am a student at the New York School of Contemporary Fine Arts, starting January. No more maybes.

What a weird day of failures and victories.

11/3 Lunchin' and chattin'

I wish you were coming home for Thanksgiving. That's how Mom started our text, then I just called her. I told her to check her earlier texts, I already told her I was coming home, but just a week late, and she practically squealed and then she was cooing again, I assume at Savannah.

"Mom, I wanted to tell you something in person, but I don't want to wait until Christmas."

"Oh, god. What?"

"Nothing bad, mom. Don't freak out." I swear I heard her brain go, PREGNANT?!?! "It's good news. I got a scholarship!"

"What?! Sweetie!"

"For school! Not a huge one, but I got one. And . . . a couple of small loans."

She screamed, "Scholarships!" and Dad jumped on the phone.

"You did it, kiddo?!"

"I wanted to tell you both in person but I didn't want to wait any longer! I'm so excited!"

More screams. A few sniffles. I told them I would email them details in a few minutes, when we got off the phone.

We said byes and a bunch of I love yous. I'm crying. I'm trying to stop, but I just want to be celebrating with them and not thinking about being fired and what's next. Life is so weird, the way it gives so much goodness and so much shitty-ness at the same time.

11/3 8:20 pm In some little park on 11ᵗʰ Street, I don't know the name, cold, had to write this all down couldn't wait

When I showed up to work on the café today before my dish shift began, Lita was not in a great mood.

"Sometimes it's a real pisser being a landlord," she said. "You can't trust anyone these days."

"What's up?" I was holding my breath, thinking she meant I did something wrong with Floor 2.

"The new tenants flaked."

I exhaled. "Wow. The ones who were gonna move in late?"

"The very ones. I told them no pets and suddenly they have two big dogs they can't live without but somehow forgot to mention to me.

"So what do you do?"

"Stir another drink. Place another ad."

I tried to commiserate with her. "Well, I lost my other job, right before I found out I got my financial aid."

"Oh? Well, that's good news, Pippin. Mazel tov."

"Well, I got it, but it's not a lot, not without my other paycheck. Right when I think I have it all figured out, kapow. I get knocked back." Is this what confession feels like? Because I felt like she was sharing her bad news and I thought I should share mine and somehow it would make everything okay.

"That's the New York way," she said, tying her hair back in her bandanna.

"Does it get easier?"

"Ha," she laughed. "You're a funny one," which kind of pissed me off because I wasn't trying to be funny, I was looking for some advice, and I sighed. "So, you're down a tenant, and I'm down a job."

"That's about the size of it."

And suddenly my brain was clicking fast, just kicking to life like my little radiator in the middle of the night. "Uh-huh," I said, stacking the tarps and cans of paint near the front door. "Interesting."

"Pippin, why do I feel like you've got a trick up your sleeve?"

I pulled up the arms of my sweater and showed her my wrists.

"No tricks here," I said. "But I think I might have an idea. Something that works for both of us."

She crossed her arms and leaned against the wall. "I'm listening."

"So," I said, thinking it through as I was saying it, trying to play it casual as Hector and the other staff were coming in for the evening shift. "What if you don't have tenants until next year? What if you let me use Floor 2 as a space that can make money?"

"Right, that's called rent. And we have Angelou's."

"Right, but you could . . . have you heard of pop-ups?"

I couldn't help but remember that Carlyle had wanted to do a pop-up show in the spring; I guess I did learn something from him. What's that saying? Steal from the best?

"A pop-up?"

"Yeah, a pop-up. We could make Floor 2 into a temporary 'underground' gallery. Like it would only be for a short amount of time, maybe one or two weekends, and I would show my work, and, and"—I was stalling, trying to think of more to offer her—"not just my work but some of my friends' work, other artists at my school, and whatever money I make, I would split fifty-fifty with you, and I'd even give five percent of my fifty to your favorite charity and five percent to a charity I like. You name it."

"Baby, you're a fast-talker."

Didn't exactly sound like a compliment, but I treated it like it was and tried to own it. I hustle, that's what Joe said. I'm a hustler. I was feeling cool. And scared.

"Well?" Dad would love my negotiation so much.

"You're gonna have to guarantee me a thousand bucks. And you still gotta wash dishes, 'cause I'm already taking a sharp loss with no renter up there."

"I can," I said. Holy shit, I don't know if that's possible. But then I think about what Carlyle was going to sell my piece for, even if the Times didn't love it. "And let's just say I don't?"

"Then you're dishwashing for free through the new year."

I thought about it, pacing the space. I could see it.

"Oh, and another thing, the pop-up has to be finished by Thanksgiving."

"That's like three weeks! What about until the end of the month?"

"I'm gonna need time to clean it up before December, then show it in a very slow month for rentals, and I have a full roster of holiday events. Do you know how many parties we're hosting downstairs?"

I shook my head. I hadn't told her I had bought a ticket home for after Thanksgiving, but maybe Dev would be ready to wash dishes again by that time. Dang. Had to figure that out too without pissing her off.

"Almost every day next month. So. You still wanna make a deal?" She smirked at me but it didn't feel mean. She was challenging me. I knew it.

"Yes," I said. "I can do this. I know exactly what I'm gonna do."

I have no clue what I'm going to do. I guess first step is touch up any last-minute spots. Second, get to work on pieces to show. I don't know if I'll have enough actually good pieces to show, but I did promise friends. So, I could get Si to say yes, make him prove we're cool. Maybe Mo? Maybe. Maybe even Joe, once I see his work. Yeah!

Andy Warhol said, "Making money is art and working is art and good business is the best art." Maybe I'm living my best art life now. I think he would approve!

Between Halloween and Silas and Joe and Carlyle, and suddenly having to put up a gallery show, and somehow get people to know about it, and oh yeah, also have enough art for it, and give Lita $1K on top of it, I'm freaked out but EXCITED too!

Texting Grace to see if she's up.

11/4 4 am

I don't know if there's some kind of best friend award I can hand out to Grace, but she deserves all the trophies. I just won't tell Kit, or maybe I'll just get her one, too. ☺

G met me at Magnolia Bakery after I texted her and we pigged out on expensive cupcakes, a real bad $$$ idea, but I just lost it. She got me to take some calming breaths in between stuffing my cheeks and we made a plan.

"I can help you with press releases."

"You can? But I can't pay you anything, at least not yet. But I will!"

"I'm a writer. I'm used to not getting paid." She laughed. "It's okay for now. Maybe I can get Eileen June to put out the word to her people. She loves supporting 'emerging artist' types, especially women. I'll vouch for you. What's the date?"

"The 23rd."

"Of November?"

I nodded my head, wiping crumbs off my mouth.

"This month?"

I nodded because I was still swallowing.

"Can you actually mount a show in a few weeks?"

"Sure," I said. "Well, I don't know, but I can't back out now. I've got to do this. Yes. I can."

"Okaaay." She let out a whistle and wrote some notes to herself. "We're going to have to use all of your connections. Who do you know? Besides me, obviously."

"Well, there's Silas, and Mo."

"No, we're gonna need to think much much bigger." She laughed. "We need the IT factor, the COOL factor. The Carlyle people."

"I could ask Benz and Abril to spread the word, even if they're . . . them. I have their numbers."

"Yes to them. And we need Rashida and Kennedy, obviously."

"Maybe just Rashida."

"Kennedy's connected, though."

"Yeah, and he and Carlyle just fired me. So no."

She tapped her pen.

"Maybe I could ask Silas to ask his mom. She's an art dealer? And his dad . . ." I stopped for a second and Grace looked at me. "His dad, I think, is some rich importer or something, and really connected in the art world, but Si's pretty over him. But I could ask him to ask them, anyway, and we can get him to be a part of the show, too. What do you think?"

"Yesss!"

"And I'll follow up at the Webster and check with Maria, see if anyone in the building is 'someone.'"

"It's gonna be hard, so close to Thanksgiving."

"I know, but it's the only time Lita is willing to do it."

"Okay, then we'll make it work."

"Yeah?" I asked.

"Yeah."

She popped the rest of her cupcake into her mouth and licked her thumb. Love this girl.

We started talking about Halloween and the whole Joe and Silas thing again. "I don't see what the problem is," Grace was saying. "You never promised to be Silas's girlfriend. Also, I'm pretty sure he's into me." She winked.

"It's not about the girlfriend thing. Si doesn't want anything remotely romantic with me, obviously." I stirred my hot cocoa and winked back. "But he sees me as a traitor. Picking Joe as a guy I hang with is like, major treason to him."

"Well, that's his problem, not yours. Do you have a real reason to hate Joe?"

"Nope. And I've tried, trust me, to come up with any excuse. All the awful things I've heard about him are from Silas. It's just that I spent my whole summer emailing with Silas and we have—had—"

She saw me trying to explain in a way that was honest but not awkward for her and she put a hand on my shoulder. "It's okay. It's not there and it's okay. You need to move on. It's what I had to do with Evan, too. It's not comfortable but it's right. If he's wrong for you, you're wrong for him, that's a fact."

Grace is so good at life truths like that. "I can see why you liked him over email," she continued. "He's a good writer."

"You mean our emails?" Had he shown them to Grace?

"Well, he slipped me some of his short stories. After my last reading, he told me he had been working on little vignettes, some poetry and short story mash-ups. I figured you knew about them."

"No. He didn't mention any of that." I felt a little clueless.

"Maybe he thought you wouldn't be interested? Maybe he wanted to impress you. And he didn't think his words would."

"But that's what did impress me, his emails. Why else would I have kept emailing?" I felt doubtful and possessive and mixed-up. I didn't want Grace to have seen Silas's writing before I did. It was hard enough dealing with feeling weirdly lonely here, and then feeling left out just added to it.

Then that's when the text from Joe came:

Joe: Hi! We okay?

I put my phone down.

"Who is it?" Grace asked. "Is it him? Or the other him?" She laughed, wicked.

I showed her my phone.

She typed back: OK.

"Thanks," I said.

"Anytime. You really can have both, you know. A friend and a boyfriend."

"How do you know?"

"Because I'm alive right now!" She sighed at me, kind of exasperated. "Piper, just be true to yourself and what you want. Be with the one you want to be with. If Silas is your real friend, he's going to deal. You don't have to fix this for him."

I gave her a huge hug. She just makes so much sense.

"And you guys are getting together, too?"

"Anything could happen," she said. There was a little smile across her lips, but she was fighting it. If she would just say yes, I think I would feel less like a friendship-betrayer.

11/4 11:30 am Getting my last remains from Carlyle's studio

I'm packing up my brushes and extra paints, though I don't know if they technically belong to me. Carlyle probably won't even miss them. I would say I'm going to miss this place, but I have F2 now (at least for this month!) and it's so much better in every way. Not every goodbye is a sad one.

Si is bringing lunch here in between his classes. After sending enough texts, he's finally agreed to try a truce. I'm supposed to feel oh so lucky but I feel nervous and a little pissed that I'm jumping through so many friendship hoops for him.

He's here now.

11/4 3 pm F2 studio

My shirt and arms are splattered in black and blue and gold-yellow and gray and silver and bright moonlight white, the color on the F2 walls, but also now on my jeans and all over the old NY Times newspapers covering the floor so I don't mess up the wood. I started a new canvas that I'm going to use to tie together all of the little #NYSeen drawings for my show. It's a big modern NYC palette, a blur, a big fat and fast-slashing blur, like an extreme close-up of New York City out a cab window, or a flash of lightning so you only see a bit of the sky for a second and then you're blinded, or when I stood at the front of the A train and watched the tunnel we entered, the urban den, feeling like we were zooming into a mechanical cave.

I've been lost thinking about the convo Silas and I had before I got here and the more pissed I got the faster I painted.

We had talked over bagels.

I said, "So, you hate me?" And he said, "No" and then I said, "But you want to?" and he said, "I don't want to hate you." He was being calm and quiet as I tried to get him to do more than just answer my questions and have an actual conversation with me.

"Grace told me about your writing. How come you never showed me?"

"How come you never told me you're with Joe?"

I started to say, "Silas, we're not—you and I—are friends" and he interrupted me with, "Friends tell each other the truth!" and I said, "Yeah, well here's two truths you didn't tell me, that you're an amazing writer, and that you would flip out about the smallest things!"

He took a bite of his bagel so he didn't have to talk. It looked like his eyes were about to tear, or he was just squinting because of the sun.

"Look, I'm sorry I kissed him, okay?"

"Really? Because I think you're sorry that you were caught, not because you were kissing him."

I was so irritated and I sighed but what I really wanted was to scream my head off at him. I was trying to be understanding.

"Okay, you got me. I won't kiss him again if it means we can still be friends."

Mouth before brain. Didn't know what I was hoping for there, because even as I said it, I didn't mean it.

"Well, no. Don't do that to me. I'm not the Kissing Gestapo. If you want to be with him, do it. But just so you know, you're probably temporary, another one of his "concepts.""

I tried to stay calm but I felt like we were going in circles and that somehow Silas was gaslighting me—telling me what I wanted to hear but also telling me I was crazy if I did what I wanted.

I started off slow. "Look, Si. To be totally honest, I do want to kiss him again. I do want to hang out with him. I like him. I don't know why. I'm drawn to him and he is to me, but I'm not going to marry him for Pete's sake. It's just . . . new . . . right now and it's not bad. He's nice and he's funny, I love his laugh"—Si looked like I had slapped him—"but you wouldn't know that because your competitiveness, or whatever it is, keeps you all locked away with jealousy. He's not trying to steal Robbins away from you, or anything like that. And not every-thing comes as easy for Joe as you think, I'm pretty sure, and in any case I'm allowed to make a new friend. I just got here, for fuck's sake. And if he breaks my heart, I'm the one who has to deal with it, not you."

"Well, I guess beggars can't be choosers."

"Dude!"

I threw a bit of bagel at him.

"You're making things so hard! I wanted to see you because I wanted to clear all this up because there are bigger and better things than all this, this"—I waved my hands around—"relationship bullshit. I need you, Silas."

He gave me a weird look. I think he was scared I meant romantically.

"I need your brain, and I need your work!" I tried to make eye contact with him when I said that. "Look, I'm putting on a show—public, obviously, not at school—and I want to include some of your photos, and your digital message board project. It's going to be this month. I'm using a bunch of the pieces I've been sketching and drawing. It's a lot to explain, but if you don't want to work together, if you're not interested in showing your work, the work I saw and loved, because you're so upset that I'm hanging with Joe WHILE YOU ARE STARTING SOMETHING WITH GRACE, then I'll save my breath. You just tell me what works for you." This was so not how I intended to have this conversation. I was spitting the words at him, but he was being so fucking rude and frustrating AND I still needed his pieces. Mostly I just wanted to get through to him that I wanted him to be cool with me and give Joe a fair shot.

He seemed to get that and let out a deep sigh. "So, explain your show to me."

I told him all the details and how Grace was involved. I hoped that would make him more willing and he said he needed more time to think about it.

"What's there to think about?"

"My school load that's kicking my ass?"

"Well, you have 24 hours to let me know," I said.

"Or else?"

"Or else I move on," I said. I hoped he wouldn't call my bluff but I was sick of working around his feelings. He either needed to get on board or not.

So we left it at that. He's going to text me in a day and I'm glad to be away from him for now. That beggars can't be choosers bullshit is still under my skin.

11/5 9:15 am The Webster

It's late in the morning, so the caf is almost empty. Lucky for all of us, the lights are low. Of course, Jasmine, carrying her yoga mat, just walked through and she looks like she's been up for hours. Ugh.

Grace asked me, sipping her coffee, "How's life outside of Carlyle World?"

I told her what happened. "Si can either get on board with Joe and me or he's going to lose our friendship. He's doesn't get to call the shots anymore. Still, I offered him the show because I really do want him to be a part of it. I hope he'll say yes."

"I'll talk to him." She shook her head. "He's such a decent guy but he's gotta let this Joe grudge go. I'm not going to be with him if he's holding on to some male ego pride thing."

Grace is coming with me to F2. She's writing and planning the email campaign and I'm working on my #NYSeens and sketching.

"I love that we can work alone—together," she said. She just gets me so much. I love her.

Si showed up today when Grace and I were at F2. She had texted him that we would be there after he asked her if she wanted to hang out.

It was REALLY NICE before he showed up. I had even been hopefully picturing how I would use his work in my show and how that might bridge something between us.

G was sitting and writing on a futon mattress on the floor, and I was reading comments on #NYSeen, seeing which drawings people liked most and trying to figure out a pattern. Most people liked the funnier ones.

The drawing of metal detector guy? 11,000 people liked it. The drawing of the Statue of Liberty dude? Over six thou. I can use these. They're okay. They're better than okay. They're fun. They're sad. They're . . . good? I think I have one superfan, @LwyerBklyn, who likes and comments on every single post and chats it up with the other commenters.

I was just writing on my to-do list to stop by that shop on 9th Street, The Source Unltd, and print out the drawings and either redraw all of them or consider using some prints if they're strong enough, when Silas showed up.

No hello, no hi.

"I'm in, I'm gonna do your show."

Well, that was fast. That's what I wanted to say. But I stayed zipped.

"I have to deal with my shit. I shouldn't have said some of the things I said. Okay?" SOME of the things? But, fine. He did that nervous thing where he brushed his hair back when Grace looked at him. He sounded rehearsed but I liked that he was making the effort. And having Grace there listening made me want to be strong.

"That's cool," I said. I wanted to tell him I had just been contemplating how to use his work, but what came out was, "Thanks, Si. I know this has all been weird. It's been weird for me, too." As much as I was feeling calm around him, I guess Grace picked up that I was still pissed and tense because she asked, "Thanks, Si," in the kindest voice imaginable. "So, Pipes and I are going to keep working for a while."

He looked between us and I looked at Grace, sitting there like some kind of magical bestie Buddha, and took the cue.

"Okay. Well, I have to go anyway," he said. "Bye." He waved and left, and we heard him run down the stairs. We didn't say anything until we heard the downstairs door shut.

"Now who's Dr. Phil?" I laughed and she said, "Honey, I'm Oprah!"

"It's like you just wiggle your fingers and everything works."

"You can't negotiate with bullies, romantic or creative ones."

"He's not a bad guy," I said. "He's just being weird."

"I wish he wasn't such a good writer." She sighed. "That's my other Achilles heel."

She tilted her head and looked at some of my sketches spread on the floor. "That one has two smudges. Smear it all or kill it. It's gotta be all or nothing."

Feels like life right now. All or nothing.

Going for pizza with Joe tonight. I texted him. On purpose. Think I need a break from all this drama, and besides I want to see his beautiful face.

11/6 3 am

Joe said he was waiting for my text. He thought it was never going to come and I told him I had some things I had to take care of, but now my brain was on right. He put his knees on the outsides of my knees under the table at the pizza place—super cheap! My kinda place!—and squeezed mine. A knee hug.

I told him about the gallery show, my first time doing something self-produced!, and told him I was thinking about showing some of Si's work as well and he pulled back just a little and I said, "It's art, don't make it anything it's not"—what is with these guys???—and he said, "You're the boss, boss." He big-teeth grinned at me. My brain bounced back to Enzo and Kit and I wondered if I could show their work too if they could maybe send me some ASAP. I scribbled a note on a napkin and stuffed it in my bag to remind myself to text them when I got home.

"And if you just happened to need another artist, let me know. I'm cheap, and I'm really cute." He winked and maybe I should have thought it was wormy but I didn't.

"As a matter of fact, I have been thinking about adding more. But I haven't seen ANY of your work yet, which is kind of absurd, right? And anyway, you should know, I can't pay you."

Somehow I just knew his art was better than what Si was saying, especially if he was on a full-ride scholarship. The school doesn't just hand those out to nice students. They award them to deserving artists.

"I offered. And I'll give you any piece you want if we can go on another date."

"Hmmm." I was grinning hard. He makes me do that. "I'm gonna have to see something, like tomorrow. And no promises. If I don't like your work, I don't use it."

"Deal." We started to shake hands and then he kissed my knuckles. He's so super sly.

Then we had this awesome night where we just walked and talked and walked and talked. It's one of the things I like best about the city—walking everywhere, especially when it's cool out like this. It's the kind of weather that when I'm walking by myself makes me feel lonely, especially when I see happy couples snuggling nearby, but when I'm with someone, like I was tonight, I just feel cozy, like we can't be close enough, like we're a walking Gap ad.

Joe asked about my family more and I told him about Mom and Dad. I felt guilty mentioning anything that felt like a big deal—next to his mom dying, what was so bad about my life?—and I was going to hold back, but before I knew it, I was telling him everything, how Marli cast a spell over my whole life, how I thought here I could escape her shadow and how New York was going to be just for me and my new memories, not for her. I hadn't told Si everything because he was so wrapped up in his Robbins drama.

But Joe had his mom. Everybody is dealing with something. He made me want to tell him. Si never had.

Being open about Marli with Joe made me feel more raw than I expected. My throat was constricting and I was trying to breathe normally and the more I tried to be myself, the quicker the tears fell. I tried for so long to be strong because of my sister, when really I'm still filled with hurt. Deep down I'm still raw and tender when I really think about her, how she'd been cornering me and trapping me all my life. No wonder I try so hard to not let her back into my life and work. As much shit as NY throws at me (or under my feet!), I feel safer here than I ever did living with my sister. God, I hope going back to Texas won't be a disaster and undo the new me. I don't want any more screaming matches, any more bruises, or any more fights. Period.

What a great date I turned out to be for poor Joe. I was shaking. But his eyes were soulful and understanding. No tricks, no mysteries. No games.

"You seem too good to be true," I said and he pushed a piece of my hair behind my ear.

"I'm just me, Piper." He tucked his hands in his jeans pockets, and I kissed his cheek.

I found a few Polaroids (two women hugging, a dog, the dog and one of the women) left on a telephone post on Broome Street and stashed them in my purse.

"What are you going to do with those? You don't know them."

"For the show."

"Mysterious woman."

I felt cool but I have no idea how I'll use them yet.

We found a club on Houston (which I heard out loud for the first time—it's pronounced HOW-ston, but it's spelled Houston. Home/not home). Anyway, the club had a dance floor and someone was spinning disco and nineties pop and it didn't have a name or at least we couldn't figure out what it was. There were only a few people on the dance floor.

He said, "Do you like to—?" and I said, "I thought you'd never ask!" and pulled him onto the floor.

It felt so so good to be there with Joe and we did some silly crazy moves—he started to disco dance OMG but he didn't care and everyone around us started clapping and whistling!

We did our own thing, danced alone and danced together, and dancing with him got me charged and we ended up making out in a booth, but also laughing A LOT, and dancing more and leaving just a little while ago.

I'm so happy. I think he is, too.

Finally went dancing at a club in NYC: ✔

I'm so inspired!!

11/7 11 am

"You want art? You get art!"

Joe and I met at CFA early this morning, after spending all last night together. Like, we've only been apart for 5 hours. We were at the 4th floor student gallery when it opened at nine.

"Come with me," he said. "And by the way, if you hate it, you still have to like me." He laughed, but it made me nervous. "Don't look so serious, Piper. It's only art."

After everything I had heard, I really REALLY didn't want to hate his work because I know myself, and I know hating his art would be enough to make my stomach churn and not be into him anymore. But he was being so cool and I tried to act like I was as cool as him.

We walked by a few sculptures, not super special, and some glasswork and then into a tiny room where there was a projector showing a film of Joe himself, no shirt on, building a wall with red bricks. I watched the film, waiting for some amazing moment. Then the wall was built, a little taller than him, and it looked like the film was bubbling and burning, but that was an intentional part of the film (I found out afterward) because the film started back up and the second half was Joe taking the entire wall down, brick by brick.

We watched it twice.

"What do you think?"

"Honestly?"

"I can take it."

"Well, if I'm getting it, it kind of feels like you're saying some-thing about pointlessness? Like what's the point if we have to keep doing and redoing the same things over and over again? It's very . . . is this considered slow-movement film?" I had read that term at the Whitney and hoped I was using it right.

"No, this is life! We shot in real time. It's everyday life! Right! And yeah, you do get it. That's the point. We wake up and do the same shit every day, only to redo it, rebuild it. What we do isn't precious. Life as a whole is precious, but the things that make it up are basic. All those basic things add up to one precious thing. Do you feel me?"

I thought of my collage, Seurat's dots, stars and snow, the mountain of trash becoming an entity. Yes. Meaningless things can add up to a meaningful thing. In the flicker of the projector, I could see his image behind him on the wall, shirtless, and said, "Yeah, I feel you."

We watched it again.

"I heard you did something about an art gallery, but there was no art in it. What's that about?"

In the dark I could see him raise an eyebrow and smirk.

"Oh you did, did you? Gee, I wonder who told you about that."

I shrugged. "Word gets around."

"It was a great piece, despite what you may have heard. I'm proud of it. I thought it was funny and it is, or was, but Robbins really helped me understand the level of my satire and how much more I could push it. That's just the beginning, really—"

"So, you're against the art world but you're an artist?"

"I like making stuff. I like manipulating and changing things. But all the garbage around art? The jargon, the parties, the price tags? It's not for me."

"I guess I haven't spent enough time around the art world to hate it."

"All that Carlyle time?"

"I didn't hate it. Not really. It's just weird."

"Well, I don't like phonies."

"But some people would say conceptual art is phony." I was hoping I was using "conceptual art" in the right way.

"Fair enough. I can't tell people what to think."

"So you agree?"

"No, I think they're wrong. But it's not my job to convince them. It's my job to keep making and their job to keep up."

I liked seeing him fired up about his work and I liked him defending it and I didn't hate his film and not just because he was shirtless in it. I still wasn't sure how I felt about the empty gallery exhibit piece, especially because I didn't see it for myself, but having Si's words in my head wasn't helping me be 100% objective.

"I want to keep up with you," I said, stepping closer to him. "I want to understand your work."

"Do you like it?" he asked and I said, "I'm on my way." And he said "How close?" and I said "Closer" and then he pulled me to him in the dark, his hands on my lower back, and we kissed against the wall in front of the projector, his film distorted and stretching across us, until a student monitor walked by and told us we had to leave.

I'm definitely using his film in my show. It works.

11/7 1:45 pm Floor 2 LUNCH BREAK!!!! I'm starving

Texted with Kit and Enzo about my first NY show and K said: YOU are taking over and I wrote back: EXACTLY! I NEED YOUR

HELP—YOUR WORK, ASAP! and E said: What can I send you? *swoon*—my first Manhattan show! and K said: I'm not sure and I wrote: I wish you were here and please send me at least one piece and she didn't answer me and said instead: Are you using the #NYSeen pieces? I told her, Of course & I'm going to show work from some friends from up here, too.

Kit wrote, You're the #ArtBoss now, dawg and I said, I learned from the best.

11/7 10 pm Another date with Joe because we can't stay away from each other

The Staten Island Ferry is a thing, a free thing, the most wonderful thing. Joe and I are snuggled on it together, right now. It's cold! He's watching me draw, and we look like this:

What do you think, Joe?

Notes from my meeting with Grace early this morning.

I showed her my #NYSeen followers.

"It's like a real hashtag thing. Look." I clicked through.

"That's me!" Grace said, and pointed. "Those are my words!"
Commenters loved her line "We are in the business of being."

14,561 hearts.

"Yeah, I sketched you the first time I saw you read and I included
one of your lines. I hope that's okay. I wanted to show you, but I
left the original sketch in the bathroom. I hoped someone would
find it. I redrew it in my journal."

"That's so cool."

"Yeah, and it has me thinking, G. I think you need to do something at the show."

"Like what?" She turned a little green.

"Like read a poem or two? Write something for the show?"

"I dunno."

"Why? You look nervous? You do readings all the time!"

"Yeah, but in the café, where I know most of the audience. The
art crowd is . . . different."

"You've only been to Carlyle's show. I guarantee it will be different at ours."

"How? You don't know that. We're inviting a lot of the same people who were there."

She made a good point, but I knew I had to have her voice for the show. "Look, if Silas is going to have a piece in it, you need to do something, too. I want all kinds of art in this show. Your voice, your sound, your words add another dimension. If you don't want to read live, then maybe we could record your voice. You could be the soundtrack of the show."

She cocked an eyebrow at me and bit down on her smile.

"Look, if Carlyle's show was about how he saw New York and the outside, I want my show to be about New York and how other New Yorkers see it and feel it and live it. It shouldn't just be my show. It's our show. New York's show. Every voice matters, right?"

"You're too much."

"I'm just enough," I said, sassy, and threw my shoulders back like I was Beyoncé. "Be the words. Please."

"Fine."

I stuck out my hand and she shook it, shaking her head and laughing. "And just so you know, I'm getting Mo's art, too. And Joe's."

"Joe and Silas at the same show? Do you think that's a smart idea?"

"I've now seen both of their current projects. I like them. There's room for all. Oh, which reminds me, my friends from Texas, the ones I told you about, Kit and Enzo, they might send something up here for it, too. I think they're working on a piece together."

"But this is a New York show, meaning experiencing and living in NY, right? Have they ever lived here?"

I shook my head. "But they've read a lot about it and watched a lot of movies, and we all have <u>some</u> idea of the city, right? That's part of what New York means."

"It's not the same, though. You know that."

"So you don't think they should contribute? I already asked them."

"It's your show," she said, using her Grace Buddha voice. "I just . . . I know you love them, but consider how much you can take on. Maybe you don't want to cram the show. It might muddy the vision."

"I know them and their work, they wouldn't muddy my vision. I know how they see New York because I saw it the same way."

"But do you still see it the same way as them? You're here now. They're still getting it from books and movies."

"No, and that's the point! The show is going to be PIPER PERISH AND FRIENDS, right? Who am I to think that only my New York is the right New York? This isn't a solo show."

She held her hands up like she was surrendering. "Okay, okay, I was just playing devil's advocate. You know how to put on your show."

"I'm not trying to be a bitch."

"NEVER apologize for being an artist with an artist's vision." She pointed at me. "You know what you're doing."

"Yeah, I do."

I thought I pissed her off but she had a cool smile.

We went back to scrolling after G agreed to do my show.

"Read what they're saying. Everyone's trying to find out who started #NYSeen. Like you're a big unsolved mystery running around New York. They want to catch you like a Pokémon!" She cracked up.

"Someone called the account the 'scribbling storyteller of New York.' We gotta use this for the show, right? #NYSeen matters."

"I told you your sketches were good! This is going to make spreading the word about your show so much easier."

"But all of these people don't live here," I said and she said, "That doesn't matter. We only need some of them, and their money." She laughed. Grace got to rewriting her press releases— she wants them out by the 10th at the very latest—and told me to focus on art production. "We need a startling image, something people can't get over, so get on it. If it's something you've already made, let's pull it from online, then get it ready. I'm the brains, and you're the drawn," she said, flexing her muscle, like brawn. Girl loves her puns.

I know I want to use the blue-black-yellow oil painting I started. I know that's the one. For now, it's City Untitled, but we'll find the name.

She's off to work for Eileen June now and I'm in the studio until dish time. Time for tunes and curating #NYSeen prints and more sketching and texting Mo and emailing Kit and E and figuring out the best way to use G's voice for the show. I like the soundtrack idea, the never-ending voice like the never-ending noise in NY, but I also want her to do it live. She puts the power in her pieces.

11/9 1:15 am

I'm freaking exhausted, but Si wanted to meet up and I agreed, so I finished my shift and after dropping three plates (Hector said he wouldn't tell on me but I'm gonna tell Lita myself— that's right, I'm grown up now), I put on my tennis shoes and ran out the door to meet Si.

We were supposed to hang in Union Square but it's cold and raining again. We ended up sitting in Jivamuktea Café. It's in a yoga studio that Silas knows about from his mom. Glenda is a member of the studio, called Jivamukti, and according to Si, it's where she "peaces out." I was happy to peace out there too because a cup of tea and sitting still sounded great for a few minutes.

He started first.

"Thanks for seeing me. I know I was a real shit. Out of line."

I nodded.

He let out a sharp breath. "I'm sorry. I just have to say all of this at once or I won't be able to say any of it." He inhaled and his shoulders rose up. "Okay, here goes."

"I was a bad friend to you and a bad student mentor and I feel embarrassed. Not just for what happened on Halloween, but this year has been very complicated for me. My family. School. Trust issues. And I blew up and blew it. I understand if you don't want to be my friend anymore. I'm going to therapy. I thought you should know."

Wow. I was totally blown away. This was like, a real apology. Plus, he was finding a real way to deal with his pain. I had never respected him more. And I never thought I would say that.

"Jamie Silas." I said his full name out loud because it was serious. "Thanks for being honest with me. Thank you for saying you're sorry."

Now he nodded.

"And thank god you're in therapy." I poked him and he cracked a smile.

"It's basically a rite of passage on the Upper East Side. I'm probably the last one to try it."

"I'm gonna get real with you, too. Okay?"

He wiped his eyes with the back of his hand and nodded.

"After the kiss with Joe on Halloween, we didn't talk for a bit because I felt bad. The last thing I wanted to do was hurt our friendship—yours and mine. But, Silas"—I sucked in my breath, it was now or never—"he and I are officially hanging out now. Officially something. And you know and I know all things add up to you and me being together, except the truth: you and I aren't great together."

He laughed. "I hate that math."

"Me too." I took his hand across the table. "But we have us and whatever we are, and I'd like you to try to understand about me and Joe, the way I do about you hanging out with Grace?" Thought I'd slip that in there, give it a shot, and he blushed! "That maybe I just connect with him. And I'm sorry you see him as Enemy Number One. He doesn't see you that way, by the way.

302

He doesn't know what you have against him. He doesn't know about your dad, you know? And he gets critiqued just like you do. You've built it up in your head that he's some untouchable prankster god, but he's just a sophomore trying to figure out his shit, too. He's no Banksy." I laughed. "Sometimes he gets good feedback, and sometimes it super sucks. According to him, he's been ripped to shreds by Robbins and plenty other faculty, too."

Silas smiled. A little too big, but what can you do.

"He's not better than you," I said. "He's just different. You need to get that through your thick, stubborn, annoying skull!"

He laughed a little and looked up seriously. You didn't tell him about Robbins? Be honest."

"I would NEVER do that to you!"

He sighed.

"If you want us to be real friends," I continued, "you have to accept that he and I are kind of together, at least for now. You don't have to hang with us or anything, but I really hope that you'll still be my friend, because a) he's also going to have a piece in my show and I don't want you guys fighting there"—he sighed—"and b) I need my student mentor now more than ever."

He looked up. "Why?"

"I got financial aid. I've been dying to tell you."

A huge smile on his face. "Ah! When?"

"A couple of weeks ago. I'm definitely going to have to work part-time or something, but yeah, I did it. I'm coming."

He clapped, and I liked outwardly happy Silas. I clapped too. The people at the other tables, all very quiet and "peaced out,"

303

looked as us like who let the animals in?, but I didn't care what they thought.

"I'm officially enrolled! And I need my real friend, the real artist who made me believe I could be one too, to help me. And I need more than that. Tell me I can still use your art in my show even though Joe has a piece in it. Tell me you'll work on it and get it ready and that you believe in the show as much as I believe in you and our friendship and your art. Because I do, Si. I really do."

As hard as he fought it, he smiled and agreed. His dimple was back in place, back where it belonged. He was beaming when I left him. The best.

Like a fool I hoofed it through the hail back to the Web and had to stop under store awnings when the rain was too much. Soaked but so happy.

11/9 10:40 am The Web

I got called to the front desk. Maria said, "Good morning, sleepyhead. Package."

Mom sent me a care package!

- Two sweaters and my denim jacket, not warm enough but I'll take it!

- Stove Top stuffing

- Cranberries

- A can of pumpkin

- I don't know where she thinks I can make all this stuff, but she doesn't know I don't have a kitchen.

304

- A bag of Halloween candy, 50% off. Classic Mom. Always buying Halloween candy 11/1 and V-day candy 2/15.

- A bunch of Savannah pics. She's so cute!!! The one of her in the tub crying with wet hair—stars and faves!

- My sweaters smell like our laundry. I miss home.

When I went to put the box up in my room, I saw Grace in the elevator and she came with me.

"Your room is so empty," she said. "It's depressing and cold, P. Why don't you put something on the walls?"

"It's not too bad. It's cold, but when the radiator comes on, probably like yours, it becomes my toasty cozy little cave and I don't want to leave. There's so much out there." I pointed to the window. "I've kind of gotten used to it in here. It's quiet but in a good way."

"A blank canvas," she said in a dramatic voice, clutching her heart. "For the artiste!"

"But of course," I answered her in a bad French accent. "One day you shall see my millionaire's château filled with Old Masters oil paintings and we will eat all the fancy cheeses!"

"Oui! Oui! But can I bring all of my fancy dogs and writer friends?"

"Only if they are millionaires, mademoiselle!"

"Mais bien sûr!" G said, laughing. "Are we done here? You have to see something!" I trailed her to the rooftop in my pjs.

OMG.

SNOW.

THERE WERE BEAUTIFUL WHITE
SNOWFLAKES FALLING ALL OVER THE CITY,
AND ALL OVER ME!

My very first snow. I had to wait 18 years to see this!

I held my hands out, and the little flakes landed wet on my fingers, melting before I could hold them.

"THIS IS SNOW? THIS IS SNOW!"

Grace was all smiles and flying hair from her scarf's static electricity. "I thought you would like this!" Snow to her was like humidity to me, she saw it all the time in Utah and it wasn't a big deal. But standing on our rooftop in our city, seeing it fall for the first time, made me feel connected to New York, to the world, to everything in a giant, goofy way. I was leaping in the flakes, jumping around like an idiot, and I didn't care. I asked her "When can we build a snowman?" and G said, "Pipes, this isn't nearly enough, all we can make with this is a tiny New York snow roach," and I threw a little roach-sized snowball at her and she laughed at me and was like, "You're crazy and I love you, Pipes" and I was like, "What would I do without Grace! SNOOOOOW!"

She told me we had a lot to talk about and we would catch up when we were both home later tonight. She went to work with EJ and even though I was hungry and cold, I stayed on the roof, in that magic snow. The sky was Seurat dots. I always thought he was so corny in school, but now I got it. It was nice to see a softer world.

I was so tired and so wired this last week. But now, I felt softer and awake.

Nothing is permanent. The Discarded wasn't. The snow isn't.

306

Everything melts away. But the snow . . . this singular moment in life? I will never have a first snowfall again. I love the Web and the world and the rooftop so much I want to burst. I'm so awake it hurts. I love this place so much.

1/9 1:15 pm Still snowing

Staying in pajamas for as long as I can. I should be working. I hope it never stops snowing again. It's really really cold outside and I keep coughing and the wind keeps making my window rattle. I wish I didn't have work at 5. I need to motivate and go put the final touches on my oil painting. I still don't know what to call it, and in last night's dream (racing around in a cab, everything a blur) I figured out something else: I'm going to adapt my very first #NYSeen sketch—it's the city, the way I saw it, fresh off the plane, but I'm adding leaves and snow, and breaking it into the two seasons I've been here. I can do it.

1/9 4:45 pm

I pulled out my copies of the #NYSeens and started placing them around my original NY sketch, trying to place them in the approximate areas where they would have taken place. I have to redraw all of them because even though I printed out the originals, they just look like photocopies. What was I thinking? Of course they all need to be new and fresh.

The more I look at how these sketches connect, the more I know I've made something real. I hope if anyone comes to the show, they'll think so too.

Grace and I are going to call it an early night, which is good because I'm achy and think I'm getting sick and she has work to do.

She's sending the press release out to all of Eileen June's contact list, with EJ's blessing, as well as listing on local sites like Time Out New York, and she wants to do a big announcement with the #NYSeen tag. We agree to wait one more day, and send it out the 11th, so we can get to the studio tomorrow and take photos with better lighting. Silas is going to take the shots and she's going to direct.

Also, just in time for the not-weirdest news in weird history:

Grace and Silas ARE FOR SURE A THING. A THING-THING. A THING SO MUCH SHE'S WEARING A RING. (Not engagement but still!!!!)

It's only weird because I saw it coming and they did too but wouldn't admit it for so long. Why do we have to make love so complicated?

Grace sat down on the side of my bed as I sneezed and coughed.

"You might freak out when I tell you this." She bit at her thumbnail and that's when I saw the sweet rose-gold trio on her thumb.

"Is that a new ring from Ev? Are you moving back to Utah? Please no!" For a split second, I thought they had made up.

She shook her head and then took a breath, kind of laughing. "Don't be mad, okay?"

"Why would I be mad?"

"Because Jamie."

308

"Silas."

"You're mad."

"No." I laughed now. "I knew it. Thank god it's NOT Evan! FINALLY! Spill it!"

"So, he came to me for writing advice."

"Oh my god. You fell for that?"

"No." She laughed. "I could see through that. But he is really good, Piper. Like really really good. And we kept talking, we stayed out until 7 am, I had to go straight to Eileen June's for an 8 am breakfast and I looked like hell, but I didn't care."

She nodded. "He's also a really good kisser. And he gave me this." She wiggled her finger in front of me.

"Girl, you can't stop being engaged!!!!" I said.

"Oh god, no! I'm not, not at all. But he gave it to me because he said he saw it and knew I should have it and I love it."

"Is it like a promise ring?"

"No," she said. "Just a . . . gift?" She took it off and showed it to me. It looked like three rings, but it was one. "He said it's from an old-school family friend jeweler."

"Sounds like a promise ring."

"Well, I'm not promising anything to anyone anytime soon. The whole Evan thing has made me want to slow my entire life down. And Si gets that. This isn't . . . this is . . . like I think this may be actually serious, but he's in no rush and neither am I. It's just, we get each other. There's nothing we can't talk about. Like, he told me about his dads. What is it with some guys? Why can't they take responsibility?" She shook her head and got a look on her face that I could tell meant she was thinking about something I knew nothing about, something Silas knew and she knew and I didn't, and I remembered feeling that exact same way about the exact same guy. It's weird to share the same feelings for the same guy and to see what could have been. Except it couldn't have been. And then there would be no Joe. And they're perfect together, it's obvious. But it's weird. If I knew this summer that I wouldn't be dating him . . . Grace and I talked about this John Lennon lyric when we were at Strawberry Fields: "Life is what happens to you while you are busy making other plans," and like, yeah. For real.

"If it wasn't for you, I would never have met him," Grace said, hugging my knees.

"You two better not be all couple-y," I told her. I didn't want to lose both my best friends, not when I just finally figured out how one of them worked.

"Oh god, we won't, I swear. Besides, who knows? Maybe it's just a fling."

"Maybe," I said. But I doubt it.

11/9 11 pm

I texted Joe and he showed up downstairs a few mins ago with matzah ball soup and crackers and ginger ale for me. Grace met him in the lobby—they are both so nice I feel like crying— because I forgot to tell him the Webster rule that guys aren't allowed upstairs, which is so archaic and dumb and sucky but I guess I'm glad because I look horrible so it saved me this time. My eyes are puffy and hurt. The last thing I have time for is being sick or getting anyone else sick.

It's the first time Si and Grace and I have been together in the same space since it's official that they're hanging out, but it's all good, because it kind of feels like normal, they're not groping each other or being some super couple, they're just being them, and Mo's here so that helps, too. I tried to get Joe to come over today but he's got his work-study until six at the library. Anyway, they brought a muslin backdrop so we can make sure my piece will be lit perfectly once it's in front of it. I guess it's a good thing Si and I are on the same side of things now because I admit after we looked at a few of the photos he and Mo shot, my work looks so much more professional than it does in my phone's pics. Si and Mo are going to do a little Photoshop to make the shots look the best they can.

They're eating sandwiches and I just finished more soup and don't feel great, but powering through. G's drafting the emails tonight and sending tomorrow so peeps will open them first thing in the morning. Kit and Enzo and me had screen time. Amazing to see their faces!!!! Can't wait to see them at the end of the month IRL. So, they're collab-ing on one piece and it's going to be small, but they're going to work on it day and night to get it here on time. They won't tell me much yet except that they're calling it Fishbowl. Also, Mo is creating something really cool just for the show—it's not like anything he's been making at school. He's totally out of his comfort zone, he said, so who knows what he's going to show me. I'm so excited!

"There's no turning back once we do this," Grace says and I nod, nervous. We both check the wording again. "#NYSeen: Piper Perish & Friends, a Floor 2 Pop-Up Art Party, 11/23 7:00 pm.

Do good with art: a portion of the night's proceeds will go to Housing Works and God's Love We Deliver."

The most I can hope for is I sell some or all of my pieces, and I keep getting to make art here. More art. Art begets art, as Adams would say. Energy makes energy.

I never want to leave this city.

11/11 7:02 am

Grace sent the emails, we posted the social media assets— Grace's term—all over the internet. We've had 13 likes in one minute on the hashtag. Will anyone come to this thing? Will I be able to pay Lita back? Will my fever ever break?

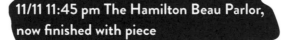

11/11 11:45 pm The Hamilton Beau Parlor, now finished with piece

I met Joe at our pizza place and we just chilled, walked around. He said we could go back to his place but then we'd be with his entire family and I wasn't really ready for that because I was still getting my brain back from the fever, and still kind of green-gray-white and I wanted to meet his dad when I was perfect, not cough all over him. We could only really go back and hang in the beau parlors at the Web if we wanted to be somewhere warm and cozy, so we did.

He told me he got me something for pop-up good luck, and then he pulled out a silver necklace with a paintbrush charm on it.

"I love it."

"It's not cheesy? My sister said it was corny AF."

"OMG, tell your sister I already love her, but no, it's the cutest. Help me put it on!"

He held up the little bit of hair that was touching my neck. His cool fingers felt soft and I was tingly. I felt shivers, the good not fevery kind.

Then he let me lean back against him, my back against his chest, and our breathing was the same, and I felt so relaxed.

I caught him up on everything about the pop-up so far.

"It's going to be so cool, P. I can't wait to see it. I'm really stoked you thought my film was a good match."

Even though the top of my head was tucked between his collarbone and neck, I could feel his cheeks rise, smiling. A good match. That's us.

11/12 4 pm Angelou's

Lita hosted an early Thanksgiving lunch/party for the whole staff today because a bunch of people go out of town on the actual day and week. It's party season for Angelou's, which means busier than usual with rentals—and extra dishes!!!—but she paid us holiday pay today too.

"But today's not the real holiday," I said.

"We'll be closed on Thanksgiving Day." She shrugged. "I don't know what to tell ya. Mort wants me to give you holiday pay now. You don't want it?"

"I just wasn't expecting it."

"Mort works in mysterious ways." She blew a kiss to the sky. I was starting to wonder if Mort had ever been real or if he was just her word for god. Either way he made me love Lita.

So it was Lita, Hector and his whole family, two of the busboys/servers who barely talk to me, Sean and Darius, and me.

Lita's prayer: "Let us all be thankful for the blessings big and small in our lives. Let us not forget those less fortunate. Let us thank this turkey for giving his life for us and leaving his turkey family behind."

I thought, Thanks, turkey fam!

"Let us thank the potatoes for growing, and green beans for sprouting, let us thank New York for trying to keep the subways running."

Lita thanked a few more things—the sweet potato casserole containers, the pumpkin patches, the cranberry bogs. And then she finished up with, "Let us thank our café and the namesake of our café, our guiding force, poet Maya Angelou, rest in poetry. And now, let's eat."

The food was damn good. A real-deal Thanksgiving meal with what felt like a real-deal family.

And now I'm about to wash everyone's plates before my actual shift begins and I'm in a total food coma. I would do anything for a nap upstairs. Oh well, at least I'm getting paid double.

11/13 11 am About to run with Grace

I still feel so full. I think I am 80% gravy now. Grace is going to run with me even though it's freezing outside and she wants to sleep in. She's been writing nonstop, a poetic memoir about distance and heartache. I can't wait to read more of her work, but when I asked her over coffee if I could sneak a peek, she said, "I'm still in it. Not yet. It's way too sentimental right now. Just emotion, no structure."

Been there. I feel like most of my pieces I do for myself are almost total emotion. But then she said, "I feel guilty. Indulgent. Eileen June would definitely say I'm not contributing to the world with it."

"But everyone's experienced heartbreak, right? Like that's universal? What about reflecting a universal truth? Isn't that a contribution?"

She nodded but I can tell that's not enough for her.

11/14 4 pm

We ran all the way to see the Christmas tree at Rockefeller Center because we thought it was already up but we were off by a week, so then we just walked around midtown, looking at the amazing department store windows, each decorated with its own holiday theme. Kind of made me want to be a window dresser. Then it started snowing again! THIS is what I have been missing out on living in Houston—snow when you least expect it!

Off to Angelou's and F2. Gotta do some major layout work today and place my #NYSeens against my blue-black-yellow piece and see what works and what doesn't. I need to research how I price everything and talk to Grace about confirmations to see if we are getting any press to come to our show and check our VIP RSVPs. I've seen a few responses to the mass email, but she's the one with the press and publicity list. And Silas is supposed to bring over two of his pieces. How do I know what my work is worth, especially if The Discarded never really sold? Sending Si a text, maybe he knows how all this stuff works 'cause of his mom. I really want to text Kennedy, but I just know I can't. No way.

Joe met me at F2 after my shift and we made out nonstop, neither one of us wanted to stop, so we didn't, and IT WAS SO GOOD, JOE IS MAGIC and then we sat around looking at my work, and he kept kissing my neck and everything was just right-right-right. I only want to hook up in art studios from now on.

Anyway, we were looking at my art, he was pointing out sketches that made him laugh, the ones that made him think, and then we kept kissing. I asked him if he knew anything about pricing because I hadn't heard back from Si yet and he said, "Charge as much as you can" and thanks, not helpful, because I actually have to make money. Seeing Silas later today because he couldn't stop by yesterday, so when he brings his pieces I'll ask him more about pricing and I think he'll help me here, way more than Joe.

#NYSeen Pop-Up Meeting Notes

I can't expect to make the same money as Carlyle because I'm not him. (Duh, but still a good reminder.) Si suggested I start with $200 a sketch, and more for the oil painting? Maybe an auction, and with the benefit/charity aspect, I'll get more?

I didn't think about real lighting for the F2 space and what Lita has in there is apartment overhead lighting. Not great.

Mo is going to make a playlist for me because he's the best with music, and he's going to add in some of Grace's recorded poetry. Also, he brought his piece to me. He painted a cardboard box, originally for a refrigerator, and now it looks like four connected brick walls. He's hand-painted old-school graffiti, though it looks like he spray-painted it, and the four sides all say something different: "Weapon" and "Tool" and "Announcement" and "Art." I love it, he did an amazing job with it, and it's going to pair great with Joe's wall film. I like that depending on which side you're looking at, you get a different message. That's very NY, I think. I told him I love it and I do.

I need snacks and drinks. Maybe Lita will help us out with wine? Peeps won't show up if there isn't free stuff!

Our two charities that we're going to help are Housing Works, my new favorite charity, and Lita's charity of choice, God's Love We Deliver, the food-delivery service for people with severe illnesses, with 5% of all proceeds going to each. G's going to contact them to let them know and hopefully get some reps from both organizations to join us that night.

I should have a mission statement prepared, something I can toast the crowd with. I asked Grace for help and she wants me to take a stab at a first draft, and then she'll smooth it out. She said it has to be from the heart first or it sounds like performance.

Kit and Enzo's piece is so cool and they promised to ship it with a lot of bubble wrap. I'm terrified it will crack before it arrives.

They sent me pics of it in the different stages and are sending it this week and I can't wait to see it IRL. Basically, they are constructing a mini-NYC inside a large-sized terrarium. It has nine panes of glass faceted against brass metal frames, and each panel is about four and a half inches in length, so it's a good viewing size. They're using dollhouse-sized furniture and structures. Kit is painting grains of rice to look like cabs. It looks really polished, not too crafts-y, and Kit said she's working on it night and day. I know she's working on it more than Enzo because of his school sched. When I said they're calling it Fishbowl Grace snarked that the title was very appropriate. I wish she would 100% trust I know what I'm doing with their work but whatev. We might just have to disagree on this one. I'd change the name if it's okay with them but for now, it remains Fishbowl.

Si and Mo think I should have a street team to put flyers up all around town, and I think I'm gonna do that, with my own drawing and our event info—get it printed up and post it everywhere.

Si talked through all that pricing with me at the Web, and then he asked me and Mo if we wanted to join him and Grace—they were going ice-skating.

So, we went skating in Central Park and it was SUPER FUN!

Maybe not the smartest thing since I don't know how to ice-skate. It was like five seconds before I tipped over, tripping Si and Grace on the way down.

"I'm so bad at this," I said. "It's my first time ever on skates, I'm sorry." Grace said, "Spot the Texan!" and Si said, "You should come with warning lights!" and Mo skated right past us, that jerk. ☺ They helped me up, over to the railing, where I stood to catch my breath. Snow was falling again and I said, "You guys are the best." Grace and Silas held on to each other, even though they were both balancing just fine, and then Mo flew by blowing kisses at all three of us.

After, in the subway and waiting for the train—too cold to walk—we watched a guy on the platform singing Frank Sinatra songs off-key, passing out candy canes. He winked at us and said Merry Chanukah. His nose was drippy. Everyone in New York has a cold right now.

My body is tired and bruised from the falling, but the rest of me is all Christmas carols and ho-ho-hos and genuine joy. I feel buzzy and free and I'm NOT missing Carlyle and Kennedy at all. Surprise, surprise.

11/16 10 am The Web caf

I was designing my flyer—which should already be out holy shit the show's a week away—then I saw Maria and waved her over to my table. We talked about her newest bracelets and then had some real rent talk.

"Carlyle has paid through New Year's, right?"

"That's right. You still want the place until December thirty-first or you out on the first?"

"Oh god," I said, putting my Sharpie down, "Yes. I definitely want to keep it after the thirty-first. What's the rate?" I don't have any place but here but I didn't say that to her.

"Okay, well are you taking over the rental contract? It's $274 a week. It's a sliding scale, but that's as low as you can go."

I raised my eyebrow and she said, "That's the rule. You don't like it, you take it up with management."

"Aren't you management?" I smiled, hoping she would be a little more chill.

"Upper management," she said, crossing her arms. She looked tough except her arms were covered in holiday bracelets that looked like wreaths and candy canes.

"I'll keep it. Please."

Okay, so I owe Lita $1k. I have no more checks from Carlyle, but that gives me almost two weeks to save and not spend, except for on my show, and I'm still getting paid from dishwashing. And when I go to Texas, I won't pay for anything for a week. I'm just not going to think about failing because I can't. Not an option.

I'm saying yes now, because I have to.

If I say yes enough, I can believe it.

If I say yes enough, I can make it all happen.

Yes to my rent, yes to my loans, yes to school, yes to Lita, yes to New York, yes to Joe, yes to the now. This is all there is, the yes and the now.

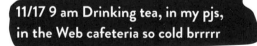

11/17 9 am Drinking tea, in my pjs, in the Web cafeteria so cold brrrrr

Yesterday I printed the flyers and posted them near the Angelou, in the parks, on Wooster Street, and in Chelsea and of course by the Webster mailboxes. I'm freaking tired today. It's harder to do things here when it's soggy and slushy out. My feet were wet like 99% of yesterday.

I stopped in Hamid's for soup and a warm-up and to be honest I missed him and wanted to see his face. He hung up one of my posters and gave me a lentil soup (for free!) and let me sit on his stepladder to eat it and warm up by his space heater.

"I have bad news for you," he said. "Freddy is engaged."

"That's okay," I said, slurping my soup. "He's happy, right?"

"But look, she's horrible. So much makeup." He waved his hands in front of his face, like he was trying to wipe it off, then he pulled out his phone and showed me a pic of Freddy and his new love. After all this time, I finally see that Freddy IS CUTE. But still, too old. And his girlfriend is super pretty.

"They look happy," I said and he said, "From your mouth to the gods' ears."

11/18 1 pm Café A

Benz and Abril both agreed to post about the pop-up and they have big followings, which means Rashida and Kennedy will both know for sure. It's not that I don't want Rashida there, of course I do, but I don't really want the Kennedy-who-fired-me to be there. That's bad juju. And if he thinks my work stinks, then he'll feel extra smug and right and I'll feel extra embarrassed. He's just going to make me nervous. Can't go there in my brain.

Today I'm framing and hanging the pieces because unlike Carlyle, I don't have an entire crew to hang my work for me so I can micromanage and snark at them. I asked Hector from downstairs if he would help me and he said he costs $15 an hour minimum and I said, "Fine, can you help me for two hours" so he's meeting me at 2:30 pm today and I'm going to pay him. I need someone else there and Hector may not be an artist, but he's honest, and I need an honest eye.

Grace and I did online stuff all last night, answering questions, promoting #NYSeen like crazy. We're now four days away and my brain feels shot. She's collecting RSVPs from the peeps on EJ's mailing list and we've been watching the responses to Abril and Benz's posts. Rashida retweeted and reposted some of them to her following, but she hasn't reached out to me directly. I assume she's coming and I'm going to wear the earrings she gave me and my paintbrush necklace from Joe as good luck.

Joe got released from classes early. I gave him a preview of things and he seemed genuinely in awe. He loves the wall where I'm projecting his film and he liked seeing it in there. I have to screen it in the darkest space in the room so that people can actually see it, but it works. And since the pop-up's at night, it will naturally be darker in that corner.

Btw, nobody should look that hot in a navy cable-knit turtleneck. Wow wow wow.

"Dang girl, this is tight, so profesh." Then he looked at my drawings and said, "There's not one of me!" He touched his heart and pretended to wipe a tear from his eye, which was super cute, then we kissed a bunch, and he said, "Piper, draw me like one of your French girls!" and I said, "Do you really want that?" and then he smiled and I told him to lie on the futon, and I drew him. My muse. One of many, I guess. :)

I needed a break, and he dragged me out of there, and we did our usual walking thing, even in the cold and wet, and all I could think was I didn't know relationships could be this fun, this easy, this uncomplicated. We were holding hands and even through our mittens and gloves, I could feel our heat. There's no bullshit between us, not like Enzo and me, or stupid CJ and me, or even what could have been Silas and me. I like the fun of me and Joe. He's like me and I think I'm more like him, too. If nothing is what it seems in this weird city, I really hope he is what he seems. I like him so much.

Maybe I believed too long in that crap that if you're two artists in a relationship, the relationship is doomed to be tortured, like Frida Kahlo and Diego Rivera or like Jackson Pollock and Lee Krasner or Andy and all of his crew's relationships. Maybe Piper and Joe can exist without all the drama. Maybe we can just be us.

11/20 Noon: lunch meeting with Grace in Web library

Kit and Enzo's Fishbowl arrived this morning and we had to do some reassembling because it was jostled in the packaging, but nothing broke and it looks even better than all of the photos Kit was texting me. Even Grace thinks so. "Hhhm. This actually works."

"Of course it does," I said. I knew they would come through.

G was checking her phone and then pulled the pencil out of her bun and added names to her clipboard. She told me we have at least 75 people confirmed for now. Is that a lot? It doesn't feel like it. Then again, Carlyle didn't have that many—but as he would say, his audience was very "select." But our graduating class my senior year was 500+ so this just feels small. I'm worried. Please let 75+ be enough.

Silas said his parents are going to come and that his mom was talking to Robbins. What if he comes?

I reminded Si that Joe is going to be at my show, that he has a short film in it, and to please be okay with it, and he sighed, "It's your first show. I wouldn't screw you over" and I said "Even though—" and he said, "No, Piper. I told you I won't screw you over, and I mean it. I would never sabotage your work." And that's the Silas I love.

I promised Silas his photo, 20-20 Double Vision, and his digital message board are working perfectly and might even steal the show. "We'll see," he grunted, but I could tell he was happy I said it.

I don't want to spend a lot on snacks, but they have to be good for my first gallery. Want to go cheap at Trader Joe's but I think I should go fancy, like Dean & DeLuca fancy. Grace said no, go cheap, no one cares if it's free.

Also, what am I going to wear besides Rashida's earrings and Joe's necklace?

11/21 11 pm

Two texts:

Kennedy: Hi, Piper. Give me a call when you get a chance?

Me: I'm busy.

I didn't call him. What could he possibly have to say to me? He's already fired me. I feel, I dunno, ashamed, like I let him down. Augh, I can't go there right now.

Kit: So excited! YOU?

Me: Nervous AF. I wish you could be here. I love your piece. It's perfect. You have no idea how perfect.

Kit: YASSSS! OMG, me too. I want to see everything. Enzo and Phillip and DJA and me are going to toast you IN PERSON when you're here next week!

Me: I really wish you were here. I need you.

Kit: No you don't, you got YOU. And we got your back down here in Houston, too. ☝ I L U. Now go kill it.

I feel like a bag of jacks, all shook up.

11/22 1 pm TO DO:

❋ get cups and napkins! I didn't get cups or napkins for the table!

❋ make the price stickers. Decided on $200 a sketch, like Silas said, and then $1,000 for the oil painting OBO (Grace told me that means OR BEST OFFER).

❋ send a blast to remind everyone of the time and our chosen charities, follow up on any social media questions

❋ go check that all the work is still hanging correctly

❋ double-check everything with Lita—how long can people stay in the space

❋ avoid Kennedy's calls!!!! He's texted twice more and called but didn't leave a message

✺ try not to freak out try not to freak out try not to freak out

✺ think positive/call Mom and Dad

11/23 8 am

Dear god or gods or Mother Nature or Universe or Whoever Is Out There, please don't let me fuck this up. I didn't sleep and I won't until this is all over. Please let me be able to pay Lita. Please let me be able to pay rent. Please let people like #NYSeen. Please let my art matter. Please let it mean something to someone besides me. Please let people see themselves in my work. Please let it help people and please people and be something for them. Please let us be able to help Housing Works and God's Love We Deliver with donations, even if it's just $50. Please.

What I'm wearing tonight:

✺ black dress (H&M, what would I do without you)

✺ paintbrush necklace from Joe, earrings from Rashida, natch

✺ purple tights

✺ black Mary Janes

✺ a light purple lipstick

✺ hair pulled back in a baby bun—it's long enough now!

Checked myself in the mirror again, then stood on a chair so I could see the bottom half and kind of crouched down so I could try and see it all at once. I like what I see. Not trying to be anyone else, not now or ever again. My outside matches my inside now. I'm seeing the real me.

326

!!!!!!!!!!!

I am so excited! I am bouncing off the walls! Yesterday yesterday yesterday!

Yesterday worked!

About ten minutes before we opened, Grace stood outside in front of the Café A door with a list, kind of like a bouncer, and kept texting me, People are lining up, people are here! and I was pacing upstairs, Mo was trying to get the music going, and Si was putting the little stickers near my drawings, telling me which ones he thought would sell first, which ones wouldn't (thanks for the honesty, Si!), etc. Lita let me borrow two fancy white tablecloths so that it looked fancier and she said, "Pippin, it's gonna be great, stop sweating it" and she took a cloth napkin to my forehead. She also put some yellow flowers (NYC gold-yellow—again!) on the other table near a mailing list sign-up and a notebook for purchases/donations. Okay, so I did pick up a few tricks from Carlyle's gallery show.

Right before G let people in, I drew a picture on a cocktail napkin, signed it #NYSeen, took a quick pic of it.

In the comments, I wrote:

I see you, New York! Happy Thanksgiving from #NYSeen, Piper Perish. I tagged the location Café Angelou, and watched the likes explode!

Grace opened the doors right at 7 and we had people immediately. I overheard some of them asking to meet the artists behind #NYSeen and someone else say they've been following online since the first post. I was geeking out and didn't introduce myself right away because I wanted to keep hearing what they had to say. There was a group of girls who brought their own sketch books and were drawing at my event—super meta #NYseen!!!—and I went over to them and asked them what they were doing and when they told me, I told them I was the artist behind the tag. They freaked and we took a bunch of pictures together. LOVED IT. I have some new friends, I think! ☺

Some people went straight for the wine and cheese, some of them stayed in their little groups, chatting and looking for places to hang their winter coats and I went into panic mode because we didn't have a rack, so Si ran downstairs and asked Lita if we could borrow a couple of chairs and we just stacked coats for people there.

By 8, F2 was packed. Eileen June brought a bunch of people and Grace introduced me to them and more importantly, to Eileen June herself! I told her I had come to her and Grace's readings and how wonderful I thought she was and she said, "Grace tells me I should be a fan of yours, too. I'm always happy to meet a fellow female artist." She shook my hand and I swear she transferred some superpower to me. I stood a little taller and looked her in the eye and said, "Me, too."

I didn't know it, but Lita had invited old restaurant customers and new café regulars, too, and she took me to them, to make sure I thanked them for coming. "Look who's here!" Lita kept saying. "It's Peter and Andy from the gelato joint!" "It's Louise from Murray's!" "It's the record store guy, Josh!" Everyone was just so freaking nice and funny and in good moods, maybe just because it was holiday time and we had free snacks, I dunno, but it genuinely seemed like everyone who came wanted to really be there. They wanted to see #NYSeen and they were accepting me into their little Cornelia Street village, too. I felt like I really belonged. I had my own little village in F2!

I was busy being party hostess with the mostest and artist and talking to the peeps I knew like Rashida—who came with Abril and Benz, who immediately demanded, "Booze?"—and a bunch of their friends (Ricardo, Joseph, Ivy, I didn't meet them all). And then Rashida pulled me aside, and said, "Girl, be your fearless self and go talk to that guy in the hat and scarf." She was giving me serious eyes.

I walked to him and my heart started racing when I saw who it was.

"You came," I said.

"Yes," Kennedy said. "But I was beginning to think you didn't want me here because, ahem, you're not very good at returning calls, doll."

"I thought it would be weird," I said. "You fired me, remember?"

"Carlyle fired you. Look, if you were still working with Carlyle, you wouldn't be doing this. When one door closes, you bust open another one. Like you've done here. But you should have called me back. I would have reached out on your behalf, brought some of my contacts."

"I'm sorry." I hung my head, feeling kind of dumb.

"No hard feelings, girl. We don't have time for that, do we? Now go and do your thang." He gave me a hug, that warm kind he gave me when we first met and I said, "Thank you, Kennedy. You're the best" and he said, "I know" and walked over to the wine. We didn't talk for the rest of the night, but I felt better about the split from Carlyle than ever. I need and want to keep Kennedy in my life.

Oh oh oh—and this was amazing—I saw Robbins talking to Silas in front of one of Silas's photographs, Robbins had his hand on Silas's shoulder and he was pointing to Silas's work and they were both smiling and nodding in the same way and talking a lot and it looked so positive! I almost started crying right then and there and I so badly wanted to know what Robbins was saying to him, but I knew Si had to have that moment, not me. But from where I was, it looked so good, so right. They did look so much alike. Now that I knew the truth, it was hard to unsee it. It was what Si needed and my heart was blowing up—if I did one thing right this whole night, it was that freaking moment!

Then without telling me she was doing it (smart Grace not to tell me, to keep me from getting even more nervous), Grace turned down the volume on her own poetry pumping through the speakers and tapped a glass with a spoon and said the artist, Piper Perish, would like to say a few words.

I walked over to where she was standing and thanked everyone for coming and told them how grateful I was and reminded them that some of the night's proceeds would go to Housing Works and God's Love We Deliver, so that even if they couldn't pay the full asking price, I'd take best offer for the sake of the charity, and that it was my first show in New York City, EVER, and I couldn't thank them all enough for being there, old friends and new.

"What I really want to say, to confess really, is that New York has changed me in so many beautiful, funny, smelly ways (I got a laugh), and I've only been here a few months. I've never lived anywhere but with my family and I thought I had problems back home and that New York would be an escape"—everyone laughed like they felt similar or understood—"but here my eyes have been opened to the bigger world, the real world, where people are hungry or scared or sick or just need help, and need art to be a voice for them when they don't have a voice, and for art to be food for them when they need nourishment. We need to make art to protest for our brothers and sisters and protect them and save them when they're cast away. They need art to make them laugh. They need art that reflects them so that they know they are seen. We're supposed to take care of each other and notice each other and reach out a hand to each other, not just to shake hands, but to help each other up. That's what I want to do with my art. I want it to matter. I want your art to matter, too. If you're making something, if you have the privilege of making something like I do, then we owe it to ourselves and each other to do better, make better, live better, not just for us, but for everyone. Art matters, but what matters must also be in art. We create so that the invisible becomes visible. It is why #NYSeen means so much to me and I hope to you. It's my artistic mission. Let it be yours, too. Raise a glass if you're with me!"

And everyone was raising glasses and I didn't realize it at the moment, but I was crying. People said "Cheers" and "Brava" and "Hear, hear" and we drank and Mo bumped the tunes and the pop-up was back in swing. Strangers stopped me and thanked me and even Kennedy hugged me as I went over to Joe, who was wearing a white t-shirt, black vest, dark-wash jeans, black fedora. Cute Overload. As if the night couldn't get any more weird-tense-exciting-wonderful.

"Hi."

"Hi," he said, giving me a quick kiss on the cheek in front of everyone, including Silas, who was near us.

THEN, in like a super-confident way, he just stuck his hand straight out to Silas!

"Jamie," he said. "I'm Joe."

Silas looked at him, then at me, then Grace was in between Si and me, whispering something in his ear.

And then Silas shook his hand. "My friends call me Silas."

So incredibly awkward. But so incredibly awesome!

They didn't talk to each other for the rest of the night, but that was a start. Joe asked, "How'd I do? Think he still hates me?" And I held up my fingers like just a little and we both giggled. "He's trying, too, I think," I whispered. I gave him a quick kiss on the ear, even though all I wanted to do was debrief with him about everything about the night (and get back to our futon).

People stayed until almost 11, then we had to clean up. All the snacks were gone and the table was a hilarious mess. I don't think I bought enough to eat, but nobody complained.

In total, I made $2,225, which was way more than I expected! This morning, I finally mustered the courage to look at my notebook I had left on the table, where people had signed their name to buy certain pieces and next to the main piece was Glenda Silas, $1,000. Almost half of the total had come from Si's mom. I called him.

"Hi?" I said. "Your mom bought my work! Did you tell her to do that?"

"No, I swear. She told me this morning."

"She's amazing! Can I talk to her?"

He said hold on and then after some jumbling, he put her on the phone. She sounded groggy, but it was after 9.

"Good morning, Piper Paris," she yawned.

I giggled. "It's Piper <u>Perish</u>."

"It's early." She yawned again.

"Mrs. Silas, I can't thank you enough. I can't believe you bought my oil painting!"

"Consider this a very small investment in your future."

"Thank you, thank you! I can't wait to see where you hang it!" I wondered if it would be in their home or if she had an office or what. I wanted to see it up in the wild!

"Hang it?" She laughed. "It's going into storage."

Your work's going into storage—just what every artist wants to hear. I mean I was happy she bought it and everything, but way to burst my bubble.

"Oh."

"It's an investment piece, Piper. It's not ready for the world. But one day, when you're known, well, it will be priceless."

"Sure," I said, trying not to be disrespectful. She did just buy my piece.

"Nobody wanted Picasso's line drawings. Then everybody wanted them. Catch my drift?"

"Yes, ma'am," I said.

"Being seen, isn't it? Isn't that the hashtag thing you were doing?"

"Yeah—it's like the city being seen, through everyone's eyes, I guess."

"Okay, then," she said. "You achieved that—being seen— eighteen years old! Color me impressed. I remember Carlyle telling me you were one to look out for when we met backstage."

Carlyle said that?

"So, I did watch out for you. Then Jamie told me about your show, and well, I had to see it for myself. You should still consider changing your name, though. Piper Paris is better."

I just laughed.

After thinking about it the last few hours, I'm glad it's going to be in her hands. She bought it, and with the other money coming in from other buyers, it means I'm in the clear for paying back Lita, donating to our charities, and my rent for December.

I'm almost done with this journal, my last page, but my mind can't-stop-won't-stop, like a million fireworks going off all at once. I have less than two months until school now. I have a month to make more $$$ and see fam and explore everywhere and who knows what else? Anything could happen. Everything could happen. I'm so ready.

New York is everything I thought it would be and nothing I expected.

334

The now—this now—my now is bold and bursting and perfect.

It's brighter than the streaks of taxi gold-yellow.

It's bigger than the moon over the Hudson.

It's sweeter than the snow on the roof.

It's this shimmering, shiny city.

I'm here in this now.

I'm home.

ACKNOWLEDGMENTS

My tribe is filled with so many extraordinary people, and I would be a real turkey if I didn't thank them all. So here we go:

John Cusick at Folio Literary Management, my encouraging, compassionate, and witty agent, I'm so glad I landed with you. Molly (Jaffa) Cusick, thank you for introducing me to him, and transferring me from one amazing advocate to another. I'm so lucky to have you both in my life. Thank you for getting me.

Taylor Norman, I am indebted to you. Your insight, patience, humor, and push make me want to be a better writer for you and our readers. I couldn't have made Piper the boss she is without you. Thank you sincerely for being my editor, my friend, and my guiding light through the last few years.

My Chronicle Books team of superheroes: Ginee Seo, Amelia Mack, Jaime Wong, Lara Starr, and Laura Antonacci, thank you for believing in Piper from day one and working so hard to bring her to the world. Hannah Moushabeck and Sally Kim, thank you for your early contributions as well.

The artists behind Piper's art, Luke Choice and Maria Ines Gul, thank you for sharing your skills and gifts in our story. Your art colors Piper's journal with humor and enthusiasm.

My mom, Carolyn Solomon, and my family, the Gluckmans, thank you for your genuine love and support. You have given me the foundation to be fearless and stand up for what I believe in. Mom, you give the best hugs in the world and there's not a day that goes by that I don't need one.

My husband's family, Korky Vann and Ellen Grusse, as well as the Cagans and the Granatos, welcomed me to their tribe and have always made me feel like one of their own. I love being one of you.

Vanessa Napolitano and Leila Howland, you are my sisters in words, my comrades in gossip, my critique partners in the trenches. Thank you for your laughs, your honest evaluations, your accountability, and your talent. I'm so glad we haven't stopped meeting, even if we're on two continents now.

My creative muses and hilarious friends: Richard Robichaux, Natalie Robichaux, Meredith Mundy, Sherine Gilmour, Tiffany Hodges, Marshall Mintz, Deborah Hetrick, Matty Groff, Carly Fisher, Paul Davis, Sharon Gonzales, Manuel Gonzales, Tress Kurzym, Jordana Oberman, Maggie Klaus, Amy Spalding, Bryan Mason, Holly Reeves, Brandy Colbert, Lori McLeese, Dave Melito, June Alian, Laura Birek, the Doubleclicks, Molly Lewis, Joseph Scrimshaw, Sara Scrimshaw, Clarke Wolfe, Mike Montiero, Erika Hall, Jen Leavitt, Lorna MacMillan, Sylvia Rodemeyer, Denise Kuan, Hope Larson, and Sean Hetherington, you are my gems, my touchstones, my rocks. I love you.

Librarians and teachers who have been supportive of my writing since my debut in 2017, thank you. Your emails and encouraging posts have meant everything to me. Special shout-outs to Kelly Wadyko, Melissa Cunningham, Elaine Baker, Karyn Lewis, and Jennifer Haight for welcoming me so generously into your worlds.

And lastly . . .

Josh A. Cagan, when you say we will always be New Yorkers, my heart speeds like an express train. I love you to Brooklyn and back. "'Cause everyone's your friend in New York City/ And everything looks beautiful when you're young and pretty/ The streets are paved with diamonds and there's just so much to see/ But the best thing about New York City is you and me." —TMBG